HURD'S CROSSING
A WESTERN DUO

LAURAN PAINE

SAGEBRUSH
Large Print Westerns

Copyright © Mona Paine, 2008

First published in Great Britain by ISIS Publishing Ltd.
First published in the United States by Five Star

Published i   Large   ISIS Publishing Ltd.,
7 Cent emead, Osney Mead, Oxford OX 2 0ES
           by   with
Golden West Literary Agency

All rights reserved

The mo   or has been   serted

British Library Cataloguing in Publication Data
Paine, Lauran.
  Hurd's Crossing.
  1. Western stories.
  2. Large type books.
  I. Title
  813.5'4–dc22

ISBN 978–0–7531–8753–1 (pb)

Printed and bound in Great Britain by
T. J. International Ltd., Padstow, Cornwall

Table Of Contents

HIDDEN VALLEY

CHAPTER
ONE

An old man named John Flores first told Arch Sutherland the story when they went out for the autumn gather and Arch's father had paired young Arch off with Flores, who was a top hand. Arch's father had never taken his son on a big gather before, not entirely because he had hesitated over subjecting his child to the hardship of living out of a wagon camp for two weeks, but also because when Ben Sutherland did any kind of serious work he had no patience for novices. Ben had grown up behind cattle in an era when not only a man's livelihood but also his life depended upon experience, and the experience of the men he rode with. Largely those more hazardous times were gone now, but Ben had been shaped as a reed, and now in his sundown years he remained oakenly unchanged in his beliefs and habits.

They got along well, Ben and this thirteen-year-old son, but John Flores had something in him that made it easier to be around him. He laughed often, and was understanding. Mistakes, he once told young Arch, were things people had to make so that now and then they would look foolish to themselves. It kept a man from becoming too superior.

They had combed through the upper hills west of the plain where there were meadows, some small, others quite large. While no range cowman felt easy when his critters were up in there, warily co-existing with catamounts, bears, buffalo wolves, and other meat-eaters, the cattle usually left Longlance Plain when the heat arrived to seek better feed and cooler temperatures in the hills and mountains.

John Flores explained it as he rode along by attributing intelligence to the cattle. "They figure things about like we do. When you get too hot, you think of a cool place and you go there. When you're hungry, you think back to where you know there'll be plenty of decent feed, and you go there, too."

John was absolutely correct. Ben would have called it pure animal instinct. Maybe it was. Arch suspected that it was, but he had listened to Flores ever since they had been teamed up, and now he was beginning to wonder if even creatures as limited in so many ways as cattle were could not in fact actually think. That was only one of the riddles John Flores left Arch wondering about. The one Arch remembered longest was that story Flores told him when they were brushing out the upcountry where Arch had never been before, came out of the trees upon a gritty bare knoll, and halted to rest their saddle stock.

Northward was a great serrated, uneven skyline of gray stone veined with white quartz, no grass at all, only a few scrubby rock pines, and an aura of sad emptiness that the boy felt, and he was at least fifteen miles southward. John looked up there for a long time, then raised a gloved hand to gesture left and right. "Big bowl under the rims," he announced. "Maybe thirty miles long and maybe ten miles broad. You got to ride uphill for a long time before you get to the nearest southerly top out." John's hand dropped onto the other one on his saddle horn. His lean, mahogany-bronzed profile looked grave under the shadow of his hat brim. "It's all by itself, that big park. There's nothing like it on over and down the yonder side of the ridges, nor anywhere else up there. The first time I sat up there looking down, I thought maybe once, a long, long time ago, it was maybe a big lake. But now it's grass to your stirrups with trees to the east and west, and southward . . . and northward, those darned stone bluffs risin' up so's you got to prop your head far back to see their tops."

Arch looked up there. All he could see was the nearest pine tops, a huge, wide void, then the cliff face and saw-tooth him.

"Have you been up there?" he asked, then amended that since John Flores had obviously seen the big bowl. "Is it hunting country?"

Flores looked around, dark eyes stone-steady, then he smiled a little. "Ghost country," he said, the smile leaving Arch half ready to believe he was being teased. John turned back without the little smile. "I never hunted up through there, but I camped in there a few times. You never saw better feed in your life."

"There must be wapiti and deer, then, and bear and all," Arch said.

Flores faintly nodded. "Yes. And grouse and quail and pigeons. There's something else up there. I guess some time back there was a band of Indians lived up there. What's left of hide houses and teepees, meat-dryin' racks and fire rings are scattered around near a little fry-pan lake at the upper end of the bowl." He stopped speaking, perhaps with his thoughts drifting to Arch's father, that granite, substantial man of no-nonsense and hard work. Flores shrugged thick shoulders, then said: "Folks don't believe in things they can't see or touch." He shot a slightly bemused, almost apologetic look at the tall stripling beside him.

Arch said: "What else, John? What's up there?"

"Lots of different names, Arch. The Portygees who ranch over in border Texas call 'em *costegas*. The Texas Comanches call 'em *pukutsi*, if I remember right, and the Mexicans call them *espectro*." Flores sat a moment, beginning to get that expression of mild apology again. "Ghosts," he said.

Arch at thirteen neither believed nor disbelieved. Like a great many things he had encountered, he did not know what to believe. But perhaps instinct as much as scraps of things he had heard left him with little doubt about ghosts; whether they existed or not — and he knew the Mexicans believed they did exist — the Sutherland hard-headed common sense told him they had no place in the cattle business. Moreover, he and John Flores had been sitting there long enough. He reined westerly off the gravelly little wind-burned hill. They did not discuss that secret high meadow again,

6

until the autumn of the last year John Flores rode for Rafter S.

Arch was nearing eighteen that year. John Flores, according to Arch's father, was probably crowding seventy. "They last a long time," Ben had told his son on the porch after supper one hot summer night. "Maybe it's all those hot peppers they eat."

Arch was incredulous. "Seventy! He doesn't seem any different to me now than he did that first gather I went on . . . and you teamed me up with him."

Ben was no longer young, had not been young in many years, so he knew about those things. "He may not look different, Arch, but he feels different."

"What'll he do? What will happen to him?"

Ben pushed out thick long legs and sat loosely in his old chair, gazing down across the big ranch yard. "You've seen them over at Ganado. They all got relatives, or married children, or brothers . . . they move in with their kin. They're more clanny than we are."

Arch sat a long time in sad thought. He had indeed seen the bent, gnarled old men over in Ganado, faggot-gatherers, threadbare old derelict grandfathers left to mind small children or hoe a squash patch. But he showed none of the resentment and bitterness he felt that John Flores was now going to become like that. The reason he kept it to himself was because his father, fair and honest though he was, viewed protests of that kind as whining weakness.

He was almost six feet tall this season, lean and tireless. He went out the very next day with John

Flores, both of them feeling sad and neither willing to mention it, or its reasons, but when they halted to tank up the horses near a willow-lined little sluggish waterway, John smiled and said: "Maybe now I got the time, I'll go up there to that big bowl under the rims, and loaf away the summer."

Arch said: "The ghosts'll get you, John."

They both laughed, then Flores sat for a while gazing at the ground before he said: "You remember when we rode up to that granite hill and I told you about the place up there?"

Arch remembered. "Just like it was last summer."

"There is something I didn't tell you. Maybe I shouldn't tell you now . . . except that you aren't much of a hunter. There's a little band of buffalo hidden away up there."

Arch's heart quickened. He had seen pictures, had heard endless stories of hunts, had felt buffalo robes, and even knew of the bizarre relationship the Indians had with the bison. But he had never seen anything nearer to a live buffalo than occasional bones. The pot-hunters and hide hunters had swept away all those hundreds of thousands of huge beasts before Arch had been born. He looked steadily at John Flores. "Really, John? Did you see them yourself, up in there?"

"I saw them. Not more than maybe twelve or fifteen. Mostly cows and one big old scarred bull. Arch, it's a secret. You know, there are men all over the territory who would saddle up tomorrow if they knew they could still kill a buffalo. It's a secret place and the buffalo own it." John's dark eyes remained fixed upon Arch's face.

8

"I'm going now. You and I have been *companñeros* . . . good friends for a long time. I share my secret with you, and we will keep it between us. All right?"

Arch smiled, accepted John's scarred, thick hand, and squeezed it.

CHAPTER
TWO

Ben Sutherland died in his sleep at Christmas. Claude Havens who had been riding for Rafter S for seven years and was the oldest hired hand on the ranch, wagged his head and said: "A hell of a time for a man to die." Maybe it was; it certainly ruined Christmas for the men, and for Arch, who was now in his mid-twenties, but if there was a good time to die, no one seemed to know when it was.

Arch had been ramrodding Rafter S for the previous three years, practically by himself, so the transition was not a problem, although it would be a long while before he got over the habit of making critical decisions until he talked with old Ben. And that spring there was an outbreak of death camas on the range, which kept everyone busy. Arch hired Mexicans from over at Ganado to ride the countryside pulling up the plants, sacking them, and fetching them to the ranch to be burned. He paid according to the sack full. It helped, no doubt of that, but as a neighboring cowman, Will Lutz, said, it wasn't possible to get them all, and unless it was a hot dry summer the damned little weeds would flourish right on up until the first black frost. It was always around, like other poison plants, but some years death camas became especially abundant. Lutz, who was as old as Ben Sutherland would have been if he had lived, maintained that warm, wet springtimes made death camas proliferate. He was probably correct, but there had to be other factors that also contributed, because, as Arch told Claude one evening on the way back to the ranch, hot, wet springtimes should also cause the other poisonous plants to proliferate.

All Claude said was: "Hell, I've burned so many carcasses lately I can't get the stink out of my nose."

That same springtime Rafter S had eleven sets of twins born to red-back cows, not an unusual thing, exactly, except that commonly there would not be that many twins born. Badger Plumber, who had ridden for Lutz the year before but who had signed with Rafter S this season, said it had to do with the position of the moon. Maybe, but along with their own duties they had to ride every day to make certain the cows fed both twins. A cow couldn't count and because generally they did not birth but one calf, often they would abandon one calf. It usually did not take long, a week or two, then both twins would be strong enough to keep up. By then, too, most cows accepted the second twin. But until the men were satisfied, they rode every day to be sure one little calf did not get abandoned and either starve to death or become wolf or coyote bait.

Arch had little time that springtime to miss Ben. At night, though, living alone at the main house, the solitude bothered him. His mother had died the second year of his life. He did not really remember her at all, although there were times when he had a dim

11

recollection of a woman, but that could have been imagination, something he had unconsciously adapted from things his father had occasionally said.

It was a good spring, that year. The rains were spaced and gentle and steady. Grass flourished even in the far foothills where an underlying strata of what the Mexicans called *caliche* prevented deep roots from reaching down. The cattle turned dark, shiny red, even the old cows with big sassy calves at their sides.

Occasionally someone would ride in wagging his head; another bloated carcass had been found where the death camas grew. Arch sent Claude to Ganado to hire more *mestizos*. Sometimes they arrived in horse-drawn two-wheeled *carretas* and tumbled little children out as they drove along, each with a sack. That way a family could bring in more full sacks and hence make more money.

One afternoon Badger came back with a team and wagon from filling salt logs, and did not say a word to anyone even at supper, when ordinarily the talk flowed like water. Frank Guthrie, who usually paired up with Badger, told Claude Havens he thought Badger was coming down with something. Arch was told and went to the barn where Badger was forking feed to see if Badger would like to remain around the yard the next day.

Badger was a dutiful range man. He had been at his trade for many years. He had never achieved top-hand status, but he was sound in his judgments, knew livestock as well as he knew the back of his hand, never hung back, and was loyal to the brand he rode for. He was a husky, medium-sized man in his middle or late twenties, and, when Arch walked into the barn, Badger was standing in the rear barn opening, leaning upon a pitchfork, and gazing far out. He heard Arch and turned, then, having finished his chore, walked over to drape the fork from its pair of wall pegs.

When Arch asked if he would prefer staying close the following day, Badger gazed at him a long moment, then said: "Naw. What for? I'm all right. Well, sort of all right." He walked over to the laden saddle pole and leaned on it gazing directly at young Sutherland. "You ever think of marrying?" he asked.

Arch, having come down here because Badger was probably off his feed, blinked, then stared. Marriage didn't have much to do with being ill. "No," he answered simply. "Well, I reckon we all get notions now and then. Badger . . . is that what's eating you?"

The other young man let his gaze go past to the deepening dusk beyond, then began his recital in a quiet, matter-of-fact voice: "I took bags of salt out yonder like I was supposed to and filled the logs. There was Mexes scattered farther out. I could see 'em in the distance. Some was little kids draggin' old tow sacks, lookin' for the camas weed. I heard some talkin' Spanish over beyond a little land swell. Sounded like someone was either mad as hell, or excited, but sometimes with those people you can't tell. I don't speak Mex. I can understand a little, but not when they're talkin' a mile a minute like these folks was doing, so I climbed to the wagon seat and drove around the swell. I'm here to tell you . . . well, there was four

13

little kids with those big sacks, and a girl with 'em, and they was playin' some kind of game. Laughin' and talkin' . . ."

Arch shifted position. In some ways he was a little like his father. Ben wouldn't have been this patient. He'd have growled for Plumber to get to the point. This notion crossed Arch's mind, but evidently Badger was already there, so Arch moved, got more comfortable, and waited.

"I never saw a woman like that before in my whole misbegotten life, Arch. Never. And I've been down across the line a few times, an' I've been to the towns here and there."

"What did you do?"

"I stopped the team and just sat there. She . . . aw, hell, I can't describe her. She had skin the color of . . . I guess sort of like new cream. And hair down to her shoulders, thick as the mane of a stud horse . . . and black. So damned black the sunlight made it sort of bluish. You never saw such a woman. You likely never will, neither."

Arch frowned. "This is what's bothering you?"

Badger raised his head a little. He gazed in an almost pitying way at his employer. "Botherin' me . . . for Christ's sake, Arch, if I live to a hunnert . . ."

"What did she say?"

"Nothin'. She stopped playin' and the little kids run up close like chicks runnin' to an old hen. They stood there lookin' up at me like they was about to run for dear life. I smiled and taken off my hat. I couldn't think of one damned thing to say."

14

"And . . . ?"

"She took the little kids and walked away, walked off in the direction of those other Mexicans a mile or so out. I watched her go. You want to know something? I'll tell you this but don't you tell no one else, 'specially Frank Guthrie nor Claude. It was like . . . the damned sky had fell on me."

Badger stopped speaking and stood there, looking glassily at Arch Sutherland. For a moment nothing more was said, then Badger roused himself and straightened up off the saddle pole. "I've got to find out her name," he said, and turned to leave the barn.

Arch went out front, leaned on the hitch rack, and rolled a cigarette. His father would have had something knowledgeable to say about this, but Arch had never encountered it in quite the same intensity. All the men talked about women now and then, not always chivalrously, but women did not interfere with them at their work, and Badger wasn't going to be worth much for the next few days. Anyway, good or bad, what with the death camas, twinning, and the myriad other responsibilities and worries of operating Rafter S, Arch was not going to become involved, or put up with a lot of nonsense if Badger didn't shake it off.

Claude Havens ambled over, also smoking his last cigarette of the day, leaned on the rack, and said: "Is he sick?"

Arch considered his reply while exhaling smoke. "No. Maybe off his feed for a day or two. Otherwise, he'll be all right."

"Did somethin' happen to him today out on the range?"

Arch squirmed, stepped on his cigarette, and shrugged wide shoulders. "Tomorrow, Claude, I've got to ride to the foothills and see if the feed'll hold up for a month, and, if it will, we'll take some cattle up there and get 'em off the good grass down here for a while. You can take Frank and Badger and begin sifting out some steers and barren cows for taking up there. I'll check with you at suppertime." Arch nodded and walked off in the direction of the main house, leaving Claude leaning there looking after him with an expression of skeptical concern. For some reason Arch had cut him off about whatever was ailing Badger. He straightened up, considered the lights at the bunkhouse, and headed in that direction, but not with any intention of pushing this subject. In a land where men went armed, it was easy to grow up being prudent and discreet.

Arch thought about the conversation in the barn while he was preparing for bed. By then, his reaction was different; he was irritated. He had a hunch his father would have muttered something about this being springtime, the sap was commencing to run again, and let it go at that, so Arch did the same thing. In the morning, when he saw Badger at the cook shack, he acted as though there had been no confidences exchanged, and afterward, over at the corrals while he was saddling up and Frank Guthrie also came out there to snake out a using horse, Arch reiterated his plan for the day, and nothing was said about Badger at all.

It was a beautiful morning, bell-clear to the horizon with a lacing of pale clouds to the east, otherwise without a blemish in the heavens. He rode east toward the foothills astride a spotted-rumped four-year-old he had put in the hackamore last autumn, and wondered how much the horse remembered since being turned out after the work had been finished last year. Appaloosa horses were not his favorites, but this one had come right along. He didn't fight or shy, and, when Arch lifted him over into a lope, the horse did not make a bobble. He was a little taller than most spotted-rump horses, which was in his favor, and he had a better head and rump. In fact, as Arch bucketed along, he decided that the conformation that had attracted him last fall, along with the even, dependable disposition and easy gait, made the horse worth keeping and riding.

The Mexican weed gatherers had little smoky camps here and there, usually near a creek, and they waved big hats as he loped through. He waved back. They were, in the main, a likeable people. Emotional, maybe, and sometimes treacherous, but, hell, those things could be found in any roomful of other folks, too.

He thought of old John Flores. It was like reaching back down into the distant past, and he wasn't even thirty years old yet. John had been special to Arch. He had meant a dozen times to ride to Ganado to look John up. He never had, and after Ben's passing even the intention rarely returned. One of these days, though . . .

There were a few head of cattle northward, off on his right a fair distance. Evidently the arrival of those weed gatherers had upset the herd. They did not ordinarily run from mounted men, but a man on foot for some reason scared the hell out of them.

The feed was good all the way to the foothills. It was also thick and rich up there, just not as tall, but then in shallow soil native grasses usually did not grow tall, and they headed out earlier. The thing to do with *caliche* country was graze it over early because the grass cured quicker than deep-rooted feed.

He nooned at 3:00p.m., ate several biscuits he'd raided at the cook shack, sat within hearing distance of a creek they called Rattlesnake for some reason he did not recall, and let the spotted-rump horse drag his reins and graze along.

Marriage! What the hell was someone like Badger Plumber thinking of? Married range riders were as useless, his father used to say, as teats on a man. They wanted to head for town every few nights, where their womenfolk lived, or else they wanted to bring their women to a ranch, and extremely few cow outfits had facilities for the wives of hired hands. Rafter S had no such facilities. As far as Arch knew, his father had never hired married men. And married riders usually had their women calving in the springtime, too. Hell!

He arose, dusted off, and went over to stand studying the quiet, handsome Appaloosa gelding. A man in the range cattle business could find all he had to admire in a fine-looking, sound, using saddle horse.

They started back with the sun turning red on its downward course toward the blue-hazed far rims, and started up a small band of wild horses that were evidently passing through, because Ben Sutherland had

18

cleared out all the mustangs years ago, his reasoning being the same as it was with every other cowman. There was feed for cattle, but none for worthless, inbred little wild horses, regardless of how colorful they were. A man couldn't pay his bills with sentiment.

The horse knew in which direction they were going — toward home. He stepped out with long strides. Arch laughed at him, but at the same time he admired the length of the horse's walking stride. That was another point in his favor. He could walk a hole in the daylight. Yes, he'd keep this one, spotted-rump or not.

There was a thin stand of cooking fire smoke rising straight up in the windless afternoon to the right, over where Rattlesnake Creek carved its uneven route southward. Willows over there hid the camp. It occurred to Arch that whoever those campers were, they were a couple of miles farther upcountry than any of the other weed cutters, and maybe it wasn't weed cutters, so he reined over there, rode easily and loosely while trying to see some kind of human activity in among the shadowy creek willows.

A horse whinnied. He could not see him, either, probably because he'd been hobbled upon the far side of the creek, but that whinny brought someone to the outer edge of the willows, where he stood gazing out at Arch approaching.

Arch rode within a couple of hundred yards, then raised his gloved right hand in greeting. The man in the tree shadows did the same. Otherwise, though, he did not move.

The last two or three hundred feet did not take long. Arch swung to earth and led his horse until he was close enough to make out the still, silent form of the man among the willows, then he halted, staring.

"John?"

The old man walked out where daylight mantled his head and shoulders. He was smiling. "*¡Oyé, vaquero!*"

Arch almost ran the last dozen yards. He grabbed old John Flores in both arms, something his father never would have done, and in fact something Arch wouldn't have done, either, normally. He was now a head taller. Maybe it was not that Arch had grown that much; maybe it was that John Flores, who was an old man and for the first time in his life looked it, had shrunk a little.

They grasped hands and clung to one another. John's dark eyes glowed with a wet, soft, sad light, then he freed his hand and turned with a gallant gesture. "*Mi casa es su casa, patrón.*"

His *casa* was a Spartan little camp with several threadbare old rugs on the grass beneath the willows, a cooking ring made of round rocks from the creek, a pair of *alforjas* from a worn-out old saddle hanging in a low limb, and two bedrolls.

"Coffee," he said, inviting Arch to be seated upon the better of the old rugs. He studied Arch. "You are a man now. You are as tall as your father was. Someday you will be as broad, too, but . . ." — John shrugged — "you look more like your mother."

Arch's head swung upward. "John, you never told me you knew my mother."

20

Flores squatted to fill two tin cups from the coffee pot, his leathery, bronzed profile gently pensive. "You were a little boy, Arch. Little boys have pain enough just trying to understand growing up. Why should anyone bring them more pain? Here, this is not the best coffee . . ." Flores shrugged expressively.

CHAPTER
THREE

They reminisced, and there was much to recall, beginning with that first trip out for Arch, up until this year when he was sole proprietor of Rafter S. It took until well past sunset even to bring them up to the present. Occasionally old John would turn and look beyond the creek, but since there was a horse hobbled there, Arch assumed that was what Flores was interested in.

It wasn't. They were warming stew in a small three-legged iron pot when a rider coming in from the west made Arch look up and made John Flores smile broadly in obvious relief.

He said: "Well, it takes a long time to fill a sack. Especially when they don't always work, but play, too."

Arch was more curious than interested. "You've got a helper, John?"

Flores nodded into the little sparkling fire. "We've gathered three sacks of camas, Arch. My helper wanted to fill one more. Well, my knees don't bend as easily as they once did. Today I stayed here."

Arch heard the rider across the creek caring for the horse, then coming on through the willows. He was looking up when she walked into the firelight and stopped dead still, surprised to find someone with her uncle.

Arch's breath ran shallow for a couple of seconds, then returned to normal. Without a clue of any kind he knew who she was — the beautiful woman Badger had seen yesterday.

John Flores raised his eyes to Arch, turned slowly toward the magnificent girl, said nothing for a moment, then in a voice as dry as old cornhusks introduced them. "Maria, this is the *patrón* of Rafter S, Arch Sutherland. Arch, this is María Teresa Obregon y Flores, my sister's girl. I am her uncle."

Then John became busy looking for a third stew bowl. "It's here," he said to himself, rummaging. "I saw it here last night . . . María?"

The statuesque woman turned toward the hanging pack bags, turned back with a bowl in her hand, without a word handed it to John, then avoided Arch's gaze while she moved around her uncle to the opposite side of the little fire, and sat down.

She was tall for a woman, perhaps five feet five or six inches tall. She was lithe and round and muscular. Badger Plumber, for once again in his life, had not been even slightly inaccurate in his description of something.

John Flores leaned to refill Arch's coffee cup. He said: "María, this is the little boy of Rafter S I have told you of."

The girl's perfect features came up, with a hint of an impish smile. Her laughter was inward, though. All she said was — "Yes, *Tío*," — and, when Arch's gaze met her glance, he saw, and understood, her amusement. He was tall and lean and weathered, for a little boy.

They ate, and, if John had not kept a conversation going, it would have been a silent, uncomfortable meal. Arch finally got back to recalling earlier times, and after that it became easier for them all, but María Teresa moved soundlessly, cleaning up after the small meal, rarely looked at Arch, and did not say ten words.

Arch was conscious of the time. It was getting late. Claude would have expected him back hours earlier. They still had to discuss moving some cattle to the foothills. Arch arose finally, nodded to the magnificent woman, and her uncle walked out to the Appaloosa horse with him. Out there, Arch said: "John . . . are you going to be out here for a while yet?"

Flores was gazing at the spotted-rump horse. "Another day, maybe. Another two days. We have three, maybe four sacks. In another couple of days I'll be able to go out with María. We should gather another couple of sacks full. You never liked those horses, Arch."

The younger man turned. The horse was standing patiently. "This one's special, John. He's no Indian pony. He's bigger, and he's got a perfect disposition." Arch walked over to test the *cincña*. "We're going to drift some cattle to the foothills in a day or two."

Flores smiled. "I thought of that. There should have been animals up here before the grass cures on the stalk and turns bitter."

Arch swung up and sat there. "What can I bring you?"

John Flores spread his arms. "Nothing. We have all we need."

For a moment they looked at one another, then Arch leaned to extend a hand, and after the clasp he settled straight in the saddle and pulled on his roping gloves. "John, this has been the nicest evening since Paw died."

Flores stood watching the spotted-rump horse lope away. He smiled into the settling night. It had been a pleasant evening. Not many things could make a man forget the aching knees and sore knuckles, make him re-live other, better times, make him feel younger, but it had been this way for the past couple of hours.

He turned at a sound. María Teresa came up and looked out where there was nothing to be seen, but where the diminishing soft sounds of a loping horse still lingered.

She said: "Your little boy is a grown man, *Tío*."

Flores eyed her. "He's not the one who was on the wagon yesterday and stared at you?"

"No. That man was the same age but thicker and not as tall."

Flores shrugged. "Well, little boys become men." In Spanish he also said: "If I had told him, he would have gone with us."

María Teresa turned beside her uncle and walked slowly back to their creek willow camp. "He has this big ranch to run, *Tío*."

"I told him of the ghost valley years ago. It was a shared secret. He wouldn't have forgotten."

"They can't just stop supervising their big cow outfits to go with someone into the mountains for weeks at a time, *Tío*."

John squatted back at the little fire and rattled his coffee pot. There was barely enough. He filled two cups, but María Teresa did not touch the second cup as she sat across from him. "*Tío*, he is old enough to have a wife."

John did not look up from the cup in his hand. "Women think of things like that more than men who are busy from before sunup until past dark." The coffee was too hot. John set the cup aside.

"Does he look like his father?"

"No. Well, he looks more like his mother. She died when he was small."

"What was she like?"

John Flores tried the coffee again. It had cooled a little but not enough. "She was a pretty woman, tall with fair hair. She was quiet. I think she came from Ohio . . . some place back there." John shrugged. "I rode for the ranch that first year, but the next year . . . when she died . . . I was trapping horses on the Borrego Desert. Arch . . . she was not so quick to speak as her husband . . . Arch is more like that. In other small ways he reminds me of her."

"*Tío*, when you told him of the meadow, did you tell him of the buffalo up there?"

"Yes. It went with the rest of the secret."

"Then they are probably gone now."

John looked up quickly. "What do you mean?"

"He's a range cowman. He wears a gun. He is the kind of man to hunt."

"María Teresa, all men are not hunters and even fewer are killers. No, no one from the Sutherland Ranch will have gone up there to kill buffalo."

The coffee finally was cool enough. John tasted it, smiled at his niece, and she picked up the other cup, the one she had declined earlier. Their eyes held across the diminishing small fire. Later, she said: "Did he say anything about you being out here like the other weed gatherers?"

John's expression briefly reflected pain. "María Teresa, men are friends, or they are not. When they are . . . one can own a big cow outfit, the other can pull poisonous weeds." He shrugged as though the difference would not affect comradeship among men.

She smiled at him, drank her coffee, and said: "I'm glad of that . . . for you, *Tío*." Then the smile faded. "My mother used to say if you had only learned a trade in Ganado and had raised a family . . ."

Flores's eyes twinkled. "You're not the only one she said that to . . . every Christmas, every birthday, every Cinco de Mayo, in fact every chance she got. Well . . . some men are suited for that, and some men are not. Go to bed."

María Teresa nodded. "How many more sacks do we need?"

"One. Two if we are lucky. That should give us enough money for the flour and coffee to take up there with us." He paused. "María Teresa . . . why do you want to go up there with me? Speaking of people who should be raising families . . ."

She sprang up. Her bedroll was slightly away from the campfire, over in among the creek willows. "Someday, *Tío*. I'm like your friend, the *patrón*. I have too many other things to think about. Good night."

John leaned comfortably at the fire alone with his thoughts, warmed and fed. It was a pleasant early night. This time of year it would remain pleasant until just ahead of dawn. There were necklaces of stars across a blue-black sky as far as the curving far horizons. There were some things age could not deprive a man of. Perhaps the finest was his ability to appreciate beauty. Another might be his desire to behold beauty.

John stirred ash over coals to dampen and hold his fire until morning and turned to his blankets. The moon was low, there was a hushed wonder to the night, as there had been all John Flores's life when he had slept on the ground like this.

CHAPTER
FOUR

Claude listened, nodded understanding, then said: "We gathered maybe three hunnert head yesterday, Arch, but we didn't finish cullin' out the ones we don't aim to take up there . . . some bulls and a few gummer cows with calves. I figure we can drift them out as we ride, let them go back. I thought you'd be in about suppertime last night."

Arch was watching Frank Guthrie saddling over in front of the barn. "Didn't make it," he replied, and looked back at Havens. "John Flores is out there with the weed gatherers. Farther north than the others. Not far from the foothills."

Claude smiled. "Leave it to old John to figure where the best place is to find them damned bushes. Sat a spell with him, eh? Wish I'd been along. We could've done some memorizing." Claude lost his smile. "Him out pullin' weeds. Jesus, I hope I don't live too long when my time comes to quit."

They left the yard as a foursome with Claude pointing the way. The gather had drifted, of course, but not far because the riders had held it until about sundown, and they were all getting out there again this morning just after sunrise. Some of the beasts hadn't bedded down but most had, and the ones that hadn't, mostly steers, were easy to get around and turn back.

Arch saw a number of animals he did not want to take north. As Claude had said, they would sift them out and let them go back. It was turning warm by the time they had the animals pointed properly in the direction of the foothills. They let the cattle choose the gait, which was slow because they had not eaten yet this morning so they grazed along as they went.

The business of cutting out continued until a little short of midday. Then, Arch rode back and forth seeking other animals he did not want taken off hard feed, but there was none, so when they broke the drive alongside Rattlesnake Creek and swung off to loosen saddles and hobble mounts, eat what they had brought in small amounts from the cook shack, they had their drive shaken down to what it would be for the balance of the trip.

Badger Plumber sat in willow shade with his legs crossed and his hat shoved back, eating. He seemed to be his normal self again. He did not mention the beautiful girl. In fact, he seemed to have perhaps at least for the time being put her out of his mind. He talked of horses, the quality of the springtime feed, the condition of cattle, all the things range cattlemen endlessly discussed, perhaps because in their insular world there was nothing else to talk about. There certainly was nothing else they knew as well.

For Arch, whose private thoughts kept sliding past into the softness of the night before to María Teresa, things seemed perfunctory, almost mechanical. He

30

knew what had to be done. He was doing it. And tomorrow when they got back from the drive to short-grass country, they would start riding elsewhere, watching, doctoring, tending, mucking out water holes, keeping salt logs filled, "chore-riding" his father had called it, the minor but generally quite necessary riding that occupied most of the late spring and summer range country people from morning until dark.

There would be nothing pressing, actually, until after the first frost in autumn. Then they would begin making up their beef drive for rail's end, their annual cattle drive to the railroad yards where ready, big fat steers, as well as old cull cattle, would be entrained for places such as Kansas City and Chicago. Then winter feeding, wood cutting, tending until spring arrived, and the entire cycle was started over again. Arch leaned back, tipped down his hat, and closed his eyes. All his life he had lived with that cycle. He understood it perfectly, understood the necessity for doing everything in its proper season, was confident of his ability to organize it and order it exactly as his father had done for half a century. And up until now it had been enough. The responsibility, the challenge, the worries, and the triumphs. It was all he had thought about.

He pushed back his hat, sat up, and rolled a smoke. Now it wasn't enough. He lit the cigarette, listened indifferently to the drowsy, desultory talk of the men close by in the grass, and smoked to ease the restlessness. He knew exactly what was happening to him. Knew it as surely as he had recognized the identical symptoms the day before in Badger Plumber, after he had walked from the barn to lean on the hitch rail. Hell! The sap was running!

Claude arose, dusted off, and said: "Let's go or the birds'll be buildin' nests in our hats."

The gather was sluggish from here on. With full bellies, half grass, half creek water, and with the sun across their backs, they moved stodgily but they moved, and, as Frank Guthrie encountered Arch on the east side of the herd, he pushed off sweat with a frayed cuff, then spoke.

"I been talkin' like a Dutch uncle since yesterday morning."

Arch looked around.

Frank's lean, bronzed face split into a tough grin. "Badger. Him an' what was ailin' him the other night when he come back with the team 'n' wagon."

"The girl he saw?"

"Yeah. I've been ridin' his hump like a tick bird. What'n hell's he thinkin' of . . . a wife, for Christ's sake. A man can ride or he can get spliced and sweep out saloons in town the rest of his blessed life because he don't have no town trade. He can by God be a free individual, go an' come when he wants to, loaf and drink and gamble an' laugh when he wants to, or he can sell himself right smack dab into bein' a genuine slave for the rest of his life."

Frank kept bobbing his head to emphasize the purity of his logic, the utter irreproachable wisdom of his pronouncement. Arch looked across the shimmery backs of his cattle to the far side where Badger and Claude were dustily visible.

32

"Someday," Frank said, emphasizing the word, "a man might find himself a banker's daughter, or maybe a storekeeper's daughter. Then it might not be too bad. But all my ridin' days I've seen some downright decent men stick their necks into a yoke, and every spring, when it's time for the rest of us to quit the settlements and fan out, they stand back there, on foot, lookin' sick. If they got a bank job or a store job, maybe it's not too bad, but Badger don't know any daughters of storekeepers, and he don't know anything but riding. You agree, Arch?"

Arch nodded because it did not make one speck of difference whether he agreed or not. "Maybe, Frank. I'm the poorest authority on earth about something like that."

"Well, by God I'm not. I'm older'n you, Arch, and I've seen some awful good riders ruined all to hell by female women. I told Badger . . . I said . . . go into the settlements now an' then and spend a few days. Then get back into your saddle and don't even look back. That's the only way to do it."

Arch pointed. "We should have cut that cow back."

Frank squinted, then said: "I saw her earlier. She'll be all right up there. She's barren, sure as hell."

Arch stood in his stirrups. They were approaching the foothills. If it had been a herd of horses, they could have busted them out and got up there within an hour. These weren't horses, so he sat back down and studied the background, distant peaks with their shiny, everlasting sheets of dirty ice.

Frank dropped back to goose the drag. There were some lazy critters back there, and some footsore ones. Someone had to keep them up with the main body of the drive. Arch rolled a smoke and told himself that there had ought to be a law against authorities on the things they denounced and had never even come close to doing themselves.

They plodded the last few miles, bored and warm and dusty, then they were within the low curve of grassy hills and it was cooler, although there was little shade once they left the creek. Because air troughs down from the snowfields miles away came southward along the forested slopes bringing air that had not been warmed yet by the time it reached the foothills, it was cooler. Here, the cattle were allowed to fan out. Here, they would stay because everything they required except salt was at hand; they knew where the creek was, for water, and the grass underfoot was ripe and strong.

Badger was standing with his bridleless horse as the animal drank when Arch walked up also to slip the bridle and stand waiting for his mount to tank up. Badger smiled through a sweat coating of dust and said: "Nothin' like short grass, for as long as it lasts. I grew up near the sand hills in Nebraska. We raised some of the best beef in the country on this kind of grass."

Arch searched for some sign of Badger's recent travail, and found not a single trace. Either common sense or Frank's crowing had made the difference. Arch cleared his throat and looked down at his drinking horse. "We've got to bring up a wagon and some salt in a day or two," he said.

Badger was agreeable. "First thing in the morning is fine with me." He waited, then also said: "Won't be anyone up this far, will there?"

They exchanged a knowing grin, then hauled their animals around to be bridled.

If they rode steadily, they would be back at the home place after nightfall. Or they could lie over. They were equipped for one overnight camp, and Arch did not really care either way, so when they came together behind the grazing cattle, he left it up to the riders. No one seemed to want to head right back, so they went down along the creek to a gravelly ford, which was wide enough to have shallow water, and started making a dry camp. They did not have coffee, or anything else that required a fire, but they had enough to take a few pleats out of their hungry stomachs at least for tonight, and a mouthful or two for morning.

The sun was going, but it would be a long while before dark, so they loafed. Claude went downstream and took a bath. Arch thought about it, but he was strung out loosely in the shade and didn't want to move right then.

Claude came back with his hair plastered flat and said: "There's been some campers down yonder. Not too long ago. Maybe yestiddy or the day afore."

No one was very interested.

"They had some pack mules along. Looked like maybe four or five mules."

Frank Guthrie looked around. "How many in the party? With that many mules it wasn't just wolvers or pot-hunters. Not down this low."

35

Claude spread his salty saddle blanket and sat down before answering. "I don't know. I'm no Indian. But I'd guess there was maybe three, four men."

Frank frowned in concentration. "Three or four men, four or five pack animals. They'd also have three or four saddle horses, too, then. That's got to be wolvers."

Badger spoke drowsily from his flat position using his saddle seat as a hard pillow. "Wolvers! When was the last time you saw any wolves down here, Frank?"

Guthrie yielded without arguing. "Hunters of some kind, Badger."

"Hell," exclaimed Plumber, "it could've been some fellers just passin' through! This time of year men'll team up for company and . . ."

"With four or five pack mules?" asked Claude sarcastically. He pointed upstream. "They left tracks on the far side of the pool down yonder where I cleaned up. They was riding for the mountains . . . straight as an arrer."

Badger had the answer to that. "Pot-hunters, then. Arch, any pot-hunters come around to get permission lately?"

Arch, who had been listening and half dozing at the same time, said: "No. Up this far, if they're strangers, they wouldn't know who to get permission from. I hope they're bear hunters, or wolvers and catamount hunters."

The heat lingered, but up this close to the mountains, with those troughs of mountain air coming down into the foothills, it was pleasant. The men ate sparingly, then Arch finally yielded to the nagging in the back of his mind and also went down to that pool to bathe.

Drying by sunlight had to be accomplished before it turned dusky; none of them had towels along. Nor, for that matter, did they possess a cake of soap, but leaf bathing was satisfactory, particularly when a man was sweat sticky and dust itchy.

The pool had indeed been the site of a recent camp. Sign was all around, and at least one of the horses or mules was a cribber when tied. He had chewed bark off a full-size willow.

Arch finished in the water and went out into sunlight to dry off. He was on the far side of the creek where most of the sunlight was. There were low-heeled boot marks over there. Maybe Claude had not crossed the creek. When he had bathed, there had been plenty of sunlight on the west side.

There were also signs of men having gathered livestock over there to be rigged out. Someone had leaned a rifle or carbine against a willow, then had rocked it forward to lift it, leaving a steel butt plate imprint in the trampled earth. Arch bent to look closer. The plate was longer and much wider than the butt plate of a saddle gun, or, for that matter, of any of the rifles they had hanging in various buildings back at the home place. Someone, he concluded, was sure loaded for bear. He got dressed as the final rays of red sunlight fractured upon a serrated ridge, spilling runnels of dark brilliance outward and downward.

Frank and Badger had a game of mumblety-peg going at the camp when Arch got back. Every time one of their knife blades struck a stone, one of them would swear, but they did not abandon the game. Arch sank down near Claude, who looked around to ask if Arch had seen the sign down yonder. Arch had seen it, but only one thing stuck in his mind.

"Across the creek someone set down a rifle with a big, wide steel butt plate. I never saw one that broad or thick."

Claude squinted. "Across the creek? I didn't go over there." Then he said: "Buffalo rifle."

Arch sat a moment gazing at Havens. Someone's knife blade behind him grated over rock and a man's disgusted profanity erupted.

"Buffalo rifle, Claude?"

"Yeah. Didn't you ever see one of those things? They shoot a ball as big as the end of a man's thumb. Slug tumbles end over end through the air, an', when it hits, it rips a hole you could shove your first into." Claude carefully whittled off a slice of chewing tobacco, cheeked it, then frowned. "What in hell would anyone need one of those things for if he's after wolves or maybe wapiti? Damned gun weighs nearly as much as a horse."

Arch rolled a smoke in silence. When he lit up, he twisted to gaze northward into the far mountains. "You said their tracks went toward the upcountry?"

"Yeah. Straight as a beeline."

Arch sat smoking for a while, then stubbed out the cigarette and shook his head. "I'm going to ride over a

38

couple miles to old John's camp. I'll be back sometime before morning."

Claude started to arise, smiling, but the expression on Arch Sutherland's face restrained him from suggesting that they both ride over and visit old Flores. As he sank back down, he got two deep creases across his broad, low forehead. Sometimes Arch could be as impossible as an Indian to figure out.

Badger howled. This time when his knife blade had struck stone it had broken off the tip. Clasp knives were hard to replace among men who visited settlements as rarely as did the riders of Rafter S. Nor did it help that Frank had ended up owning all the pie-shaped pieces of ground inside the mumblety-peg circle, the undisputed winner. He looked around for challengers but Arch was saddling up and Claude wasn't interested. He reared back in surprise. "Where's Arch going?"

Claude answered shortly: "John Flores's camped over a ways. He's goin' over there."

Guthrie straightened his shoulders. "Hell, old John! By golly, let's all ride over and visit the old cuss."

Claude shook his head. "I think Arch wants to go alone."

Badger had dug up the piece of veined white granite that had cost him the tip off his castrating blade, rubbed it clean on his trouser leg, then bleakly began grinding and honing a fresh point on the knife. "Bad enough there's hardpan under the grass, but there's white granite, too. No wonder the Indians never put up much of a fight over this damned country."

Dusk arrived softly, those runnels of cool air turned a little colder, and the men wrapped blankets around their shoulders as they sat comfortably at ease waiting for the time to come when they could decently roll in.

Frank Guthrie, with old Flores in mind, told a couple of stories he recalled, and Claude did the same. "There are not many left," he said in closing his remarks. "In another couple, three, or four years, there won't be none left at all. You know, when I first come to this country, the best range men was Mexicans . . . only they wasn't really Mexicans. John Flores wasn't a real Mexican."

Badger had to abandon the knife sharpening because of failing visibility. As he pocketed the knife, he said: "You mean John was Indian?"

Claude looked annoyed. "No. He's no Indian. They were Spanish."

Badger snorted. "Every Mexican I ever talked to said he was Spanish."

"Not like John and those other old-timers," stated Claude, stubbornly persevering. "They're the grandsons and so on, far back, of the real old-time Spaniards who first come to this country. Yeah, they really are. They aren't Mexicans at all."

The distinction eluded Badger Plumber who categorized all people with dark hair and eyes and dark skin as either Indians or Mexicans. "Looks Mexican to me," he grumbled, and arose to go in search of his other blanket so he could roll in for the night.

Claude sat there wagging his head.

CHAPTER
FIVE

It was not particularly late when Arch got over where Flores had his camp, but the fire had been banked, and, when Arch reined up and swung down a short distance out to halloo the camp, there was no immediate response. Not until he had called twice, then John's voice came forth roughly, as though he had been sleeping.

Arch went on up, left his horse at the camp's edge, and hunkered by the fire, stirring it with a dry twig, then putting the twig atop coals for light.

John came out of the willows fully clothed and with a carbine, but when he recognized his visitor, he left the carbine leaning against a tree, walked ahead, running bent fingers through his hair. He sat down, nodded, groped for the little coffee pot, and placed it over the fire. As he put in more twigs, he said: "When I was your age, I never bedded down before midnight." He smiled. "That was long ago."

Arch offered tobacco, which John declined, and in turn accepted a cup of lukewarm coffee. "Years ago," he said to the older man, "when you told me of that punch bowl up below the rims, you said there was a band of buffalo up there."

Flores nodded.

"John, that was pretty close to ten years ago."

Flores nodded again, waiting.

"Do you figure they're still up there?"

"I know they're still up there," answered Flores. "I was up there last summer, alone. I was going back this summer, alone, but María Teresa thinks I'm too old. She didn't say that, but that's what she thinks. That's why she's going up there with me. As soon as we sell you the sacks of camas weed and have money for coffee and flour and sugar, we're going up there. I want her to see that place, Arch. I maybe won't see it again after this summer. It's a long ride, mostly through hard country. But I want her to see it so she'll have something to remember . . . a hidden place that hasn't changed."

"Some fellers passed through heading into the mountains a day or so ago, John, with several pack mules. One of them is carrying a buffalo gun."

Flores sat steadily gazing across the little stone ring. "Did you tell anyone, Arch?"

"Not a soul. I didn't even tell my paw. John, ten years is a long while. You said that was a big meadow up there. Men could come over the rims in that length of time. Or maybe some other old-timer knew about the place, and the buffalo."

Flores reached for his cup. "You are too young to know much about buffalo hunters." He sipped thoughtfully, then lowered the cup. "I've seen bones you could walk on for five miles and never touch the ground. They'd take the hide, the hump, and the

42

tongue. The rest would lie there and rot." Flores sipped more coffee, his weathered, smooth old bronzed face russet-colored by the campfire. "Well, with several mules they couldn't carry out many hides. But maybe this is their first trip in. Next time they'll bring along three times as many pack animals."

Arch finished the coffee and put the cup aside. "Tell you what, John. If you'll go back to Ganado, go first to the ranch and pick out a couple of pack horses, then go to Ganado, load up some grub on the pack animals, and head up there. I'll take the riding crew first thing in the morning and with any luck we might be able to catch up to those buffalo hunters."

Arch fished in a pocket, drew forth a pad of greenbacks, and tossed it over. "You're buying grub for Rafter S," he said, to forestall a protest from old Flores, "not for yourself."

John picked up the money. "You don't know the way up there, Arch."

"No, but if those men have four or five pack critters and three or four saddle animals, they'll leave a trail even I can follow."

Arch sat a moment, gazing across at Flores, who seemed to be making a gradual adjustment to this fresh situation the way older men often did — without haste or recklessness. Finally John nodded his head.

It did not occur to Arch that he should have told John to leave his niece behind when he struck out from town with the laden pack animals, until Arch was two-thirds of the way back to the creekside camp, and by then it was too late to go back. But John was certainly that knowledgeable.

Frank, Claude, and Badger were inert lumps inside their blankets when Arch finished caring for his horse and went in search of his own bedroll.

Sleep came slowly. He lay looking at the high rash of stars, thinking ahead. There was no particular reason why he and the crew might not be gone from Rafter S for a few days. Of course, there were the routine chores to be done, but they would still be waiting when the men got back. He pondered his private reaction to those buffalo hunters. There was no reason for him to have reacted as he had, except that, like John Flores, he liked the idea of a handful of surviving bison being able to avoid civilization in a secret meadow. It went with his stockman's way of life. His father had said often that range cattlemen were more like Indians in their style of life than any other people were. They wanted the land to stay unchanged.

Then he slept, and in the morning, when he opened his eyes, Frank Guthrie was over there stoking up a tiny fire to warm himself by. That cooling air from the highlands of the day before had become downright cold this dawn.

Arch washed, ambled over to the fire where his men were hunkering like old crows holding out their arms and hands to Frank's fire, and told them where he had gone last night, and why. They listened, shoved a few more twigs into Guthrie's fire, then Claude screwed up his face. "Real buffalo?"

Arch nodded. "Yeah. John Flores was up there last summer. I got in mind heading off those hunters."

Badger Plumber said: "I've been ridin' in this country a lot of seasons an' I never before heard tell of buffalo around here. Those fellers are more'n likely just pot-hunters lookin' for elk or wapiti or deer."

Claude cleared his pipes, spat aside, then said: "One of 'em was carryin' along a buffalo rifle, Badger."

The men gazed at Claude. "How do you know that?" Frank Guthrie asked, and Arch explained. Guthrie rubbed his thawing hands together and looked into the fire. "You want us to ride along, Arch, is that it?"

Arch replied quietly: "It's up to you."

Claude scratched, gazed out where their horses were standing motionlessly waiting for the warming sun, and said: "Suits me. I kind of like the notion of a few buffalo still being around. But we've got no grub."

Arch explained about Flores's agreement to pick out a pair of pack animals at the ranch, load them up in town, and head into the mountains.

Frank Guthrie stood up and turned, to get his backside warm now that his front side already was, and said: "Let's go. I don't much want to go back and commence muckin' out water holes anyway."

They broke camp, led in their animals, and saddled up. Within twenty minutes they splashed across the creek, located the tracks there, and turned toward the mountains, following sign.

The sun finally arrived, when they were close enough to make out individual fir trees part way up the dead-ahead slopes. The horses were full and fresh and willing. The men were not as full but just as willing. It occurred to Badger about the time they were leaving the foothills that none of them had a saddle gun.

Claude passed that off. "They aren't worth a damn in a forest anyway. Besides, those fellers don't know we're coming."

The uplands were cooler and remained that way except where the Rafter S men crossed an occasional lush grass meadow, then there was heat. It was pleasant riding, but by noon it would have been more pleasant when the men stopped to rest their animals if they'd had something along to chew on.

Badger made a telling remark about that. "Folks who are forever eatin' get fat. I never saw a fat range man in my life."

Creek water helped, and an occasional smoke for everyone except Claude Havens, who chewed, but when they left the creek to press along, their foremost concern was the trail they had been following. It was still easily discernible, but if there had been fewer animals, it would not have been, not to any of the Rafter S crew because not a one of them was a tracker. That was an achievement an earlier generation of range men had been schooled in; it hadn't been necessary to read sign well in twenty or so years. And forests had ways of blotting imprints like shifting sand also had. What helped particularly was that everywhere they encountered a rest halt the buffalo hunters had made, Arch found a cribbed tree, and that removed any doubt but that they were following the right band of men.

46

He tried to read something at each rest stop about those men, but failed. As he told Frank Guthrie, his father, or someone like old John Flores, would by now have had a fair idea in mind about the hunters, their horses and mules. All Arch knew was that one of the animals cribbed.

They were fairly high into the back country by mid-afternoon. Badger, who had ridden for Will Lutz for three seasons, and who had hunted these mountains several times, knew where they were and what was ahead, but he was the only one among them who did, and Badger had not been much farther than they were by late afternoon. He had never even heard of a big punch bowl up ahead, below the rims.

They came out of the trees eventually, with a wind-scourged, gravelly hogback hill ahead. It had a very slight lift to it, which was welcome because most of the day they had been riding steep country, not directly up it, of course, but even angling around it upon game trails was hard on saddle animals.

Badger dismounted to step behind a big tree for a moment of privacy. From back there he said: "This here ridge is as far as I ever been up in here. It butts against a sort of claybank barranca northwest a mile or two. After that, all you can see is treetops."

Arch thought those were the treetops he and John had looked at once, many years ago, but he said nothing except to suggest that they must be getting close.

He was right. Where the claybank cliff face arose, they followed around a slightly harrowing trail of loose gravel with a sheer drop-off southward. There were birds circling below them, and, while not a word was said as they picked their way along, they were astride good, sound horses.

At the upper end the trail boosted upward in a hillside slot that delivered them atop the same barranca they had just been squeezing around. Up here, because the last hundred yards or so had been hard scrambling, they halted, loosened their *cinchas*, and let the horses blow for a half hour.

Claude said: "An old man who was cook at a ranch I used to ride for in Wyoming told me there was no better eatin' than buffalo hump, and right now if someone would hold one of the bastards by the horns, I'd start chewin' in back and work my way forward."

Frank grinned. "I'd settle right now for one of their mules . . . roasted slow over an oak fire."

Badger looked pained. "You've been around Mexicans too long. Mule meat!"

Guthrie came right back. "The Army used to give its worn out mules to the Indians. They said it was the next best thing to buffalo."

Badger was still disgusted. "Hell, Indians'll eat dogs. I've been in their camps and seen 'em doin' it."

Arch was just as hungry but he did not get into this discussion. It interested him as it had before that Badger and Frank, who partnered up at the marking grounds, and at just about everything that required two men, who worked perfectly together, were always arguing. Or seemed to be anyway.

Arch said: "My guess is that we'll top out pretty quick now. Within another couple of miles. Then we'd ought to be able to see the big punch bowl."

Badger, still grumpy, said: "Yeah. If it's up there."

Claude pointed. "From here, unless you're blind, you can see treetops. Just treetops. That means those trees is growin' on a downslope. And beyond them, what do you see? Nothing, Badger, until you fetch up a hell of a distance off against the cliffs below the rim." Claude, having made his point, dropped his arm. "There's something up there . . . a big void of some kind, between those treetops and the rims."

They had better sign to follow from here on because for as long as they were crossing the claybank bluff there were no trees. The tracks went straight toward those treetops. Over there, at the far side of the claybank flat, they halted upon a rather abrupt drop-off. True to Claude's observation, the big trees were growing thickly down that north slope — and farther out was a huge expanse of open grassland. They sat silently awed for a long while, then Badger said: "I never would've believed it."

The men they were following had also halted up here, but it was their last stop and evidently it had been a very brief halt because there were no cigarette butts or boot marks. The trail down was hard going, primarily because neither they nor the men they were following knew this country, and therefore did not know where the game trails were. But there was an advantage to not being able to see your horse's ears very often — it was a direct route and therefore the quickest way down.

Once Frank, who was riding in the lead, straightened and swung his head. "Sounded like a gunshot!" he called back by way of explanation. "Or maybe thunder." But there was not a cloud in the sky.

They had more than an hour of that braced-back downhill riding, then reached less precipitous ground and the horses were relieved; in some ways a direct descent was harder on them than a direct ascent. The men smelled grass. Claude thought it must be ahead up here, which was right, but they would not be sure for another half hour. For some reason, the feed at this elevation seemed to make seed much earlier than the grass back down on Rafter S, and that didn't follow any rule Arch had ever heard of. Usually, grass at the higher elevations grew slower and headed out much later than the grass down at lower, hotter elevations.

Then Frank reined up out of the trees, sat a moment, just looking before he swung off and stood beside his horse, thumbs hooked, until the others came up and also dismounted.

Arch told himself John Flores had been right. This high country punch bowl was huge. Except that the air up here was glass clear, the far cliff faces below the rims would have looked as distant as they really were, and, although the huge meadow ended on their right, which was westward only a few miles, turning to gaze eastward they could barely make out additional stands of dark trees off in that direction.

50

"Hell of a distance," opined Frank, and Arch nodded. John had told him when he had been a youngster that this place was thirty miles long. Right now, he thought perhaps John might have cut it short by a few miles.

The horses pulled and fidgeted. They wanted to get out into all that grass.

Claude, eyeing the sky, said: "Might as well make a camp here."

He was correct. They still had several hours of daylight left, but the tracks they had been following to this point veered eastward, hugging the trees, meaning those buffalo hunters knew better than to ride out into the open country. What made Arch think this was a good place to camp was the doubt he had about how much farther along those other men had ridden. His intention was to come onto them before the hunters had any idea they were not alone up here. They could only accomplish that if they were very discreet from this point on.

CHAPTER
SIX

Arch took Frank Guthrie with him. They both left their spurs behind as they walked around through the trees following the tree line where those mule and horse tracks went. Badger and Claude remained with the horses. The last thing Badger said to his partner as Frank was shedding his spurs before following Arch was: "If you find those fellers, steal their grub."

But they did not find the hunters, and to Arch it seemed that the strangers were experienced at this hunting business. They were reconnoitering the south side of the punch bowl. No doubt they were looking for the buffalo, but mainly it seemed to Arch they were taking their time at familiarizing themselves with the entire area. Evidently Frank had arrived at this same conclusion because, when they paused before springing across a little creek, he said: "Arch, we could be walkin' all night an' still not find their camp."

They turned back, and, as they walked, Frank mentioned that gunshot he had heard earlier, and for which there was no other explanation since there were no clouds to suggest distant thunder.

Arch said: "They been up here at least a day. Sure as hell they found the buffalo."

Frank plucked a grass stalk to chew on as they hiked along. "I've heard it said that buffalo are dangerous critters, that they'll charge a mounted man and upend a horse."

Arch had heard the old stories, too. "I think the old-timers used to get 'em running. Stampede 'em, then, once they're running, they'd ride in close and shoot down into them."

Claude and Badger had a surprise waiting at camp. They had found a big, fat raccoon, had herded him into a small tree with sticks, had killed him with the sticks, and were now dressing him for supper. Claude looked a little anxious as Arch came up. "You find 'em?" he asked, and, when Arch shook his head, Claude looked relieved. "Then maybe it'll be safe to go back into the forest a ways and make a supper fire."

The raccoon was as fat as a sow pig, something Badger might normally have complained about, but they rendered him as best they could, then hobbled the horses, hung their rigs from low tree limbs to prevent night foraging varmints from eating the leather — because it was impregnated with salt sweat — and took their fat raccoon up a half mile where they made a clearing and built a small fire.

Claude winked at Arch as they spitted the raccoon. "Looks like a little baby with his head cut off, don't he?"

Frank picked that up at once. "You should've cut off his little feet. They look exactly like the hands of a little child."

Badger looked at the cooking carcass, then became busy in a head-down position rolling a smoke. He did not say a word.

The meat was greasy but savory. Maybe none of them would have voluntarily eaten the thing if there had been any kind of an alternative, but there wasn't, and they had been a long time between meals.

Afterward, they hung what was left in a tree, killed the tiny fire, and went back down where their saddles were. The horses had grazed out several hundred yards. They were in plain sight out there away from the trees, but no one who was not very close by could make them out in the dusk. The men got down their blankets. At this high place, the sun did not descend so much as it dropped, and those distant high rims were responsible; when the sun got low, the rims simply stood up in front of it. Within a matter of minutes the world went from light to dark.

They lay back, replete and tired. Frank said: "My guess is that those fellers got to be at the far west end of the valley. Or across it, maybe, but anyway a long ride from here. What've you got in mind, Arch?"

The answer was a long time coming because Arch did not have any plan. Up to this point, he had thought only about getting up here. He said: "Damned if I know. Find them and run them off, I guess."

"Maybe they don't run off very good," Badger drowsily said.

"We can teach 'em to," Claude Havens commented, then he mentioned something that had occurred to him earlier. "Who owns this country up in here, Arch?"

Again the reply was slow in coming. Arch had no idea whether anyone owned it at all. His own property line was back about where that barren, gravelly ridge had been, but he did not know exactly where, nor had it ever mattered. "The buffalo I guess," he told Claude. "I guess once, years back, there was a band of Indians lived up in here. John told me that."

Badger's voice lost some of its drowsiness. "You don't expect they're still up here, do you?"

Frank answered quickly: "Sure they are. By now they're likely sneakin' in to make a surround on them buffalo hunters. If they haven't already lifted their hair, you'll hear some god-awful screamin' directly."

Badger lay a moment in silence, then said: "Frank . . . go to hell, will you?"

Everyone laughed but Badger Plumber. He rolled up onto his side, his back to Frank Guthrie, and pulled down his head like a turtle.

There were wolves up here. They heard them in the settling night, and that reminded Arch of something else he had once heard. Buffalo wolves were much larger than ordinary wolves, sometimes large enough to weigh a hundred and fifty to a hundred and seventy-five pounds. And thcy had, in the old days, traveled right alongside the buffalo herds, scavengers who pulled down the weak and ailing, stealing an occasional calf when its mother was not close by. They sounded larger. Echoes of their calling came clearly to the listening range men. Badger sat up, looking out where the horses were. "If those sons-of-bitches smell our animals," he said, and did not finish it as the

55

far-away calls came again. Then, as Badger dropped back down, he turned in the opposite direction so he could look out where the horses were standing.

But he was not as worried as the horses were. They were hobbled so flight was out of the question. The next best choice was to move closer to the men, which they did, and spent the remainder of the night eating grass within scent distance of their riders.

Dawn came with the same abruptness that had characterized nightfall the day before. The sun was well up back down upon the south range, and, when it was high enough to appear over the treetops of that slope uphill from where the Rafter S men were lying, it suddenly rose with a vast outpouring of hot brilliance.

The men went back to finish their raccoon, but this morning, because they did not make a fire, even though the cooked meat tasted good, it was even more greasy. Claude shook his head and smiled: "How long before John Flores will get up here?"

"Not soon enough," stated Badger, whose face cleared on a happy thought. "But if we can find those buffalo men today, we'd get by."

They saddled up and rode westerly, but because the uphill country at their backs made a deep curving sweep, it was difficult to keep track of directions. Sometimes they were riding more southward than westward, and again, if the curving tree line moved around more, they would be riding almost northward. In general, though, they followed Arch and he was bearing basically westward.

56

Claude thought it would be prudent to put out a scout, and volunteered. He had scarcely disappeared on ahead when that rolling clap of deep sound came, twice, with an interval of perhaps five minutes between shots. Arch thought it was the buffalo rifle. The other men had never heard one before, either, and speculated about a weapon that made such a sound even though it had to be miles away.

Frank shook his head. If they didn't find those hunters soon, they'd have killed a lot of buffalo. He also said: "Every place I've been in my lifetime, folks turn their noses up at somethin' like that."

Maybe. Arch was not convinced the buffalo hunters were after the meat anyway. Maybe people had begun to scorn buffalo meat some years back when better quality, domestic meat had become available, but one thing that had increased in value as the supply of bison became less was a robe. No cowhide could turn the cold of winter as well as a buffalo-hide robe.

"Hide hunters," he said in response to Frank's comment about the meat, and Frank slowly nodded his head. He had not thought of that, but for a fact there was nothing better to keep a man warm than a buffalo robe.

They did not hear any more gunshots, but shortly before they met Claude a mile ahead, Badger caught sight of what looked like a far-away cloud shadow, and after watching it for a while, he pointed. It was moving across the plain several miles out, and passing from west to east. And there was not a cloud up there to cast shadows that dark earthward.

"Is that buffalo?" Badger asked.

They rode along, watching. Claude was sitting his horse down near the thin last stand of trees, also staring out there, when the others rode up to him. He looked around and asked the same question.

"Are those buffalo?"

They dismounted to stand beside their horses, which had also seen the oncoming mass of dark movement. But the horses, without ever having seen a bison, knew what that was out there. The men had to wait several minutes to be certain. The herd was angling northeasterly as it sped along, away from the watchers among the trees on the valley's south side, and the herd was at least two miles distant. There was only one animal that large, high, and more massive in front than it was behind, darkly shaggy and stubby-legged. Buffalo.

Claude finally said: "Hell. You know what we're lookin' at? Maybe the last herd of wild buffalo in the territory."

Arch, from lifelong habit, estimated their numbers. As he recalled now, after ten years, John had told him there were only a dozen or so of the animals. He remembered John mentioning one big bull. Now, of course, this was the natural result of being left alone up in here for those ten years. It looked to Arch as though there were about two hundred animals in that tiring herd. Clearly whatever had frightened them into a stampede was far back, because the animals were slowing, were beginning to break out of their protective close bunching. They trailed down to a clumsy trot, and slackened off on that eventually to end up in a walk that several big bulls managed with unkempt dignity. Then the bulls halted and swung about, looking back.

The Rafter S men also looked back. The valley was empty as far as they could see. If the hunters were in pursuit, they were not riding in plain sight, which Arch thought they probably would not be doing, anyway. Obviously those fired-up bison were now close enough to panic to be intently watchful.

Badger broke the long silence. "I remember bein' told when I was a button folks could see those things in herds so big they really and truly went from one horizon to the other when they was migrating."

"And they'll fight a buzz saw," put in Claude. "I heard that many times when I was a kid. A buffalo cow with a calf'll charge a whole train of wagons all by herself, and bulls'll take on a pack of wolves and fling 'em around like busted dolls."

Frank leaned across his saddle, gazing out there. "And we're fixin' to save 'em? Anything that ornery don't seem to me to need a lot of saving."

Arch made a dry comment. "Maybe not against bows and arrows, but you heard that damned cannon those men have got."

Claude left off looking out where the big animals were beginning to fan out, as they settled to grazing, and looked eastward. "Those fellers'll be coming," he said. "This might save us a lot of riding."

Everyone's attention returned to their position there, and their purpose for being there. Frank thought they had an advantage. "They've got to come around in this direction."

Arch glanced around. The forest on the upslope was fairly dense. It was shadowy dark the farther up he looked. "Ride up higher," he told them, "and scout along westerly. We'd ought to hear 'em long before we see 'em."

It seemed like sound strategy. They got back over leather and angled upslope, dodging in and out among the trees until Frank, a few yards ahead, decided they had climbed enough and set off westward again. He halted every half mile or so. They sat, listening. But there was no sound except the irate protests of birds at this invasion of their domain. The most raucous birds were large jays with dark, almost purple coloring and a pointed, tall stand of feathers atop their heads. These were not only noisy big birds, they were also aggressive, dropping to low limbs to scold and rant as the riders passed along. Nor did they relinquish their attack even when the horsemen had passed out of their territory, but skimmed along in the wake of the Rafter S men, indignantly and raucously protesting.

CHAPTER
SEVEN

There were a number of creeks up in here, and over across the big valley the riders saw a white-water drop where a large creek tumbled over an escarpment to fall what seemed to be quite a distance before it reached a large stone pool. They were the full width of the valley distant from that waterfall, which meant that even despite the glass-clear air up here, it had to be a wide stream to be discernible that far away.

Arch thought the hunters they were searching for probably had their main camp another six or eight miles westward. Those gunshots had come from over there somewhere, and so had that stampeding band of buffalo. He was also of the opinion that the hunters would follow the herd, would come around one side or the other of the valley in pursuit, and, because the buffalo band was now closer to the south side, it seemed reasonable to expect the hunters to be coming toward them, but lower down, since their main purpose would be to keep the herd in sight.

Where Arch and the riders with him erred was in thinking as cattlemen thought, which was the way each of them had learned to reason, but they were not in cattle country now, nor were they involved with cattle.

61

They were riding through a land as their fathers and grandfathers had done, with the difference being that those older generations had possessed no preconceived ideas. Rafter S's range crew had crossed a mountain chain to reach this hidden place. More than distance had been breached — time, too — Arch and his riders were in another era, almost in another time.

Frank got his first inkling of this when he pushed ahead through the trees to a small meadow of perhaps twenty-five acres and caught sudden movement from the side of his eye and halted. There were several big gray wolves out there whose astonishment at seeing the riders had halted them in mid-lope. For moments the men and big wolves stared at one another. Then the wolves exploded into wild runs in almost as many directions as there were wolves. In moments they were gone, lost to sight among the pine trees.

Badger was shaken. "I never even heard of wolves that big. That big bastard out front must have weighed as much as a weaner calf."

The men reacted to that sudden, surprising sight according to temperament. Frank Guthrie sat there peering upcountry where several of the wolves had disappeared. Claude Havens made a practical observation. "Next time I go where folks haven't been before, I won't move a step without my Winchester."

Arch said nothing until they had crossed the little meadow, with one stop to sit and stare at the soft earth midway across, looking at the wolf tracks. They were three times as large as the tracks a dog could make, the biggest dog imaginable.

As they passed back into more trees westerly, Arch said: "They must hunt by sight. They saw the buffalo run east and are loping along by keeping them in sight. I thought wolves hunted by scent."

A quarter mile farther along they heard a wolf up the slope a fair distance and far behind them give a series of yapping, sharp barks. He did that several times, did not howl, just made those incisive, penetrating loud barks one after another for a minute, then seemed to wait before repeating it.

Badger said: "He got separated and wants to know where his partners are."

It was a reasonable assumption, and as though to verify it two more big wolves barked, each from a different direction. After that there was silence again. The wolves were cautiously heading toward each other to resume traveling in a pack.

Claude dismounted when they halted to water the horses, and looked all around. "You fellers get the feelin' we don't belong up here?" he asked.

Badger suddenly hissed and held up an arm. Each man immediately took a step closer to the head of his horse, but for now the horses were only interested in drinking water.

Frank looked annoyedly at his partner. "You didn't hear anythin', Badger."

Then they all heard it. Something downslope a few hundred yards moving heavily in the underbrush near that place where the trees ended and the grassland began. Whatever was down there was probably not a mounted man; it was not avoiding small trees; it was breaking them as it moved. Every range man had the same idea at the same time. Grizzly bear! They were not as numerous as they had once been, but there were still enough of them in the high country to require extreme caution. On his hind legs a grizzly might stand seven or eight feet tall and weigh well over a ton. He had been undisputed master of the primitive country for centuries. He was the only animal Indians counted coup on after killing. Nothing could stand up to him, and even a bullet through the heart did not ordinarily bring him down immediately.

Badger said: "Jesus! And us with six-guns!

But Arch turned back from the direction of the noise to gaze at his horse. The animal was drinking, pausing, then drinking again. Bears, of any variety, smelled rank enough for other animals to detect them at a great distance. His horse was not even wrinkling its nose. Arch said nothing, though, until Frank's horse, full now, raised up and turned to peer in the direction of the noise, little ears pointing, eyes intent. The same doubt touched Frank after watching his horse.

"It ain't a bear, I can tell you that. This horse is scairt peeless of even the smell of a little cub bear. If that was a grizzly yonder, by now this darned animal be draggin' me all over the side hill."

Arch handed his reins to Claude, pulled loose the tie-down over his handgun, and started down the hill moving over spongy ancient pine needles without making a sound. Behind him the others also loosened their tie-downs, but otherwise they stood in silence, listening for any fresh sounds.

64

Arch covered a hundred yards and was moving down his second hundred when the big animal down there began moving again, slowly and massively, again, toward the area where Arch was. He stopped, though, and floundered among the saplings and undergrowth again.

Arch drew his six-gun. The last thing he wanted to do was fire a gun and have those buffalo hunters realize they were no longer alone up here. He considered turning back so he might not be put into the position of having to fire. An animal made a wet half-snorting, half-coughing sound. Arch moved behind a tree, selected his next tree, got behind it, and in this manner covered the last two dozen yards. Then, when he stepped from behind a huge pine, he came face to face with a huge shaggy buffalo bull. The animal had saliva and blood dripping from his open mouth. Another trickle of foamy blood came from his nose. He was hard hit. Perhaps instinct told him that if he went down he would never rise again, because he was weaving, occasionally staggering into trees and over brush growth, fighting doggedly to remain upright. And he had detected Arch's presence, had in fact picked up the terrifying scent of a man long before, and that was what had started him moving when Badger had first heard him.

Arch stood stonestill. They looked steadily at one another. The huge bull had been lung shot. He may have been shot elsewhere as well, Arch could not tell, but he knew what caused that blood from the nostrils. Fifteen minutes earlier the bull would have been able to

65

charge. The trees might have protected Arch, but they would never know, now, either of them, how that kind of an encounter might have ended. The big bull was dying, was standing weaving a little as strength waned, as pumping blood filled him up inside. His little dark eyes remained fixed upon Arch.

In this moment of silence except for the bubbling breathing of the big buffalo, these hereditary enemies stood gazing at each other. Arch knew death; not a season had passed since he had been young that he had not encountered it in one form or another. He was able to accept what he saw in front of him, the inevitable crashing to earth of this big animal. It wasn't the thought of death that troubled him; it was what it symbolized this time — the end of a great species. He stood holding his gun to his side, looking, and feeling sad and regretful.

The bull's gaze never wavered. It did not seem vengeful or savage; it seemed to be patiently resigned, as though the buffalo had enough intelligence to understand what was approaching, what he had to accept now. Then he fell. One moment he was braced and steady. The next moment his final reserve of strength failed and he came down to the earth with a crashing of small trees and underbrush. He blinked both eyes very slowly, heaved a big grunt, and feebly gathered his forelegs under him in a resting posture, looked elsewhere, blew out a big frothy sigh, and turned back to look at Arch.

A faint sound up the hill momentarily distracted Arch. He thought Badger or Claude or Frank, or their horses, had moved back up there. Then the big bull's head began to waver; it fell lower. The animal was no longer fighting; he was turning drowsy or weak. His head went down, his body pitched slightly to one side, and he died.

Arch did not move for another couple of minutes. Not until from a great distance he heard the wolves. Then he turned his head to both sides, and looked down out of the forest to the sun-bright, golden grassland yonder, leathered his Colt, and went ahead a short distance for a closer inspection of the big dead bull buffalo.

He had seen many large cattle, larger than ordinary cattle, but not a one of them would come close to being as large as this animal, even though the bull's legs were no longer than the legs of cattle, not as long in many cases, in fact. But his oddly humped body with its tapering away from hump to flank was massive. Standing there, he had been as tall as a big saddle horse.

Arch sighed, lifted his hat to mop off sweat, reset the hat, and turned back. There was no point in looking for the bullet hole, or bullet holes. Arch's father had told him once that when a man or a critter died, it was no longer relevant at all what he had died from. For years that had not made sense to the growing boy, but eventually it had, as now, when the dead buffalo lay back there as though sleeping. One thumb-size lead slug through the lights, or ten smaller saddle gun bullets elsewhere did not make a bit of difference. The bull was dead.

He trudged back, halting a couple of times to stand a moment, struggling against the feeling of depression that had touched him as the bull had gone down, then he pushed steadily up the hill.

Badger, Claude, and Frank were still at the creek holding their horses, which was odd, and the way they were standing, stiffly and expectantly, was even more odd. Arch wondered, pulled his thoughts away from the passing he had recently witnessed with an effort, and shoved ahead up into the scant open area at creekside. Claude looked at him without saying a word. Badger and Frank did the same.

A thin voice spoke from the westerly trees. It was inflectionless and menacing. "Mister, shuck that six-gun! You make one god-damned move and we'll blow your guts out!"

Shock like cold water struck Arch. He waited a moment for recovery, then looked down. The holsters of his riders were empty.

"The gun!" that thin voice said again.

Arch started to look over a shoulder, thought better of it, reached to lift away his Colt, and let it fall. Then he looked.

There were three of them, unshaven, faded, weathered men with carbines in the hands of the first two who stepped from behind trees. The third man was holding a big-bored old rifle with both hands. It looked heavy, and, if there had ever been any bluing to the metal parts, there was no sign of it now. Arch looked longer at that buffalo rifle than he did at the men, until all three of them started forward, then his eyes came up.

The foremost man gestured with his Winchester for Arch to get over closer to his friends. Arch obeyed and not a word was said until the three strangers had completed their study of their latest captive.

The man with the nearly falsetto, thin voice said: "I'll tell you same as I told them. We got two lame horses, mister. One cast a shoe and got bad rock bruises. The other one hurt his shoulder in a fall." The lean man paused to spit amber and shift his cud. "We need your horses."

Arch said nothing. Neither did his disarmed riders. The two other hunters were younger, perhaps in their late twenties or early thirties, but that thin-voiced man was easily forty-five, and maybe older. All three of them were rough, rugged, unkempt, resourceful-looking men, and not a one of them looked the least troubled by this encounter and their clear intention of putting the Rafter S men afoot in a country where survival depended mostly upon horseflesh.

Arch finally said: "Just like that?"

The sinewy man nodded without batting an eye. "Just like that, cowboy. There ain't no law in here but the kind men pack with 'em. We got to have the horses. It ain't like we hanged you. You can start climbin' back out o' here."

Arch's composure returned. "Mind if I smoke?"

The sinewy man shrugged. "Go ahead. But if you're hatchin' some notion . . . don't try it. Like I said . . .

there ain't no law in here, an' we got no time to dig graves so the wolves'd find you."

Arch spoke as he dug out his makings and went to work. "What about your mules?"

All three hunters stared. One of the younger men, a dark-eyed, shaggy-headed man, said: "How'd you know we got mules?"

Arch waited until he had lighted up to answer. "Because you left tracks and we saw them."

The dark-eyed man grounded his saddle gun and leaned upon it. He studied Arch with a fresh interest, but the older man, clearly their leader, said: "We got to pack hides out on the mules. Besides, they ain't broke to ride."

"How many hides?" Arch asked, and got a mean, sidelong glance from the older man. "What's that to you, mister?" Arch trickled smoke as he quietly said: "Maybe nothing much. We heard that rifle being fired a few times."

The sinewy man's narrow, suspicious eyes, widened slightly. "That's our business . . . hunting."

The heretofore silent member of the buffalo hunters growled: "We ain't got all day to stand around here, Al."

The sinewy man swung his head, but the stocky, thick-necked younger man who had spoken gave Al look for look and did not yield his hard glance so Al, the sinewy spokesman for these three, faced Arch to say: "You fellers think you're goin' to steal our buffalo hides, you're wrong."

Claude Havens had been standing near Arch throughout this exchange. Now he spoke. "Take two horses," he said, in an obvious attempt to keep one horse, but Al's little mean eyes glinted with cold humor. "That's right decent of you, mister. Do we look like we come down in the last rain? We'll take all your horses . . . and your guns, an' your bridles, an' your ropes."

Badger glanced up the high, towering mountainside. "It's a hell of a long walk," he muttered, and the sinewy man laughed. Neither of his companions so much as smiled. Maybe Al was enjoying himself, but those other two were not and showed it.

That bull-necked younger man growled again: "Tie 'em up or shoot 'em or whatever you're goin' to do, Al, and let's get on down where the herd went."

When Al turned, slowly this time, to glare coldly, the bull-necked man yielded a little, to the extent of saying in garrulous protest that they only had to pick up another two hides to be loaded, then they could get the hell out of this place.

Arch calculated Rafter S's chances, thought of telling the hide hunters where that big dead bull was, decided not to for some reason he responded to out of instinct more than common sense, and dropped the smoke to step on it.

Al motioned toward the ground with his carbine barrel. "Lie down. And figure yourselves god-damned lucky we don't shoot you. Lie down!"

CHAPTER
EIGHT

Those hunters were good at tying, but they might have been even better if they had not chosen to take all the lass ropes, which left the binding of the robbed riders to leather belts that were susceptible to straining and tearing at the tongue holes. Even so it required a full hour for Frank to get his arms free and sit up to unbuckle the trouser belt around his ankles. Then he bitterly arose without speaking and freed his companions.

Badger got up rubbing both wrists, first one, then the other one, as he looked eastward through the trees, and surprised his friends by not saying something petulant. "Well, at least we're alive." He looked over at Arch. "Was that a bear down yonder?"

"No, it was a big buffalo bull shot and dying. I stayed with him until he went down."

Claude was not interested. "Afoot, without guns, and only the Lord knows how far from home . . . and He isn't going to say."

Arch turned. "How the hell did they catch you flat-footed?"

Claude was almost nonchalant about that. "Easy as fallin' off a log. We was standin' here maybe ten minutes after you'd started down yonder, looking down that way, and that scrawny bastard with the girl's voice called out from behind a tree just like he did with you."

"How did they know we were up here?" Arch asked.

Claude answered dryly: "Those damned wolves, scattering like they did, then callin' back and forth. And those big blue birds with the top knots, caterwaulin' around the treetops."

"They said all this?"

Claude nodded. "Yeah. I'll tell you one thing about those sons-of-bitches . . . if they aren't renegades, they sure as hell think like 'em."

"Or Indians," put in Frank Guthrie, leaning to retrieve the hat that had fallen from his head during the tying. He dumped the hat on his head gazing at Arch. "Now what?"

Arch had his answers in mind, had had them in mind since the hide hunters had ridden off with the horses and six-guns. "Go back to the trail and wait for John Flores. He'd ought to be along in the morning sometime."

Badger groaned. "They took our damned blankets, too."

Frank was not without resourcefulness. "Tonight we build a decent fire. They know where we are anyway, so it won't matter. What we need is another raccoon . . . or something anyway."

Even Badger did not argue with this. Hunger, among range men, was a cumulative thing; they could and often did go for many hours without eating, but then, when they finally sat down to a meal, they did not stop eating until everything edible in sight had been consumed.

They tied their saddles into trees and started trudging back the way they had ridden to get over this far. They found a pair of porcupines, fat and ugly and too dense and stupid ever to do more than whine and complain when confronted with peril. The easiest animal to kill was a porcupine. Wolves and coyotes had trouble because an imperiled porcupine tucked his feet under, pulled in his head, and waited with spines all over, but most dangerous because of his tail which he would slap an annoyer with, using speed and accuracy surprising in such a dumb critter. But men had no trouble. They got two sticks, rolled the porcupines onto their backs, exposing the unprotected undersides, killed both animals, then very carefully set about skinning them. Badger worked in strong silence. Any way a man looked at a porcupine, alive or dead, unskinned or skinned, it was a repulsive little animal.

They made a fire, roasted the meat on green pine limbs, ate most of it, abandoned what was left, washed at the next creek they encountered, and continued on their way, mostly quiet, mostly grim.

Frank finally put his crystallized feelings into words. "Arch, suppose one of us hangs around the trail where old John'll be comin' and the rest of us go after those sons-of-bitches?"

Badger looked disgustedly at his partner. "Them with guns . . . us with sticks in our hands?"

Frank scowled. "Badger, use your skull, will you? It'll be dark directly. Those fellers'll have to make a camp.

74

An' we won't try an run over the top of 'em. We'll try and get back our horses and drive off their animals at the same time."

Claude took spirit from this idea. "Sure. And the feller who hangs back can make a fire so's they'll see it from their camp and know where we're supposed to be sittin' all hunched up, despairin' and cold in the night."

Arch was agreeable. He had been trudging along, trying to find a solution and none had come to him, except the obvious one of striking out back over the mountains to the home place for fresh horses and carbines, which would not only be a prolonged, uncomfortable procedure, but which would allow the hide hunters to collect their last couple of hides and be well on their way.

When they reached the place of that first night camp, they were leg weary. None of them walked any more than was absolutely necessary, ever.

Badger agreed to stay and await the arrival of John Flores. The others rested, had a smoke, discussed their predicament the way men would who were bitter and grim, but not disheartened by it, then Arch, Frank, and Claude went in search of the trail left by the horse thieves. It was not hard to find. The hunters, being men in a hurry, remained down along the forest border of the grassland, obviously riding along in search of the buffalo herd.

It was out there, scattered into individual animals, twos and threes but it was a long two miles out into open country. Arch thought the hide hunters would probably make a camp and await nightfall. Otherwise, there would be no way for them to stalk in close enough without being seen. He had no doubt but that the hunters would also be watching their back trail. Maybe, in their view, the dismounted range men would start hiking back out of here, but those three had not impressed Arch, Frank, or Claude as the kind of men who would be careless.

They found where the men had halted in the final fringe of huge old trees, had dismounted, according to the boot tracks, and had either rested their stolen animals or halted in order to study the distant bison and formulate a plan. It was an easy trail to follow. The hunters were leading their own animals, two of which limped, and were riding the horses they had stolen.

A mile farther along Arch thought he detected sounds on ahead and gestured for silence. It was three lobo wolves; they had been startled by something up ahead and were loosely trotting directly toward the three dismounted range men, looking over their shoulders from time to time.

Frank Guthrie shook his head. "There's more darned wildlife up in here than a man can shake a stick at."

The wolves came within a hundred yards before either scent or instinct made them come to an abrupt halt and peer intently ahead. Frank removed his hat and waved it. The wolves did not even wait this time; they spun and went straight up the southward hillside. Frank put the hat back on. "Wonder what they'd have done if they'd known we didn't have anything that'd shoot?" Then he grinned widely. "They'll maybe cut west again . . . and scare the hell out of ol' Badger."

Even Arch grinned. It was the one amusing thought any of them had had since being robbed and left bound on the ground.

The day waned, afternoon arrived, pleasantly warm in the forest and downright hot out beyond, across the vast valley floor. The men alternately watched ahead, and northward, out where the bison were, but the buffalo clearly had not as yet picked up either movement or scent. Claude was of the opinion that, rank as those hide hunters smelled, they were experienced at their work. "Those big brutes won't know a blessed thing until someone starts shootin' into them."

Arch said: "Come to think of it, I'd hate like hell to have someone aim at me with that buffalo rifle."

Claude made a good guess. "Unless he was real close, he likely wouldn't be able to hit you. That thing looked to me like it was so old and shot out the rifling'd be gone out of the barrel."

None of them was a good tracker, but they did not have to be to figure out eventually from the length of stride that the hide hunters had begun to lope. Arch halted to mop off sweat, then stepped down past the trees and cast a bold glance on around where the uneven tree line went. There was no dust, no visible movement, and not a sound. He stepped back and looked at his companions. "Those bastards are goin' to make this hard for us. They're widening the distance all the time."

Frank said: "They better. They better widen it ten miles, an' even then I'm not goin' to quit."

It was a grim statement of resolve, but a mile and a half farther along Frank began to limp. Boots were not made for walking; they were made for riding. Frank had developed a blister. He sat down at a little warm water creek, removed the boot, examined his blister, and said — "Wish I had some of that porcupine grease." — as he tore a piece off his handkerchief to make a bandage.

The limp was less from here on, but Arch wondered how long it would be before he and Claude developed blisters.

A great haze drifted over the punch bowl. Clouds were sifting in from the northeast. As yet they were filmy, whitely delicate, but far back hovering over the peaks were dirtier-looking darker clouds.

Arch said: "Just what we needed. A damned rainstorm tonight. Us without slickers or even a horse to climb under."

The heat changed subtly as they went doggedly along the trail. Sweat poured, the men stopped at every creek to drink, and by early evening when they were sitting briefly upon a huge old punky deadfall fir tree trying to guess how far they had come, the air had become weighted and utterly still.

Arch looked up. The delicate sheep-herd clouds were moving southwestward. Behind them were the soiled-looking clouds. They had more body and substance to them. "Rain clouds sure as hell," he muttered as they arose tiredly to press along.

Those hide hunters, aware of what could be behind them — some bleakly stubborn unarmed range men — kept moving. It seemed to Arch that they might go to the nearby curve of the valley's east end and start circling around. If they did that, there was nothing to stop them for another five or ten miles. He looked over at Frank whose red, sweat-streaked face showed weariness compounded with pain, and decided to halt for an hour. He did not want to halt, but he did not want to lose Frank, either.

They stopped in a small clearing where a lightning strike years earlier had left broken, blackened trees rotting on their stumps. Frank gingerly removed his boots. The cloth was bloody, sticking to his aggravated blister. He soaked it in black mud, then removed the bandage, and using another strip of handkerchief made a fresh one. Then he lay back in the grass, tipped down his hat, and said: "Call me when someone arrives with roast turkey, dumplings, and dry-bread stuffing."

Claude only sat there for about fifteen minutes, then he fidgeted, finally got to his feet, said he'd look up ahead a way, and walked on.

Arch would have gone, too, but Frank needed the rest. If both his companions had struck out, Frank would have struggled to get the boot back on to go along. Arch made a smoke, lay back in the breathless warmth, watching the moving sky above their little clearing, and wondered where John Flores was about this time. Unless he had been delayed, and it was improbable that would have happened, by now John should be well into the mountains on their back trail.

With any luck at all, he might even get over the last hill and by tonight down where Badger would tell him all that had happened.

Then Arch's thought drifted completely away from his predicament. He thought of María Teresa, how exquisite she was, how she had affected him the same way she had affected Badger, and forcibly pushed his thoughts to other things, not because there was single reason for not thinking about her, but because it would do absolutely no good to think of her.

Frank stirred, lifted his hat to study the darkening sky, and sat up to make and light a cigarette. "Arch," he said conversationally, "did you ever sit in on a hanging?"

Arch laughed. "Never did, but I can sure understand how fellers would feel about catching horse thieves."

"Like that son-of-a-bitch said back yonder . . . there's no law up in here but the kind we carry along with us."

Arch looked over. Frank was dead serious. Arch knew how his father would have felt — and what he would have done if he were here with them, and they finally ran down those hide hunters. He said: "We haven't caught them yet, Frank."

CHAPTER
NINE

Claude did not return so they went looking for him along the hide hunters' trail. He was more than a mile farther along, sitting pensively on a deadfall. He had heard them coming and was looking back, awaiting their appearance. When they walked up, he was skiving off a sliver from his depleted plug of tobacco.

Claude watched the way Frank was walking, popped the chewing tobacco into his mouth, and said: "There's a lame horse up ahead in a clearing. Hurt shoulder. Tucked up, rode down, and abused."

Arch digested this. "Too lame to ride?"

Claude nodded as though surprised Arch would ask. "No other reason for 'em to abandon him, Arch." He spat, then also said in the same conversational tone of voice: "And now they got the mules with 'em."

Frank and Arch stared.

Claude arose from the tree and led the way southward where visibility improved the moment they got close to open country. He showed them the tracks, and sure enough there were mule shoe imprints among the horse tracks.

Arch frowned and looked around. "Hell, how did they manage that? The mules weren't with them when they robbed us."

Claude said: "My guess is that maybe they had a second camp over in here somewhere. For all we know they might even have had their main camp over here." He looked at Arch. "We didn't backtrack 'em after they robbed us. We came eastward after them. No one looked westerly. We just assumed they come from that direction."

Frank was wagging his head. "I don't believe it, Claude. That shootin' we heard yesterday and today came from far off to the west."

"Sure. Because the buffalo was down there," stated Claude, who had evidently used the time he had sat waiting considering the significance of this fresh development. "Frank, they wouldn't leave their mules tied to trees over here . . . a full day's ride from where they was shootin' . . . would they?"

Arch stopped the discussion by starting ahead toward the small, grassy glade where that lame horse was. The animal was tall, and at one time had been a handsome beast. Now he was rough-coated, shrunken until his ribs showed, and never put his weight on his right leg, not even when the three men walked into his glade and he sucked back, rolled his eyes, and snorted at them.

They walked around him. Claude swore with feeling. "Any man who'd treat a horse like this ought to be shot."

Frank was matter-of-fact with his retort: "All right. Just point me in the right direction and show me one of 'em."

Arch looked off eastward as he said: "When we come back, we'll rope this one and take him back with us. Otherwise, the wolves'll pull him down sure as hell. Let's go."

They were running out of decent light to see by when Claude's theory was proven correct. They came upon an abandoned camp where several men had lived for some little time. It was close to the fringe of the grassland, had water at hand, and enough tall, thick feed to support a number of animals for a long time. There were indications that hides had been pegged out in this place. There were scraped low tree limbs men had used to hang things from, and there was a slight pit where ash and dead coals lay.

Frank shook his head, having trouble coming to grips with this new idea. He, like the others, had been convinced the hide hunters had had their camp miles to the west. It took Frank a little time to adjust to, and also to accept, any new idea. He poked around the camp as his companions were doing and paused to look at something underfoot, scuffed away dust, trampled grass, and fir needles, then leaned with an outstretched hand. The object was a tip off someone's bridle throatlatch. It was metal, and, where the pin had held it to the leather, there was an enlarged hole where the small pin had dropped through. It was nothing of much importance but he stood studying it, then walked back to his friends, and they also examined the thing.

Arch had been thinking. As he handed back the metal tip, he gestured across this upper, narrow end of the punch bowl valley. "They went on around sure as hell. They got a better chance at the buffalo from the opposite side." His arm dropped, his eyes narrowed. "After dark, instead of wearing ourselves out walking three or four extra miles, let's just head straight across on a westerly angle which ought to put us over on the far side maybe after midnight." He looked around. "If I'm wrong, when we get back, you two can have a week off with pay."

Frank, who had been wilting a little at the prospect of all that walking, brightened at once. "Done. Claude?"

Havens nodded. "Done." Then he also said: "Westerly had ought to put us pretty close to where the buffalo was the last time we saw them."

Arch smiled. "That's the idea. Those bastards'll camp where they can make their best approach."

Frank sat down where someone, probably one of the hide hunters, had made an Indian chair out of twigs against a scraggly bull fir tree. It had a latticed backrest but no seat. He fished out his tobacco sack, squinted at its depleted condition, then went to work creating a very thin cigarette.

Claude found a gob of animal fat and brought it over. Arch and Claude watched as Frank removed his boot, salved the dried-on caked bandage without trying to remove the cloth, then wiggled his toes and looked up. "Buffalo fat," he said.

Claude shrugged. He did not know what kind it was but the easiest conclusion was that it was, indeed, fat from one of the scraped hides.

84

Frank wiggled his toes some more. "Supposed to have great curative powers," he said, watching his toes. "Indians figured it was big medicine, anyway."

Arch sank down in the still, heavy air. Claude did the same, and after listening to his stomach for a while told the others, if he didn't get something to shove down into that thing directly, he was going to roast his hatband.

The heavy clouds were gradually overrunning their high world of dwindling daylight. They brought with them a definite scent of rain, but Frank said: "They're moving. As long as they keep doin' that, I'd say there's less'n fifty-fifty chance of 'em openin' up and droppin' water on us."

Arch had seen moving clouds deluge a country many times, but he chose not to argue. He was tired all the way through. He lay back, killed a big black ant for biting his neck, then closed his eyes.

Not until Frank was shaking him did he open them again. There was an occasional star visible straight up; otherwise the sky was dark, and even those few visible stars seemed obscured, their weak light diffused.

Claude was down at the edge of the forest, waiting. Frank's limp was less pronounced as he and Arch went down there. Claude grinned, showing big white teeth. "You get your sleep out?" he asked Arch, then without waiting for an answer raised a pointing hand. "That'll be northwest," he said, and started walking. Frank went fifty feet, looked at Arch, and groaned with exaggerated dismay.

"The reason I took up the ridin' trade was because I didn't like walkin'. I'll tell you one thing . . . I'm not goin' to walk back, not even if I've got to make one of those horse-thievin' bastards carry me on his back."

It was warm. Not a breath of air stirred. Sounds were audible a fair distance away, and those feeble stars above seemed to wink off, then wink back on again, as though perhaps the high rain clouds had rips in them as they passed along. Maybe Frank was right, maybe it wouldn't rain, but when they halted after an hour of steady trudging, Claude said: "It's goin' to catch us out here without even a tree to get under, sure as I'm born. You know why? Because nothing's gone right today, that's why."

They were well out into the open, perhaps a third of the way across, when Claude, still out ahead, abruptly halted, raised a hand, then sank soundlessly to one knee. Arch had heard nothing, but he also knelt.

Whatever was out there did not make any more noise. Claude turned, looked at his companions, then shrugged and got to his feet. "Maybe I imagined it," he said, and walked on, but with greater caution and with more wariness to the way he peered ahead and listened.

The second time they all heard it, and dropped down. The sound was like a painful grunt followed by sounds of something writhing against the ground. Arch knew what that was up ahead, without ever having seen it under these circumstances. He started past Claude slowly, and, when the three of them were much closer, Arch stopped and pointed. A large, shaggy dark mound was sitting up, looking back in their direction. It was a

86

buffalo, another ginger-colored big animal that had not entirely shed off yet and had mats of loose hair around its massive, upper body.

Frank quietly said: "She'll get one of us sure as hell." He meant the big animal would jump up and charge them.

Arch shook his head. He did not think she would and with good reason; she was calving. In fact, she was at that point in the birthing process, brief though it was, when someone could walk right up beside her with complete safety.

She dropped back on her side as a spasm arrived, raised her little tufted tail, raised the high side rear leg, and threshed with her head against the ground as she strained. They saw small pale hoofs appear, close together, then part of the head, wet and shiny as the cow paused for breath, then strained a second time.

Arch jerked his head and led the way past. Within minutes, maybe even moments, the calf would be ejected, and within another moment afterward that young cow would be on her feet. That would be when she would be most dangerous. Anyone who had watched range cattle calve would know that the time to leave, if they were on foot, was exactly the moment Arch led his companions onward.

They lost the calving buffalo behind in the night, but now that they knew the other bison were close, they went more cautiously. They had in fact reached the eastern end of the herd. Most of the animals, the more herding ones, were off on the left closer together. That calving buffalo had gone off a short distance to be alone and undisturbed during her time of birthing.

They smelled the bison, and Arch gave a little more ground. The last thing he needed right at this point was to walk onto some cud-chewing ton of belligerence. Maybe they could elude a charge in the darkness, but if man smell roused the herd, it would make enough noise to be heard a mile off in this still, warm night.

It was slow going, but that did not particularly trouble Arch, either. They were at the eastern end of the big valley, at its narrowest place; they had the entire night ahead of them. To the west a buffalo wolf suddenly barked a clear alarm. He had detected man scent. Arch, Claude, and Frank halted. But that wolf dog did not bark again. He was probably hightailing it back in the direction of the trees, along with any of his scavenging companions that had been out here with him. Frank, favoring his sore foot, looked back and said: "Lucky we was between that calvin' cow and those lobos."

Arch tried to estimate how far they had come and thought it was probably more than halfway. One thing that had bothered him since they had started across the grassland was a lack of a campfire on the opposite side. Of course there were ways to screen a supper fire, go back up a mile or so into the forest, or eat before sundown, but it still bothered him.

They saw several of those massive sitting buffalo on their left, and the buffalo had seen them, but long before the sighting they had detected the scent, so they were sitting there, big, furry faces turned, not chewing but not jumping up either, listening and watching. The men were too far eastward to pose much of a threat; otherwise, the entire herd would have been on its feet, perhaps forming one of those shoulder-to-shoulder phalanxes buffalo used against serious enemies. It was while they were keeping a wary eye to the left and also being very careful, as they advanced, not to walk up onto a bison dead ahead that a horse whinnied, and all three men stopped stone still in their tracks. According to Arch's rough estimate they were still not very close to the yonder fringe of forest across the valley.

Claude silently raised an arm to point in the direction of that sound. Then he stepped close to his companions to say: "Closer to the herd. Maybe a tad northwest and not too darned far from where most of those critters are." Claude suddenly dropped his arm, a thought having struck him that had not occurred, yet, to the others. "If that's one of those horse-stealin' bastards and he's sneakin' in for a shot . . . those god-damned buffalo are going to jump up and stampede. If they head in this direction, they're goin' to go over us an' leave mincemeat behind."

Arch started moving again, more briskly this time. He altered course a little, heading in roughly the direction from which that horse had made its sound. Even if that were a loose horse, or perhaps even one that had hopped out this far while grazing in hobbles, it was something to ride. If it had a saddle on, along with a bridle, then there was a hide hunter out here, which would not surprise Arch very much. He had thought hours earlier that perhaps the best way for those

89

hunters to collect the last couple of hides they needed to have a full load would be to sneak close in the darkness for a couple of pointblank shots.

The horse did not call again. Arch thought he was walking in the proper direction. Out this far, everything looked tawny tan in a ghostly way. The far forests on both sides of the grassland blended too perfectly with the night to be discernible, but they were farther now from the south curve of the punch bowl than they had been thus far, so when Frank looked over his shoulder, he caught sight of a far-distant constricted brightness, and grunted. They all saw it. Badger was back there a long way westward, keeping a fair-size fire going.

"I hope it convinces 'em," grumbled Frank without defining who he meant.

Claude leaned, touched Arch's arm, then jutted his jaw Indian fashion to point out something in the direction he was indicating.

A large buffalo was silhouetted against the sooty sky, more tangible and dark than the surrounding tawniness. He was standing there simply watching the men. Arch gave ground at once. This one would charge. He was probably a bull. He was too large to be a cow, and there were only two kinds of bison, bulls and cows. No one altered bull buffalo calves as they did cattle.

Watching very carefully as they gave ground until they could no longer see the buffalo, the trio of range men finally halted. Claude rolled his eyes and let go a sigh. Then he said: "We're too far east, Arch."

They had to start around all over again in the direction of the horse. It was hard work, not because

90

the grass impeded progress or even because the night was cold — it was not cold; in fact it was unusually sultry and warm — but because all three of them had been traveling on stamina alone for a number of hours now, and tough, resourceful, and durable though they all were, physical capability had to be decently fueled or it just simply failed.

Frank's limp was more pronounced again, too. He said nothing, or permitted himself to delay the others, but Arch had noticed how increasingly difficult it was becoming for Frank to walk. He headed in the direction of that horse with fresh determination. If they got that animal, and, if it could be ridden, Frank would be able to ride.

CHAPTER
TEN

The horse knew they were out there; he also knew they were approaching, probably had known it since about the time he whinnied, and the fact that he had not departed suggested to the range men that he could not do so handily. They were correct, but the hobbles that had at one time constricted his ankles were broken. One hobble was hanging loosely. He was standing on it, so at least to him it seemed that he was still restricted in movement, which probably was the reason he had not moved away as the strangers approached. But he was not a spirited animal in any case. He was tough-coated, ridden-down, and lethargic when the Rafter S men walked up and stopped to look at him.

Frank shook his head with bleak emphasis. "Like I said back yonder . . . a man who'd treat his animals like this ought to be shot."

Arch talked his way up, placed a hand on the horse's neck, and made a closer inspection. Claude, thinking that there might be another horse here, walked away, and Frank stepped up beside Arch to examine their catch.

From far to the west wolves sat back and howled; the horse trembled so both Arch and Frank talked to him.

Horsemen were a breed who had learned over many years as much about horses as they had about people; some of them had learned more about horses. Arch and Frank had grown up as horsemen. This frightened, badly used horse they were standing with brought up a strong feeling of bitterness in them both. When Claude returned from his brief scouting expedition, Arch said — "Find anything?" — and, when Claude shook his head, Arch then said: "They've got to be northwest of here, or just north. Let's go find the sons-of-bitches."

They fashioned a squaw bridle from their trouser belts for Frank and hoisted him bareback. He went ahead at a walk. There were more stars now, but the night remained unusually warm. Perhaps the storm was passing, would in fact pass completely out of the area without a deluge, but as long as there was that steady warmth to the night, there was reason to suspect that, stars or not, it might still rain. But starlight by itself did not increase visibility very much, perhaps a half hundred or so yards. What added another fifty yards for Frank Guthrie was being up atop the horse where he could see ahead better than his trudging companions, and it was this advantage, or perhaps a combination of both advantages, height and starlight, which permitted Frank to locate the fitful far flashes of pale firelight.

He halted and pointed for Arch and Claude to search in the correct direction. It took several moments, then Arch caught a feeble flicker. Claude saw nothing until they had advanced another few yards. By then the licking tongues of flame were fewer and farther between.

Claude said: "I guess they decided against a night shoot. When I first heard that horse back yonder, I thought they were out here in the grass inchin' their way for a night shot, an' I can tell you for a fact it didn't set too well with me. One shot an' those critters would bust loose like an avalanche."

Arch only half listened. The stampede they had all worried about had not materialized and it was, therefore, part of the past. Arch motioned for Frank to ride on a way. He and Claude walked, flat-footedly and heavily, but with something now to keep their thoughts off their physical condition. They had a goal in sight finally, and in the first subdued excitement over this they did not reflect upon their unarmed condition until Frank halted the last time and leaned to speak softly: "I could maybe lead the horse on up, keepin' on the far side of him. They wouldn't think much of one of their horses comin' into camp. With some luck I might get us a couple of guns."

Arch hesitated. Now that they were almost close enough, after their night-long walk, something more was required besides grim determination. He was still standing there considering when Frank slid off the horse, landed on his sound foot, eased the other one to the ground, and said: "You fellers could slip along behind me. We only got maybe another couple hours of dark."

Arch, who had made no attempt to keep track of the time, twisted for a look eastward. There was nothing along the horizon to indicate sunrise might not be far off, but, as he faced back again, he decided from instinct that Frank was probably right. He nodded at Frank and was about to speak, when someone off to the left of Frank and the horse, spoke first.

"Stand still! Stand right where you are!"

Claude started and Arch turned to look out into the darkness, but Frank reacted almost as though he had expected nothing else. He said: "Hell! Not again!"

The unidentified voice answered Frank dryly: "Yeah, again. Face that horse."

They turned, and behind them a man walked up from farther off, his legs making a *swishing* sound as he pushed through the grass. Arch kept waiting to hear the other two men, but if they were also out here, they were evidently not moving in because when their captor arrived and directed them to face him, he was alone, without any indication his companions were around. It was that thick-set, stocky man, the one who had argued with the head hide hunter back at the site of the original capture. Arch had pegged him hours earlier as direct and lethal.

The thick-set man said — "Drop your weapons." — and Claude snorted: "You know damned well we don't have any." Their captor's cocked Colt drooped slightly, and he considered his prisoners with a tough, ironic look.

"You fellers must be part mountain goat. Or you sure like to walk."

No one answered.

"Damned good thing I heard the horse 'way out here and come lookin' for him." The stocky man pointed with his gun barrel. "Lead the horse and head for the trees yonder."

Claude said: "You fellers got anythin' to eat over there?"

The question seemed briefly to throw the burly man off balance. "Eat? Yeah, I guess we got something. What'n hell you fellers been livin' off?"

"Raccoon an' 'possum," stated Claude. "And not enough of that."

The captor eyed them with strong curiosity. "You must be half rawhide," he muttered, and wigwagged with the gun barrel again.

Frank went ahead, limping slightly as he led the horse. Claude and Arch were behind the horse. Arch was reaching a conclusion as he hiked, head down. If this one was alone, and, if the other two were on ahead up where they had seen that dying supper fire, then the moment Arch and his companions walked into the camp the odds were overwhelmingly against Rafter S. They might be that bad now, too, but at least there was only one gun behind them, with one man behind the gun.

Arch looked at Claude. He got back a searching glance, a gradual understanding. They walked along without a word until Frank halted, his limp more pronounced, and faced their captor.

"How about me ridin' the horse?" Frank asked. "I'm gettin' lamer by the minute. I can't keep this up."

The thick-set man considered Frank. He had noticed the limp. It was clearly not feigned. "What you got wrong?" he asked before making a decision.

"Blister on my heel as big as a spur rowel," Frank replied. "Got it this afternoon an' all the walkin' since then's made it a heap worse." Frank gestured. "That's another mile, maybe again that much, and, mister, you might as well shoot me right here because I'll never make it on foot."

The hide hunter showed contempt when he said: "All right. Get on the damned horse. But remember . . . I can shoot you off of there before that horse's covered a hunnert feet, if you get clever. Get up there!"

Arch and Claude gave a boost. As Frank settled back astride, he nodded at the hide hunter, then moved out again, holding the horse to a walk that did not offer to outdistance the men on foot.

A slight but noticeable chill was in the air now. To Arch this signified the bearing of a new day even though the horizon was still dusky dark.

Their captor suddenly said: "Where's your friend? I'll guess. We seen that fire back a few miles across the valley. You left him there to keep pushin' in wood so's we'd figure all you boys was still over there." None of the three captives acted as though they had even heard the hide hunter. But he was either savoring his triumph, or was naturally garrulous because he kept right on talking. "I'll hand it to you . . . we never figured you fellers could possibly catch up. And now I expect Al'll be for hangin' you."

Arch could not resist. "That'll be something novel . . . horse thieves hanging horse owners."

The hide hunter grunted as though to laugh, and for a while he had nothing more to say.

Arch could make out the black wall of timber on ahead. There was no longer any sign of that fire farther northward, up through the trees, but the smell of smoke was in their faces as they walked along, and the horse had his head up, eyes and ears set dead ahead. He had smelled the camp, or perhaps the other animals up there.

Claude suddenly spoke to their captor. "What in hell did you care about losin' one horse for? You got ours plus your own critters, and all those mules."

"Al told you . . . the mules ain't broke to ride, an' we had to abandon one of our horses some miles across the valley, an' we got another we're goin' to have to abandon, too. He's went bad lame in the front foot. We need every horse we got."

For a moment Claude was thoughtfully silent before speaking again. "You're willin' to be an outlaw just to be able to haul a few buffalo hides out of here?"

The man laughed out loud, and Arch winced because the sound was sure to carry up through the trees to the hide hunter's camp. If they were going to attempt anything, they would have to do it within the next few minutes. But as Arch looked at his companions, it occurred to him, without any idea that he might try reaching the stocky man, they wouldn't be much help in time. Also, one of them was probably going to die. That hide hunter was still carrying a Colt dangling at his side that was on full cock. All he had to do was tip up the barrel and squeeze.

He was trapped, along with Claude and Frank. The stocky man was never close enough for a rush to be successful against him. Maybe he appreciated the value of a little distance.

Frank halted at the foremost thin fringe of trees, placed a hand on the horse's rump, and sat looking back at their captor. "Where to from here?" he enquired.

"Get down," the man ordered, "and from here on lead the horse. Keep straight ahead. Follow your nose . . . that smoke smell will lead you on in."

Frank slid to the ground, his eyes swinging to Arch, then to Claude, then forward. Arch understood by instinct what Frank was going to do. He studied the forest terrain on ahead because he and Claude might be able to do the same thing.

That chill was less as soon as they entered the trees. The smoke smell was stronger. In fact, dark as it was up in here, little drifting tendrils of smoke came down through the trees, so apparently the fire up ahead was not entirely dead despite the fact that none of the Rafter S men had seen flame for more than an hour.

The buffalo man finally walked up closer. "You fellers hatch some notion you're going to sneak off from me among the trees . . . don't even think it. You wouldn't get two yards." He gestured menacingly with his gun.

Claude answered back, complainingly: "Right now, all I want is something to eat."

Arch knew it was a ruse. Claude never complained; Arch had been with him under circumstances as stringent as these had been the last twenty-four hours; Claude had never been a complainer. But it also worried Arch because the hide hunter was less than seventy-five feet behind Claude. If there had been a way to do it, Arch would have cautioned Claude.

Up ahead, the horse lengthened its stride. It knew the way up through here obviously. Arch half expected it to whinny to the other horses up ahead — unless of course the other animals were elsewhere.

Their captor suddenly closed up the distance even more. He walked with a strong, easy stride, no longer speaking or acting in that bantering, contemptuous manner. Their last chance to escape had gone, Arch was sure of that. The camp and those other hide hunters were no longer very distant. The captor's abrupt growl snapped Arch's wandering thoughts back. "You up there . . . hold that damned horse back!"

Arch and Claude looked ahead where the briskly walking animal was leading the way. The horse's gait did not slacken. The hide hunter swore. "Damn you, I said hold that horse back!"

Just for a moment the horse seemed to slow a little. But only for a moment, until he had squeezed past a particularly dense stand of tall timber, then he resumed his brisk walk again. The hide hunter cursed savagely and raised his six-gun. Arch, hearing the profanity, warily looked around in time to see the gun come up. Then the horse slackened his gait and this time he seemed willing to continue advancing more slowly.

The hide hunter lowered his Colt with a growling admonition to Frank. Arch breathed easier again. He looked up where the horse was, looked over at Claude, and saw the strained, anxious look Claude was directing toward the horse, and swung back in that direction again.

What Claude had seen and what had held him spellbound, and which Arch noticed now as he and Claude got closer to the horse, was that there was no separate set of legs up ahead. No one was leading the horse!

Arch breathed a shallow prayer. Frank was gone. When he had managed to step in among the big trees was anyone's guess; perhaps back yonder where the timber had been so dense the horse had had trouble squeezing through, but wherever he had done it, Frank had got cleanly away.

Claude was staring at Arch. They instinctively moved closer together to conceal as much of the horse from their captor's view as they could. They walked like machines, raising each leg and placing it down, then raising the other one. What seemed like a lifetime came to an end when somewhere behind them a man's breath gushed from his throat in a strangled great grunt.

Arch whirled just in time for the thunderclap of a solitary gunshot to half blind him as the hide hunter, probably reacting from being attacked from behind, spasmodically yanked the trigger, then the hide hunter went down in a mêlée of threshing arms and legs, and Claude sprang toward the struggling men. Arch, unable to see clearly, groped his way back, and the loose horse, panicked by that gunshot and the flash of blinding muzzle blast, lunged dead ahead toward the silent camp up through the trees.

Claude leaned to grab the hide hunter's right wrist, force it to the ground, place his foot on it, then lean with all his weight. The gun slid from flexing fingers. Arch, able to see better each passing moment, stepped past Claude, who was retrieving the gun, caught the hide hunter as the man lunged with his greater weight to hurl Frank off. He caught the man's head, twisted it, and swung. The blow should have knocked the hide hunter senseless. Instead, he sagged, then shook his head. Frank scrambled up, turned, and fired his right fist straight from the shoulder. The blow made a sound as solid as stone. That time, the hide hunter loosened and toppled sideways.

From the camp someone yelled sharply. A second voice joined. Arch recognized that second voice as the peculiarly high tone of the man his friends had called Al.

Claude was pulling Frank to his feet. Arch sprang up and the three of them fled westward through the trees. Frank did not limp; he was running for his life.

102

CHAPTER
ELEVEN

There were a number of shouts behind Arch, Frank, and Claude. There were no gunshots, which was what the fleeing men were instinctively tensed to flinch away from. There was someone charging through the trees, evidently traveling by the sound the escaping men were making. Nor was this any time to be especially concerned with silence or cleverness. That pursuer back yonder was armed.

Finally, when Arch thought his lungs would collapse, he gestured for his companions to fade out among the trees, which they did. Moments later the racket of the pursuer abruptly stopped. He, too, had apparently decided this chase had gone on long enough.

Arch waited, straining for a sound to indicate where the man was. He heard nothing for a long while, until Claude eased into sight from behind a fir tree, and gestured to catch Arch's eye. The three of them rendezvoused with Claude clutching their solitary weapon, the old gray six-gun from that vanquished hide hunter. Claude was anything but demoralized with that six-gun in his grip. He said: "We got to get back our horses."

Frank, leaning upon a tree favoring his sore foot, spoke between panting breaths: "What we got to do is get back across this damned valley, back to where Badger and old Flores are, and take the horses John brought. Then hunt down those bastards."

For a lame man the suggestion had merit. Arch, however, was thinking differently. If they could get back across the valley, which he doubted now that dawn was approaching, they would still have to go back about eight or ten miles to the place where Badger and John Flores were. During that time without any question now the hide hunters would be on their way out of the country.

He told his companions that, if they allowed the hunters enough time to recover from what had happened, they would never get their Rafter S horses back. For a moment Frank looked unconvinced, then he shrugged: "You want to go back to them?"

Arch showed a thin smile in the gloom. "Don't want to, Frank, not with them stirred up and with carbines, but if we don't, we're not a hell of a lot better off than we were . . . except for one gun."

Claude, examining the cylinder, looked up to report: "Five slugs left."

Frank eyed the gun dispassionately. "We should've busted the barrel over its owner's skull. That way there'd only be two of them left." He pushed upright and tested his sore foot. "Lead off, Arch."

They were extremely wary. Perhaps the man who had pursued them was still lying in wait, but after they had traversed a hundred yards Arch heard voices distantly, close to the camp. Two men were upbraiding a third man, which clearly meant the hunters had found their battered companion, and it also meant three hunters, not just two, were over in the vicinity of the camp.

There was a glimmer of watery paleness above the high, easternmost ridges. Dawn was approaching. Unlike night darkness, which had been their ally, morning light was their enemy. Arch stepped up the pace, mindful of what it would cost Frank to keep up, but they were now down to the point where they had to succeed.

The camp was deserted. They could see it plainly through ranks of trees. There was no sign of its occupants, and no one had stirred the morning fire to life. Arch stirred uneasily. That stocky man had no doubt told his companions that the only weapon the manhunters possessed was his handgun. Arch may have made a mistake, coming back here. Surely the hide hunters were searching for the Rafter S riders; they would suspect Arch might try to come back in the direction of the camp.

Frank pointed. Someone had left an open saddlebag lying in plain sight near the center of the camp. Someone had also left a three-quarters full whiskey bottle out there in plain sight. Frank said: "Those bastards are on across the camp waitin' for us to go after those vittles and that whiskey."

It was a reasonable guess. Claude, holding the Colt as though it were the most precious article on earth — which it may have been to these men, in this time-forgotten place — eased out flat, snake-crawled a

105

few yards to a red-barked pine, and looked around. The camp was as silent as it was empty. Too silent — there was not a bird in the treetops. Claude crawled back, shaking his head.

"Frank's right. They're baiting us sure as hell."

Arch nodded. Baiting was easier than trying to hunt down the Rafter S men through a primeval forest in poor light — when one of the Rafter S men now had a loaded weapon.

They went back, conferred briefly, were of one mind on how to handle this, and Frank agreed to remain on this side of the camp, watch for a signal, and, when it arrived, attract attention to his vicinity. Claude and Arch slipped northward on a big, uphill stalk that would lead them far out and around, and down around to the east side where the hide hunters were waiting. The cold had been steadily increasing for more than an hour, but neither Arch nor Claude felt it. They were taking chances that permitted men to think of nothing else, not even cold or heat, or food.

There were game trails north of the camp, and, surprisingly, one very broad trail a half mile above the clearing where the camp was. If the bison had made that trail, and it was hard to imagine any other grazing or browsing animal being large enough to force that big a trail, then there was probably a saltlick back up the side hill somewhere. They used the buffalo trail as far as they could, then curved southward, estimating distances and guessing they were probably well behind the ambushers.

Now they exerted more caution than they had at any time during this hunt for the men who had taken their livestock. Twice Arch passed from sight against trees in response to faintly heard small sounds. Both times it turned out to be the busy movements of small squirrels emerging after a night's long sleep, hungry and energetic in their efforts to do something about it. One of the squirrels ran up to within two yards of Claude and sat up. Claude and the small varmint gazed at one another, then the squirrel flicked his tail and was gone in a twinkling.

Arch was down to moving no more than a yard at a time, and allowing long moments to pass between. If the hide hunters were over here at all, they had to be within a perimeter of approximately a hundred and fifty yards, and they were supposed to be looking toward the camp where the bait was. Arch studied squares of gloomy terrain, did not see a single thing to indicate a man might be anywhere around, and decided on a stratagem. He leaned to whisper for Claude to go back, and, when he thought it would be safe to do so, to signal Frank with his hat. Then Arch found a good place to take his stand, and waited.

It was a long interlude. Arch saw Frank flick between two trees but was uncertain whether this was the result of the signaling, or just a voluntary movement. Moments later Frank moved again. This time, Arch was sure Frank was responding to Claude's signal. Arch blocked in as much territory as he could, and waited.

It happened! Southward and part way around the lower end of the camp, something moved. Arch did not take his eyes off that area even when Claude came along behind him. He pointed and kept pointing. The movement was brief and furtive when it came the second time. Claude let his breath out slowly, then joined Arch in studying the terrain there. The hide hunters had their backs to the open grassland, but there was a stand of smaller trees, not as dense as elsewhere, between them and the open country.

Arch backed clear and turned eastward. He made a wide, long hike this time before turning back to try and edge in among those smaller trees at the edge of the grassland. It was dangerous territory, the trees were not as closely spaced, and, since he and Claude dared not get too close, the hide hunters with their carbines had a definite advantage. That six-gun would be lethal only at close range.

Claude sighted the prone man first, brushed Arch's arm, and they both halted. The man was far beyond the range of their Colt. He had his back to them, had his carbine shoved ahead, and was intently watching the area over where Frank was. It was the dark-headed, black-eyed hide hunter, the one Arch thought was probably half Mexican. For moments they stood motionless, seeking the other man, the one called Al. If he was up in the same area, he and the stockily built one they had knocked senseless earlier, he was invisible.

Then Frank moved like a wisp between two trees, and Arch saw watery dawn light momentarily shimmer on a gray gun barrel. One of the two remaining hunters was up closer to the camp and to the left of it, westward a yard or two, hidden by a pair of very large trees. If

108

they could locate the third man, they would then know which way to move, but for as long as they stood waiting, there was no sign of the other hunter.

Arch made the decision. They started forward, crouching where there was no cover, Claude slightly to the front. The distance to be covered was several yards, something that would not normally have taken more than minutes, but in this instance was to take almost as long as it had taken Arch and Claude to get down among the fringe of tall, thin young trees.

They could not risk having the dark-eyed man look over his shoulder, but, as they stalked him, they also had to keep a watch on the hunter facing toward Frank. Arch had grave misgivings. If that third hunter was around here, and was not being distracted by Frank, he might turn toward the dark man, in which case he was going to see the dark man's stalkers. But they were committed. Arch angled to one side, winked at Claude, and moved still farther to one side, his purpose being to offer still another diversion should the dark man look back. Claude had to get much closer.

But the dark man was evidently an individual of powerful singleness of purpose. He did not move. He was crouched around the stock of his saddle gun, as motionless as a striking snake, never once taking his eyes off the yonder forest where he had seen Frank. And Claude got up within range finally, knelt down very slowly, raised his six-gun, and started to close the last short distance. He could kill the dark man from where he was, but if he could get close enough to disarm the man without firing, it would simplify his escape afterward.

Arch stepped close to a tree, scarcely breathing. Frank must have given them another glimpse of himself, although neither Arch nor Claude knew this, nor would have looked up right at this moment in any case. Claude was moving awkwardly on his knees. He got to within thirty feet of the dark man. Arch scarcely breathed. It was like watching a deadly snake stalking an unsuspecting meal.

Then Claude paused, pointed the gun gingerly, and with infinite care moved another few feet and made a low, soft hissing sound. The dark man started, twisted with a look of quick annoyance as though expecting to see one of his companions beside him, and to Arch the slow, melting expression of complete horror that spread from brow to jaw line was impressive; the dark man seemed to melt with terror, then congeal that way.

Claude did not say a word. He held out his left hand for the carbine. The dark man twisted and just as silently handed it over. Claude pointed to the man's hip holster, got the six-gun, too, then he placed a finger to his lips and pointed with the six-gun the way he wanted the dark man to start crawling. The man twisted farther, swiveled around, and began making his way like a serpent or a lizard, swinging one side of his body, then the other side.

Arch finally looked up where that carbine barrel had briefly shown from behind the tree, and now there were two barrels showing up there. Evidently Al and the burly man had rendezvoused. Arch stood watching

110

until Claude and his captive were past, in the direction of the spindly pines farther back, and began edging away to join them.

It had come off perfectly. It had also resolved the one issue that had kept Arch in knots — the location of that third hide hunter. He had evidently been up ahead, somewhere not too distant from Al, and had decided to come down where Al was to confer.

They made the dark man crawl the full distance to safety before they would even allow him to sit up. He was perspiring profusely despite the chilly air when he finally leaned an arm against a tree to stand up.

Claude handed Arch the Winchester and shoved the dark man's Colt into his own waistband. Then wordlessly they herded their prisoner farther back around in the direction they had originally come from. They neither spoke nor halted until they were a considerable distance on their return trip.

Where they eventually halted, the dark man sank down upon a shredded, ancient stump and ran a sleeve across his forehead. Arch said: "What's your name?"

Without any hesitation the dark man answered: "Josh Levitt."

"Indian?"

"Half-Mexican. Mister, it wasn't me wanted to take your horses."

Arch smiled. "Of course, it wasn't. Stand up, you son-of-a-bitch and keep walking!"

CHAPTER
TWELVE

The sun was climbing by the time they got back around where they had left Frank. The chill was gone, and, while there were shards of ragged soiled clouds overhead, most of that moving thunderstorm that had worried them last night had passed farther westward. Frank came back, sat on a deadfall, and studied Josh Levitt with cold, clinical interest. They told Levitt to empty his pockets. Among the strictly personal things was some pepper-cured jerky. Arch parceled it out among his riders. As they chewed, they asked Levitt about his companions. The hide hunter seemed entirely willing to talk. Nor was he particularly complimentary. Al, it turned out, whose full name was Alfred Clampett, was a wanted man with prices on his head in Montana and Colorado. Levitt was not sure what Al's crimes had been, but he thought they included rustling and robbery.

The stocky man was named Moe Billings. He was a celebrity among renegades; he had escaped from notorious Yuma prison, a feat unheard of among either outlaws or lawmen, and, while Moe Billings bragged often of that, Josh Levitt did not know why he had originally been imprisoned there. Neither Moe nor Al talked about themselves very much, and they talked of their pasts even less, according to Levitt.

"And you," said Claude caustically, "are just a dumb cowboy they talked into joinin' them for a buffalo hunt."

The sarcasm was not lost on Levitt. He mopped off sweat, avoided looking at Claude, and said: "I've been in a little trouble now an' then." He turned finally to look directly at Claude. "Yeah, I was a dumb range man, I guess. But there's no law against hide hunting. Robes bring more than meat from pot-hunting you got to peddle around the towns."

The jerky was like chewing rawhide, but it was flavored well and had remarkable recuperative powers for men who had been a very long while without anything better. Arch finished his jerky and asked where the hunters had the horses. Levitt pointed north-eastward. "There's a meadow up yonder. There's an old saltlick in it an' a big wide trail leading in from the west through the trees." He dropped his arm. "Al first figured we could ambush you fellers up there. You're afoot and got to have horses. But Moe said you were hungry as hell, so we set up the ambush around camp."

Frank chewed and eyed Josh Levitt. "So now, when they find that you're gone, they'll figure we got you, and the bait in camp didn't work . . . so they'll go up and start another ambush by the horses."

Levitt shrugged to indicate he had no idea what his friends would do. He looked like someone who was now beginning to worry most of all about what was to

113

become of himself. The three beard-stubbled, filthy, and rumpled men sitting across from him were not a very reassuring sight, and Levitt knew how dangerous they were, had in fact known that before they had stalked him, because he had been the one who had found Moe Billings lying unconscious south of the camp. He was struggling hard against a feeling that they would kill him. Into a period of silence he interjected a suggestion: "It wasn't my idea, stealin' your horses, but we needed 'em bad. Without 'em we couldn't get out of here with our load of green hides. But I'll make a trade with you. I'll help you get Moe and Al if, when it's over, you let me ride off."

Arch, leaning far to one side to crane upward for the sun in order to estimate the time of day, leaned back and saw Claude's rueful look. Frank was still eating jerky. He did not look at Josh Levitt or act as though he had heard anyone speak.

Arch said: "We've got three guns now, Josh. We don't need to make any trades. From you, we've got all we needed . . . a Winchester and a Colt."

Levitt's shirt front was darkening, his dark features had a greasy, wet sheen to them. "All right," he said, controlling what was obviously an unsteady voice. "I've got sixty dollars in my belt."

Frank swallowed his jerky with a visible effort, waited a moment, then looked up. "Back there where you fellers took our horses you were real *bravo*. It's different now, isn't it?" He looked at Arch. "We got time to lynch this son-of-a-bitch?"

Levitt's black eyes with the muddy whites swung frantically. Arch ignored the man to say: "We've got no rope, Frank."

Guthrie considered. "How about usin' our belts? I heard once that it's been done before. Belts or *cinchas* off saddles, or latigoes."

"No *cinchas* or latigoes, Frank, and I've shrunk so much the last couple of days if it wasn't for the belt my britches would fall plumb down," Arch said.

Frank sighed, stood up, and tested his sore foot. It was still painful; it would have been a miracle if it hadn't been. He limped over to stand facing Josh Levitt, Levitt's own six-gun sticking out in front of his waistband. Without a word Frank pulled out the six-gun, turned slightly to toss it to Claude, and he said: "If we had some blankets, Claude, they tell me a man can shove a gun barrel into a mess of folded blankets and it don't make hardly any noise when you shoot a feller that way."

Josh Levitt may have been as courageous as any of them, but prolonging this kind of thing would sap the courage of any man. He said: "What did I do? All right, I took one of your horses, but I never hurt any of you."

"Horse stealin' is enough," stated Claude, examining the gun Frank had tossed to him. He arose, saying: "Hell, when was the last time you cleaned this thing?" He walked over to show Frank. The gun was indeed battered and dirty. "You treat weapons like you treat horses."

Arch remained aside, smoking and thinking. There were now only two hide hunters left, the stocky man

115

named Moe Billings and that man with the almost girlishly high voice, Al Clampett. Now, too, although they were not as well armed as their adversaries, the Rafter S riders each had a weapon. Frank and Claude had six-guns. Arch had a carbine. He leaned, punched out his smoke, and said: "We've got to take him along. At least until we can get hold of some rope." He stood up, looked in the direction of the camp, and spoke again. "One of us ought to try an' raid the camp. The other two better go for the horses. If they split up, one watches the camp while the other one's up yonder watchin' the horses, that might be in our favor, too. We've got numbers now, as well as guns."

Frank belched, raised his eyebrows, and said: "What did you cure that jerky with, Josh?"

"Nothing," replied the agitated captive. "Just the usual stuff . . . garlic, black pepper, red pepper juice, an' salt."

Frank nodded. "I believe you. The inside of my mouth tastes like a whole damned Mex army walked through it barefoot, and the last bastard scraped his feet."

Arch said: "Frank, you want to raid the camp?"

The sore-foot range rider nodded. Doing that would not require as much walking as going up where the livestock was.

Claude looked from Arch to Josh Levitt, then growled for Levitt to walk ahead. Arch's last word to Frank Guthrie was: "Be damned careful, Frank. They've got carbines and they're going to shoot to kill."

116

Frank nodded, ran his tongue around inside his mouth, lustily spat, and made a face. That jerky was going to continue to trouble his taste buds until he got something else to eat.

The heat was building, the mugginess was gone, and, when Arch found an opening amid the treetops to look up through, those tatters of sooty rain clouds had dissipated. There was nothing up there now but clear, clean blue sky.

They located that broad buffalo trail and did not use it, but padded along above it among the trees where spongy layers of ancient needles muffled sound almost completely. Arch carried Levitt's Winchester. He had checked it for loads, and had discovered the same thing Frank had noticed — Levitt did not use his guns often, and never cleaned them, either. Perhaps that was characteristic, but most range men owned such weapons and did not take any better care of them.

The trail in bright daylight showed dusty imprints of small cloven hoofs. There was also an occasional rubbing tree where patches of dull hair had been scraped off by itching bison. Claude, feeling like an Indian, stalked through the fragrant forest re-energized by the jerky he had eaten. Neither he nor Arch knew how completely disreputable and villainous they looked. There was not much to be done about that anyway. Nor was it pertinent right at this point in their lives.

Josh Levitt knew the way with unerring accuracy, but he halted back a quarter of a mile to hold a hand to his lips for silence. Then he stepped close to say:

117

"Anywhere up in here. One of 'em could be around here any place. Maybe they're both around here. That'd be like Al. He'd want to maybe set up his bushwhack with someone lyin' among the trees to the north, an' someone else maybe lying along the trail another hunnert yards or so on this side of the meadow."

Arch, with little reason for not being skeptical of anything Levitt told them, was inclined to believe the man this time. Possibly Levitt would not have lied in any case, but the possibility was greater that he would not lie when he was out front of his captors, more vulnerable than the other two men. He stood watching Arch, awaiting a decision or a judgment. Arch ignored the man to step ahead and look around. There was nothing to be seen but trees, errant sunshine coming downward with a dusty, cathedral-like beauty here and there, the wide, dusty trail, and ahead, barely discernible, a greater puddling of golden sunlight up where a clearing existed. There was no sign of another human being other than Levitt and Claude Havens. It occurred to Arch that the law of averages was working. The hide hunters had scored against Rafter S twice. Now the Rafter S men had scored against the hide hunters twice, once when they had acquired Moe Billings's gun, and the second time when they had captured Levitt. Whose turn was it now?

Claude straightened up slightly and cocked his head in a posture of listening. He remained in that position for a moment, then straightened around as Arch said: "We've got to split up, Claude. It's two against two.

Each one of us has got to try and find one of those sons-of-bitches."

Levitt started to speak but Claude growled at him, and Levitt remained silent. Claude said: "You want to go north and circle around and maybe find 'em? I can scout up this trail and keep Josh with me as a sort of shield. Arch, you figure they're both up here?"

Arch doubted that very much, but, as he told his companion, in this kind of situation men don't get to make but one error of judgment. They parted. Levitt watched Arch fade out with the carbine swinging in one hand, then shook his head. Claude scowled. "What's that mean . . . wagglin' your head? If you let him walk into something, mister, you're as good as dead."

"No," stated Levitt, "I didn't let him walk into anything. But if it's Al Clampett up here . . . he's as foxy as a tarantula."

Claude considered this, decided there was nothing more to be done, that none of them had had any guarantees from the first time they had looked down into the big punch bowl valley, and was about to motion for Levitt to walk ahead, when that same slight movement of air, or whatever it was that he had been troubled by a few minutes earlier came again. He muttered — "Be quiet." — then turned to look back and intently to listen.

Levitt evidently had heard nothing. He looked back, then watched Claude. When the Rafter range man turned, slightly frowning, Levitt finally detected the very faint disturbance. At once his face smoothed out with understanding. "Buffalo," he said. "They're on the

119

trail, comin' this way. Must be bound for the saltlick."
He stared at Claude. "They always travel with bulls out
front. Mister, them bulls will charge. We better get the
hell uphill or downhill, away from here."

Claude, with much less experience around bison
than his captive, nonetheless had learned respect for
buffalo over the past few days, but not enough to be as
near to panic as Josh Levitt was, so he did not move.
He stood there, continuing to listen. The animals were
distant and they did not sound as though they were
moving fast; probably they were shuffling along the way
they normally moved.

Levitt said: "Mister, we can't just stand here."

Claude showed disgust. "They're a mile off."

Levitt energetically shook his head. "They're a lot
closer than that. They're walkin' along in two inches of
dust. Mister, take my word for it, they're going to be
comin' around the bend in a few minutes."

Claude turned to look, saw nothing, heard only a
slight increase to the sound of many animals shuffling
along, decided Levitt was probably correct and that he
had been wrong, and gestured for Levitt to walk into
the trees on the uphill side of the trail.

They walked without haste although clearly Josh
Levitt, if left to do this his way, would have got a lot
more distance between himself and the trail back
yonder. Where they finally halted, Claude had a
question: "What happens if the horses and mules are
up there in that saltlick clearing?"

"Nothing," stated Josh Levitt, looking westward,
gauging the sound. "They get along with horses an'

mules, unless the horses an' mules get to foolin' around, or get too close, or nose around some cow with a calf by her side."

"They won't scare 'em out of the clearing?"

"No." Levitt looked at Claude. "You was out there last night where Moe found you fellers tryin' to catch one of our horses, wasn't you?"

Claude did not answer, but, yes, he had been out there, and the buffalo had not even got out of their beds when the horse had been close among them. It was a relief to know this. What Claude, Arch, and Frank did not need right now was for the horses to be frightened out of the country.

Levitt wrinkled his nose. "Smell 'em?" he said to Claude.

There was more than bison scent in the air; there was also a rising thin haze of tan dust that lazily made its way up as far as where Levitt and Claude Havens were standing.

"They must not have smelled us," Levitt opined.

Claude was skeptical. "Anythin' that's as rank smellin' as they are . . . it'd be a wonder if they could notice any other smells." Claude looked southward. The bison were just now appearing where he, Arch, and Levitt had been on the trail. A pair of massive old bulls paced majestically past. Claude nudged his prisoner. "Go down a little closer. I've got to see this."

Levitt seemed ready to protest, then he started moving carefully southward, always keeping shelter and protection between himself and the long file of ambling big hairy animals.

CHAPTER
THIRTEEN

Levitt was more alert to different aspects of what was happening than Claude was. Levitt perhaps had more reason to be that way. But in any case he was standing beside Claude and looking back, perhaps trying to estimate the size of the buffalo band, when he said: "This is only a part of 'em. Maybe forty, fifty head. But those damned things are sort of like cattle. If the others saw this bunch start up to the lick, they'll be comin' along in a while, too."

Claude began to think of this rare sight in terms of its relationship to himself and his friends. He asked how large that meadow was up yonder, because if all those buffalo came up here to lick salt, it seemed to him they would overflow the meadow. Levitt was reassuring about that. "Maybe sixty-five or seventy-five acres. If you're worryin' about the horses, you don't have to. No one's goin' to get crowded out of . . ." Levitt stopped speaking, staring intently past Claude in the direction of the clearing but across on the south side of the trail. "Moe," he said in such a low tone Claude barely heard him.

Claude turned to look. There was a pall of dust now. There were also hordes of stinging buffalo gnats, many of which got back up where Claude and his prisoner were standing. At first Claude did not see the man. When he finally made him out in dusty sunshine, he could not determine whether it was Billings or Clampett, but he was certain it was not Arch or Frank, and that was all he cared about.

Levitt, continued, speaking as though he did not believe what he saw: "What in the hell is he doing there?" The implication was that where Billings was standing below the trail, but still close to it, was no place to be, as indeed it wasn't. By now even Claude understood the respect these hunters had for bison. Levitt stared, standing motionless. Then he said: "The damned fool. He's always wantin' to prove how brave an' all he is. He's always got to challenge everything."

But the bison had not seen Billings, perhaps because in the heat, the dust, and their preoccupation, they were not very wary or watchful. If, however, Billings moved now, the movement would attract the attention of the nearest bison on the trail. Billings knew this evidently, because he was standing there among the little spindly trailside trees as though he had taken root there.

Claude wished he had that carbine Arch had taken with him. Billings was well within carbine range but he was too far to be hit by a six-gun. Claude watched, wrinkled his nose over the smell, and only gradually figured out how to eliminate Moe Billings. When Billings finally began to fade southward a step at a time, Claude guessed he was going to try and get somewhere out in the meadow. By now, Arch might have satisfied himself there was no one around. If that

123

were so, then Arch would start heading for the hobbled horses. If Billings reached the meadow undetected and saw Arch out there without any shelter but grass . . .

Claude's worries increased each time Billings took one of those rearward wide steps, then froze in place for a moment before taking another one. He said: "What's he doing?"

Levitt answered matter-of-factly: "What he should have done fifteen minutes ago. He's backin' away so's he can get out of their sight, and maybe get the horses out of the meadow."

Claude required no more confirmation of his own worries than that last remark. He palmed his six-gun, watched the line of shuffling animals, and said: "Those things stampede real easy, don't they?"

"Easier'n horses or cattle any day of the year," Levitt replied. "And those big old bulls . . . when they're fired up an' runnin' . . . will head for anything that's an enemy in front of 'em."

Claude reached and gave Levitt a rough shove. The hunter stumbled onward, then looked back with an expression of wonder and protest. Claude said nothing, but he gestured with the six-gun, and Levitt, with no alternative went down still closer to the trail. But he was dragging his steps every inch of the way. He was also using every tree trunk he could find.

Claude forced his prisoner to go right down to the final uneven line of big trees and here Levitt's expression of fear was unmistakable. He looked around at Claude as though convinced his captor had gone out of his mind. They were close enough to those plodding behemoths to see their little eyes, their short, black little upstanding horns, and the smell was rank and gamey. Claude stepped close to Levitt: "If you move from here, I'll bust your back." At the strained, baffled look he got back, Claude added: "I've got an idea. Maybe it won't work but I'm going to try it."

He stepped away into plain sight. A string of cows was passing. None of them even looked up. He stepped down closer, aimed into the air, yelled, and, when the cows lifted massive heads to stare, Claude fired. He ran straight at the cow bison, yelling and firing. They were stolid beasts in many ways, but not when they were startled or frightened, and now they were both. They whirled away from the thunderclap gunfire, punching each other in their hurtling charge to get off the trail and into the southward forest. Dust rose in choking clouds, more animals caught the panic, even big old bulls that were coming along in the wake of the cows. They, too, tore away southward down into the forest, and except other large bulls or the biggest trees nothing could withstand them.

Within moments after three gunshots, the entire band had broken away southward off the trail. Claude could see nothing but moving, dull shaggy hides. The sound was sudden and loud; so was the reverberation underfoot as all those great animals went charging southward. Panic was contagious, more so among bison than among cattle or horses. Claude turned to look for Levitt. The hide hunter had stepped from his sheltering tree to stand in open-mouthed astonishment. When Claude turned, Levitt suddenly swung to peer down

125

where he had last seen Billings. It had finally occurred to him why Claude had caused that stampede, and, as the horror of this sank in, Levitt seemed paralyzed. There was nothing to be seen down there but more dust, heavier where those great bulls had been leading the procession, causing an occasional small tree to shiver upon impact, then go down.

Claude turned back and without speaking motioned for Levitt to start walking eastward along the fringe of trees just above the dust-choked trail. Levitt obeyed like a sleepwalker. He knew what he was supposed to do. Down where he had last seen Billings he left the trail, picking his way through trampled underbrush and small downed pines, Claude directly behind him.

He halted where dust was beginning to settle, stood a moment just looking, then he glanced back at Claude, who walked on up to look past. Billings was lying partially behind a thick fir tree that had lost its lowest limbs and had suffered trunk damage in the stampede. Levitt moved around to look further, then said: "He's alive!"

They rolled the stocky man over and Levitt used his own hat to raise Billings's head and keep it off the ground. Claude was more impersonal. He picked up the stocky man's six-gun and the carbine, but it had a broken stock and a dented barrel, so he cast it away as he knelt.

Levitt said: "He needs a priest."

Claude leaned for a closer inspection and shook his head. Evidently Billings had tried to run eastward, and he must have succeeded to some extent because,

126

although he had been knocked down and run over, if he had been back where the full brunt of that stampede had passed, he would not only not be alive now, he would be ground to red mush.

Levitt looked at Claude. "You wouldn't have a little whiskey?"

Claude did not even answer. He had deliberately engineered this injured man's end, and he had no regrets about that at all. But he leaned to place a twisted arm gently into its proper position. Billings's face was untouched but his clothing was torn, his chest and lower body had been trod on repeatedly, there was flung-back blood from his lips past one cheek to the ear. Claude thought that, if Billings lasted a half hour, he would be doing very well.

Levitt rocked back, beginning to accept the inevitable. "What a hell of a way to die," he murmured.

Claude had said nothing to this point and he did not say anything now. He turned, though, to look southward where the bison had by now burst out of the trees and were back upon the grassland where sunshine brought highlights to the dust. They were slowing.

Claude looked back at the dying man, and got a surprise. Billings was staring straight at him. Claude finally broke his silence. "Where's Clampett?"

Billings completely ignored Levitt. "Go to hell," he weakly said. Then he also said: "How bad is it?"

"You won't be goin' out of here," Claude told him.

"Where was you?"

"Across the trail northward. We saw you stand up and start easin' back southward."

"Why didn't you shoot?"

"Because I didn't have a carbine. Otherwise, take my word for it, I would have."

Billings made a bubbly cough, then turned his eyes. "Levitt, you bastard. Sold us out, didn't you?"

"No. They caught me lying flat in the grass, Billings. I didn't have any chance at all."

"You damned liar," said the dying man, his eyes shiny with malevolence.

Claude supported Levitt. "He told you the truth. He didn't sell out to us. We caught him south of your camp on his belly in the grass, took him prisoner for his guns. One more time . . . where's Clampett? Down at the camp or up here?"

Billings drifted his gaze slowly back to Claude's face, but now there was no longer much brightness to his stare. He did not speak right away, simply remained as he was, his broken chest barely rising and falling.

Claude said: "Never mind. We'll get Clampett. You got any family you want something passed along to?"

"You lousy . . . bastard . . . you," Billings said, pushing each word out with clear effort.

Claude leaned back to wait and took out the nubbin of his tobacco plug, all that was left. He carefully sliced off a bare cud and shoved it into his mouth, replaced the plug, re-buttoned the shirt pocket, and raised his eyes. The trampled man was dead. Levitt was hunkering over him, staring. Claude heard something back on the trail and whirled with Billings's six-gun in his fist. It was a better weapon than the one he had taken from Levitt.

128

Arch called, and Claude let go a big breath of relief as he stood up to gesture. Arch came down through the rubble where the buffalo had torn and mutilated the earth, saw the dead man half behind the bruised old fir tree, and moved in for a closer look.

Claude turned aside, spat, and, when he turned back, Arch was looking at him. Arch said: "That was you fired the shots?"

Claude nodded. "Yeah. I saw him down here and, when he started movin' to get clear, figured he'd head for the clearing. Levitt figured that, too. I thought you'd likely be out there in the open gettin' the horses. He had a Winchester."

Arch looked back where Levitt was coming heavily upright from his kneeling position. "The horses are out there," Arch told Claude without facing him. "Tucked up but not too bad off. The mules and a couple other horses are out there, too. One's lame as hell." Arch finished his study of the dead man and looked back at Claude. He smiled and said: "Thanks."

Claude curtly nodded. "Clampett's still loose, Arch."

"Yeah. And I think he's got a belly full of fightin' by now, so we better get the horses and mules away from here. Afoot, we can find him. On horseback, maybe not."

Levitt was looking at them. Whatever else he was, clearly Levitt did not possess their intransigence, their range-bred hardness, which, if they had lacked it, would have prevented them being where they were now, victorious, after starting out with nothing but resolve.

Levitt gestured earthward. "You goin' to leave him here?"

Claude said: "We should, the worthless, horse-thievin' bastard." He cocked an eye at the swarthy man. "I thought you didn't care much for Billings."

"I didn't," replied Levitt, "but anyone deserves better'n to be left here to be gnawed on by wolves, don't he?"

Claude did not reply. He turned toward Arch. "Anything to lead the horses and mules with out there?"

There was. "Two lass ropes hanging in a tree. I guess they used them to lead the horses up here. Cut 'em up and we can fashion some squaw bridles and lead shanks." Arch looked Claude up and down. "You all right?"

Claude's sunken eyes glinted. "Naw. I'm hungry."

They set Levitt in front and started back toward the meadow. Dust was hanging in the air like a tan pall; every breath smelled of buffalo. There was not a sound, not a bird or small animal anywhere around. Perhaps the earth-shaking tumult those bison had created was responsible, but the three men walking through dust, and in dust almost to their ankles, were utterly alone. Only when they reached the edge of the sun bright, dusty clearing and the distant horses and mules caught their movement, looked up and acted a little nervous, did they return to the company of other creatures.

The lariats Arch had mentioned were each forty feet long. Levitt demonstrated a virtue neither of his companions possessed. When he cut the ropes into lead-rope lengths, he deftly and almost effortlessly made a small braided knot at each end to prevent unraveling. When he glanced up, saw that he was being watched, he said: "My grandfather was a Mex. He could braid and plait better'n anyone I ever knew. He taught me."

Claude said: "Did he also teach you to steal horses?"

Arch was fashioning a squaw bridle. "We hadn't ought to cut both ropes or we're not going to have enough length left to hang this son-of-a-bitch," he muttered.

Levitt did not speak.

They went ahead out across the lush grass of the meadow toward those hobbled animals on across it, without having to hold the ropes behind them because hobbled animals could not escape easily, even when they saw men with ropes approaching. Unless, of course, they were old hands in the hobbles, and evidently none of these beasts was because they all stood, hunched and afraid, but made no attempt to hop away.

CHAPTER
FOURTEEN

Frank Guthrie knew they were coming. He knew someone on horseback was coming. He moved to one side with a carbine and waited, not worried as much as anxious, and, when he saw them, recognized Arch and Claude, he let them get up very close, then stepped into sight looking at that little Spanish mule with the dead man tied across its back.

"Who's that?" he asked.

The men dismounted. Levitt stepped aside to hold his horse and the laden mule.

Arch said: "The feller we knocked senseless. His name was Billings."

Frank nodded. "I heard the shooting."

"He wasn't shot. The buffalo stampeded over him. The shooting was to get the stampede started." Arch looked around. "Did you raid the camp?"

"Yeah. But there wasn't anyone over there."

Claude scowled. "You sure?"

Frank was sure. "Yes. I scouted hell out of it, didn't see a soul, and made a couple of fake passes, then went on in. Nothing, Claude."

Arch was looking at Frank Guthrie when Claude said: "Where in hell is Clampett?"

Frank had no answer, so he pointed and said: "Their saddlebags with the food, and that bottle of whiskey, are down yonder among the trees."

Claude started past, leading his horse. Three of the mules dutifully followed. Arch remained with Levitt and the laden mule. Frank, guessing Arch's thoughts, said: "I can't explain it. Clampett just plain wasn't over there."

"You went out into the clearing?"

"Yeah, finally, right after I heard those gunshots and all that other racket up yonder. Picked up their grub and this carbine and walked back . . . standin' straight up, Arch, in plain sight." After a pause, Frank added: "Maybe the shots spooked him. Maybe he wasn't never over there. All I know is that I scouted up the place real good, and couldn't find hide nor hair of anyone. And he sure as hell wasn't there. That's all."

They took the animals on down where Claude was sitting on the ground, eating, his horse and the mules looking on with fatalistic patience.

Frank went to the horse he had ridden from the home place, looked him over carefully, ran a hand down both front legs, then arose to say: "Whichever one of those bastards rode my animal didn't abuse him."

Levitt looked at Frank. "I rode him."

They offered Levitt food but he settled for one swallow from the whiskey bottle, and sat there in deep tree shade, silent and detached in manner. He finally looked up to say: "No matter what those hides'll bring, they'd never be worth it."

Arch was worried about Clampett. He mentally inventoried the weapons. He had seen that shattered Winchester up where Claude had flung it, and they had Levitt's Winchester. Now, too, Frank had a Winchester. The hide hunters had only had three. Hell, Clampett was out there somewhere with that damned buffalo rifle!

He stopped eating to look out among the trees. The buffalo stampede no doubt had upset Clampett, had perhaps sent him fleeing from its close-by sound, but that was not going to influence what Clampett did for very long. He arose, dusted his britches, and said: "Let's go. Let's get the hell out of these trees and get across the valley."

Frank was ready but Claude was still stuffing food into himself. He gazed at Arch, swallowed, then said: "He's around here, maybe?"

Arch's answer was impatient. "No. Or by now he'd have blown someone's head off. Claude, the buffalo gun is missing."

They gathered the food, the other things Frank had brought from the camp, and wished they dared linger long enough to go back over there and take the saddles as well. Riding bareback was all right for kids and Indians, but a range man without his saddle was like a bull without cows or a squirrel without a tree.

They had no trouble with the mules, and, as they worked their way down toward the grassland, they came to admire the mules more. Someone had spent a lot of time with them. Claude handed the shank of the mule bearing the dead man to Levitt, but the other mules were loose. They picked their way among the trees, following after the riders exactly the way everyone thought a good mule should do, but which few mules ever actually did.

Claude was still eating when they reached the last stand of timber and halted while Arch dismounted to walk out a few yards. They were west of the hide hunters' abandoned camp, and southward. If someone had in mind ambushing a party of riders from afoot, down here would be the place to attempt it because once the horsemen left their timbered shelter and crossed out into the open, sun-lighted valley floor, they would be perfect targets. But Arch saw nothing to make him suspicious. As he went back to mount again, though, he was worried. If they could have had some idea where Clampett was . . .

Arch went first with Frank directly behind him, and then Levitt, the mules, and Claude. But Claude was not eating now; he was riding with a carbine across his lap, keeping his head turning constantly. Not a word was said. The animals plodded along with the mules lingering in the vicinity of the led mule on Levitt's right side.

The sun was off center, the heat was full and steady, and there was a blur of haze over across the valley and southward where those forested high peaks stair-stepped their way toward a pale skyline. Arch was wet down the front of his shirt and in back across the shoulders. Not knowing was harder than knowing, he told himself, and wanted to urge his horse over into a lope. The range of a buffalo rifle was greater than a carbine; he did not know exactly how far out such a rifle would reach, but as they plodded along he was sure it could reach every one of them. But there was no gunshot, no noise from back yonder of any kind.

Eastward, over near the upper end of the valley, they could see buffalo grazing. They were too distant to be clearly definable, particularly when they were backgrounded by trees, but they moved from time to time, and that made it easier to recognize them.

Frank finally said: "If that son-of-a-bitch is back there, why don't he shoot?"

It was almost as though Frank had given the cue, but the gunshot was westward and it was not a rifle that made the noise; it was a carbine. The shot was sharp and high-pitched.

Frank straightened back from his instinctive crouch and turned. He was about to yell something when the second gunshot sounded. This time, it was a buffalo gun. The sound was heavy, deep, and left a thunderclap echo.

Arch halted and turned, facing the direction of that gunfire. The others did the same and Claude called to Arch: "That's got to be Badger!"

Arch shook his head. "Badger didn't have a carbine." He glanced at Frank. "Let's do some riding."

They left Claude out there with Levitt, the dead man, and the mules to lope westward. They made no attempt to go back anywhere near the distant forest. They were beyond carbine range, and Arch thought that, as moving targets, they might not have too much to fear from the buffalo rifle. There was another exchange of gunfire, but this time the carbine fired three times. Once, then again two more times, faster. For moments there was no answer, but when it came, it seemed to Arch that it was coming from farther back, as though perhaps Al Clampett had used the interim between the first and second exchanges to get farther from the valley fringe of trees and back deeper into the timber.

Frank reined close to offer an opinion. "Old Flores'd have a carbine, maybe. Badger borrowed it, and a horse."

Arch did not speak. He was trying to find powder smoke. That old rifle would use only black powder. But if there was gunsmoke, the trees effectively concealed it.

They halted, waited a moment, then resumed their way at a fast walk. Neither of them was afraid now that the buffalo gun would be aimed at them. Clampett had his hands full.

Frank had a question. "Don't those old rifles have a trapdoor loading hinge like the old-time Sharps rifles?"

Arch was not sure. "I think so, Frank. I never really paid much attention to them, but in the days when folks used them, that was about the only way to load. One slug at a time."

"Then Badger'd ought to get Clampett to fire, then run up onto him."

Arch nodded absently. "Yeah. Except that Clampett's going up that damned hill right after he shoots. He knows the danger better than we do."

There had been no gunfire now for some time and that worried both Arch and Frank. "If that son-of-a-bitch hit ol' Badger," growled Frank, "even in the hand

137

or foot, with one of those thumb-sized slugs, it'll be just about all over."

They cantered a hundred yards. Arch thought Clampett, retreating up the hill, probably would not be able to see them. And he was sure Clampett was not concerned about them right now, either, so he reined directly toward the tall timber.

The buffalo rifle blew apart the hush again. This time from northward somewhere, and more westerly than before. Frank echoed Arch's thoughts. Clampett was as high as he meant to go. Now, he was coming back down, but above the place where the carbine shooter had been.

They reached the trees, plunged ahead a few yards, sprang off, tied the horses, took their carbines, and started carefully eastward, but when the carbine opened up again, it was also northward, so evidently Clampett's adversary had not only also been moving, but he had guessed about where Clampett might be and was going to hunt him.

Frank's limp did not slow him now. As he and Arch turned up the hill, Frank kept up. The buffalo rifle roared again. This time they heard the ball strike dead center against a big tree to their right and up the slope. The carbine did not reply for a while. When it finally did, the sound was close to the general area where Arch thought the buffalo gun had been fired from. He said: "Badger's piling in on him."

They changed course again, trying to come up from below where they guessed the carbine had been fired from, until Frank, running out of breath, leaned on a tree and said: "Wait. He won't know it's us."

Arch paused, and the carbine fired again, one lone shot. They stood waiting for the rifle to answer. It did not do it. Frank said: "By God, I think he caught the bastard unloaded."

They waited for what seemed a lifetime and still nothing happened. They started forward again, very cautiously and slowly this time. Finally Arch could smell the burned black powder. He slowed still more. They utilized big trees on their uphill stalk. Not very far ahead someone snapped a tree limb. They stopped to listen. Someone to their right a few yards and not very far ahead up through the thick timber was moving.

Arch looked around. Frank was favoring his sore foot but his eyes were fixed upon something ahead. He reached, brushed Arch's arm, and pointed. They could see movement, a man's worn shiny old sheepskin vest and a shapeless hat from time to time but that was all they could make out.

Frank said: "That's not Badger!"

Arch had already reached this identical conclusion. He held out a hand as warning to Frank, then started up the hill a step at a time. The man up there was kneeling. Arch could make out that much. He had his back to the south slope. Arch's recollection of Clampett was that the man had been tall and spare. The thick back and heavy shoulders up ahead, as well as that old vest, did not coincide with Arch's recollection. Baffled more than curious, he stole ahead another three or four yards, grounded his carbine to lean on, and sank slowly to one knee. Frank did the same behind him, leaning out, trying hard to see.

The stranger stood up. Arch recognized him in a flash. "John!" he called, and the vest disappeared among the trees. "John! It's Arch! Did you get him?" The answer came finally: "Come on up where I can see you!"

They walked ahead, saw old Flores standing with his cocked carbine low in both hands, and waited. John turned the weapon aside, lowered the hammer, and said: "Where are the other two?"

"One's dead and we got the other one out a ways on a horse," Arch answered, stepping past to look among the trees. Clampett was on his back, looking sightlessly upward. Frank moved closer. "Twice," he said, turning as Flores came up to gaze stonily upon the man he had killed.

"I didn't know I'd winged him that first time, but he made a lot of noise goin' up the hillside and I knew he'd try to come down onto me, so I went east a little, and waited. He was sneakin' along when I nailed him." Flores turned toward Arch. "He didn't know what hit him that time." The dark eyes ranged over Arch, over Frank, then back to Arch again. "You two don't look so good."

Arch smiled. "We don't feel so good. Where's your horse?"

Instead of replying Flores gestured backward. "What do we do with him? I've only got one horse."

They took the dead man down to John's horse, tied him on, and led the laden horse back out into the open.

Frank wigwagged with his hat until Claude and Levitt saw them and started riding.

Flores offered food from his saddlebags. Neither Arch nor Frank was especially hungry right at this moment. Flores said: "Where are the buffalo?"

Arch pointed, but they were too far west to see them so he said: "They killed a few. Not for the meat, for the hides, but there are a lot of them still out there, John. How's Badger?"

"All right now. María Teresa is over there with him. He was half starved."

Arch stared. "You brought her back with you? John, we got a feller tied on a mule who was run over by buffalo. He's a hell of a sight."

Flores was watching Claude and Levitt, and the handsome Spanish mules when he answered. "Maybe we can bury him, and this other one, on the way back. I passed a lot of good deep little cañons. Anyway, María Teresa's not a child, Arch."

Claude and Levitt arrived. John Flores looked a long time at Levitt. While Arch and Claude were boosting Clampett across a patient mule, John said: "This is what you are doing now, instead of pot-hunting?"

Levitt looked forlorn. "I had the mules. They said all we'd do would be pack back six or eight hides."

Flores turned away, waited until the others were ready, then swung up across his saddle, and, as Arch set a diagonal course for the visible distant slot where their trail had come down into this place, Flores rode up beside Arch in the lead.

"I know your prisoner," he said. "I knew his mother and his mother's father. In fact, his mother's father was the old man who taught me how to braid rawhide. What did he do, Arch?"

"Helped his friends steal our guns and horses, John."

Flores rode a while in grave silence before speaking again. "Do you want to hang him?"

Arch frowned. "I don't want to, John. How well do you know him?"

John settled both hands atop the saddle horn as he answered. "He's . . . a little childish. He's very good with mules and horses. He can plait and braid almost as good as his grandfather could. But he is . . . well, not grown up in the head. He's always been that way." John kept looking stonily ahead. "Horse stealing means hanging."

Arch reached inside his filthy shirt to scratch. "Well, we got the horses back."

"Did he see that man die?"

"Moe Billings. He looked pretty sick about it to me, wouldn't eat afterward, and hasn't said ten words since."

"Maybe he learned. But I don't know. He's always been easy for people to influence. But he is very good with mules and horses."

They continued on across the open country with a lowering sun blood red at their backs. It did not take nearly as long to cross back on horseback as it had taken to get across the valley on foot.

When they reached the far side, they did not enter the trees until John Flores held up a hand, then led the way to a narrow, dark, little, brushy cañon. Without much talk they placed both dead men down in there and piled rocks atop them. When they were ready to ride onward again, Claude offered Levitt a chew from his plug. But Levitt did not chew; he did not use tobacco at all.

The food came out again. Everyone but Levitt and John Flores ate as they rode along.

Arch could smell smoke on ahead in the hazy early evening and suddenly remembered how disreputable he and his friends looked. But there was no creek nearby, nor did he have a razor, so he smiled at John and said: "She's going to think I'm an animal instead of a man."

John considered that for a while, then answered it. "If she does, then it may save you both some worry. But I don't think she will."

Claude and Frank gave Levitt a drink of whiskey. The prisoner's color returned a little. He said: "Do you like my mules?" Claude looked at the handsome animals. "Yeah. They're right nice. Did you break them?"

"Yes. And I raised them from colts."

Frank and Claude exchanged a look, then Claude offered the bottle to Levitt again. "Just one swallow," he said. Levitt obediently took just one swallow.

HURD'S CROSSING

CHAPTER
ONE

Colonel Cross was not ordinarily a pensive man, and yet there are times in the life of every man when circumstances, events, periods of a day or a night press in upon him, all the high and low points of life, bringing him down to a moment of thoughtful, relaxed reflection. It happened to Colonel Cross the night after those people arrived, dusty and troubled, seeking help for their town, saying they'd lost their third peace officer in a month to gunmen from the cow camps and from the renegade hideouts back in the forested Cordilleras. Colonel Cross was a short, burly man with coarse, straight hair and a round face. His glance was dead level and steady. He'd come through the crucible fires of civil insurrection with a finger shot off, a thin scar low on one cheek, and somewhere during those four bloody years Michael Cross had forgotten how to smile.

He stood now, after "Retreat" had been sounded, the flag lowered for the night, the Color Guard gone back to barracks, scarcely even mindful of this ancient routine he'd been a part of so many years: "Reveille", mess call, stables, drill call, fatigue; the old ways of deliberate violence acted out under rules that never changed, rarely deviated, were as old as man himself was, and perhaps even older than that. The ways of professional soldiers had come out of the mists of time, tried and proven and unchanging. The monk's life, he thought, standing there facing his parade ground. Celibacy at its most selfless, exalted best — or worst. Colonel Cross was fifty. He didn't know yet, which it was.

Ground shadows crept across the enclosed world of Fort Jackson from west to east, winking out the hot blast of midsummer sunlight an inch at a time. The air was breathless, stale, and like all desert country air, strongly smelling of dying things. Musty air, he thought, in a musty place.

Mess call sounded. Then the hard, biting tones of a sergeant hastening a troop into alignment out front of its barracks. Dust rising under booted feet, red faces looking toward the bare flagpole, beyond it to the command hut where Colonel Cross stood, not really seeing any of it, but fully aware it was all there.

The colonel turned and went back inside where the heat rolled up breathlessly over him. Where the corporal at the desk stood stiffly, eyes ahead, until Colonel Cross passed on into the little cubicle beyond, then relaxed and quietly sweated. The ancient law said no whiskey on post, but it applied to those whose high sense of duty held them rigidly obedient. After places such as Bull Run — first and second — Missionary Ridge, Antietam, Shenandoah Valley, Shiloh, the Peninsula battles right on down to Appomattox where the Stars and Bars dipped for the last time to the Stars and Stripes, Michael Cross obeyed rules automatically when they applied to tactics and strategy but beyond that his obedience was sketchy.

The bottle was there, in his lower desk drawer, and whether whiskey would only make him perspire more or not, he had his tumbler of the stuff. As Dr. Kleburg had once dryly observed, all men near fifty, or past it, needed whiskey like those under thirty needed a tight rein. He put the bottle away, kicked the drawer closed, and sank back in his chair as the flat, muffled sound of voices drifted in through his open office window from around front. They were unpleasant voices. Most voices this past year or so had been unpleasant voices. After a certain age, men only heard voices that wanted something from him. The colonel closed both eyes, waited for boot steps on the command hut porch, then kept his eyes closed as men stamped into the outer room asking the corporal if Colonel Cross was in. He heard the name Roberts, heard the dull, exasperated profanity that accompanied that name, and finally opened his eyes.

"Send 'em in!" he called out wearily to his corporal.

They entered, three raw-boned, sun-scorched men in soiled clothing, run-over cattlemen's boots, and hats as shapeless, as nondescript and weathered as their faces also were. He knew them. The stooped, ferret-eyed one was Charley Jones who had the smithy over at Hurd's Crossing. The tall man with the prominent Adam's apple and the long, hawkish features was Hezekiah Wicke, an old-time hide hunter who now operated a freighting outfit, and the third was Dutch John

149

Oberdorf, paunchy, beet-red, with pale blue eyes and small, tight-held mouth. Dutch John was a deceptive man. He was thick and massive and running much to lard now, around the middle, but at one time, so the story went, Dutch John Oberdorf had lifted a thousand-pound jack mule off its feet and held it up for five minutes. Dutch John was a trader, general store proprietor, and, also according to gossip, had earned his first competence peddling powder and shot to Chiricahua Apaches. "But only," he'd once confided to Colonel Cross, "when I was sure they were going to raid down in Mexico."

Now he sat there, feeling the pleasant euphoria that whiskey inspired, gazing at those three, thinking to himself that there wasn't a one of them who wouldn't, right now today, rob a man and dump his carcass over a cliff with a gashed throat, if the Army wasn't so close, and if the risks for such offences weren't so great.

"The Roberts bunch," he said, making a statement of it, instead of a question. "They're back in Hurd's Crossing again."

Charley Jones's little bright, glittering eyes shone upon Colonel Cross. "An' bolder'n ever," he said. "Swaggerin' up an' down through town like they wasn't wanted in half the territories between Arizona an' Council Bluffs."

"How many?" asked the colonel, feeling pleasantly detached from all this.

"Seven or eight," put in Dutch John. "An Emmett's meaner'n ever, Colonel. He come right up Main Street on his big bay horse, smilin' like he was a conquerin' hero."

"I see. But with seven or eight men behind him."

"Colonel," said Zeke Wicke, "it's all startin' up over again. We got another town marshal to bury."

"Is that so," said the colonel mildly. "How did it happen?"

"No one knows," stated Zeke Wicke, giving his long face a forlorn wag back and forth. "There was a helluva burst o' gunfire in the night. Next mornin' there he lay, our town marshal, strung out face down in the roadway like he'd been flattened by a . . ."

"Mister Wicke . . . *next* morning?"

Hezekiah looked up at the ceiling, down at his scuffed boot toes, then out the window into the gathering desert dusk. "Colonel, you know it ain't safe after nightfall to go pokin' your nose into no gunfights."

"Of course not," murmured the colonel, eyeing those three steadily. "Especially if someone could be lying out there unconscious and bleeding to death." His tone firmed up. "Possibly, if you'd gone to the aid of your town marshal, he'd be alive right now."

Dutch John shook his big head. "Wouldn't make no difference, Colonel. If they didn't kill him that night, they'd have done it the next night, or maybe the night after that."

This logic, at least, was sound, as the colonel knew. The Roberts gun crew, notorious from Texas to the California line, preyed on peace officers. It had also been known to attack and swap lead with Army patrols. One time Colonel Cross and Captain Bennington had

151

totaled up the rewards on that band; it had come to a staggering $12,000. That, the junior officer had remarked at the time, was more than most career Army officers netted throughout their entire period in the armed reserve.

"Colonel," said Charley Jones quietly, "we simply got to have help. It's ruinin' business. Folks hardly poke their beaks out o' doors any more. Travelers stop over just long enough to hear the stories, then grab the next coach leavin' Hurd's Crossing. On top o' that . . ."

"Could there be anything worse?" asked Colonel Cross, heaving upright out of his chair, straightening his tunic, and glancing at his three visitors with that totally unsmiling, dead-level gaze of his. "All right, gentlemen, when I can spare a patrol, I'll have one ride over and bivouac near Hurd's Crossing for a few days."

Dutch John looked round-eyed and threw up both hands in despair. "Colonel," he protested, "a few days? You might as well not send no men at all. And a patrol? That's six men, Colonel. Already Emmett Roberts has got seven or eight . . . not countin' him. They'd kill your patrol."

"That," said the colonel very softly, "would be the biggest mistake they could make. The Army has a pretty poor opinion of civilians who shoot soldiers."

"Maybe so," muttered Zeke Wicke, looking miserable. "But maybe they don't shoot your soldiers, Colonel. Maybe they shoot us for comin' over here an' beggin' you for help. The Army don't think that's so bad, I reckon, but we think it's even worse. What's the country without its civilian settlers an' merchants an' . . . ?"

"Mister Wicke," interrupted the colonel very dryly, "you'll have me in tears." He waited a moment, then said: "But I believe I might have a solution. Tell me, how much do you pay town marshals over at Hurd's Crossing?"

The three townsmen exchanged a quick look. They had no idea what Colonel Cross was leading to, but as town council-men they turned crafty and suspicious. Dutch John cleared his throat and earnestly looked at the lithograph of President Abraham Lincoln some earlier commandant had nailed to the wall. There appeared to be an amazing degree of veneration for President Lincoln in John Oberdorf, suddenly.

Charley Jones became involved in a fierce engagement with something that was biting him under his shirt. He scratched, peered through an unbuttoned place, and vigorously scratched again.

Zeke looked at the other two. They were leaving this matter up to him evidently. He wrinkled his nose, pulled down his already drooping lips, and gave his bony shoulders a pathetic like hunch upward, then downward. "Hurd's Crossin'," he explained sadly, "is a poor town, Colonel. We hardly got enough cash in our town moneybox to . . ."

The officer was getting impatient. It was past suppertime. On top of that, the whiskey glow was dissolving. "How much have you paid the last three men?" he barked.

"Thirty dollars a month!" exclaimed Zeke, then sighed and looked helplessly at his companions, who were glaring at him. "Thirty dollars a month, Colonel, an' ammunition as well as horse feed. But you got to understand that was only because they was outstandin' gun . . ."

"They must have been," said the colonel, walking around his desk. "They're dead, aren't they?" He opened the door with obvious meaning. The committee from Hurd's Crossing shuffled back out where the corporal had been drowsing with his booted feet cocked up atop the desk, but who was now industriously writing in the day book.

"Thanks for calling by," said Colonel Cross, closing his office door.

The committee men gazed helplessly at the corporal, who pointedly ignored them because he was so busy writing, then looked at one another.

"A patrol," muttered Charley Jones. "Six soldiers . . ."

Zeke Wicke nodded forlornly. "That Roberts outfit'll whittle them up one at a time. Killin' soldiers don't worry 'em. You boys see that piece in the Globe *Gazette* about what happened to them soldiers in a saloon over there, when one of the Roberts bunch got mad an' . . . ?"

"We saw it," said Dutch John wearily, turning toward the door. "All right. We get a patrol. You know what'll happen? Roberts will know we was over here. He won't bother the soldiers. He'll bother us."

They passed outside into the pleasant, pungent-scented Arizona night, still muttering back and forth,

154

went trudging over where their horses were tied, and clambered into their saddles. It wasn't a very far ride, and with no more to tell folks than they had after this visit to Colonel Cross, they didn't care how long it took them to get back, either.

CHAPTER
TWO

Hurd's Crossing had got its name the identical way many another frontier town had also been named. Not because it was beside a river where there'd been a gravel bar to cross upon, and not because it represented some kind of a halfway point, or crossing, from arid to lush country, but rather because a man named Samuel Hurd had made the overland crossing from Indiana to Arizona without losing his life, had built a trading post beside a well he'd dug, and had tacked up a crude sign on a tree — both long gone now — that announced to the world that Hurd had made the crossing. No one now recalled whatever had happened to Samuel Hurd. There was even some dispute about which of the old log-mud buildings around town had been his original trading post. But in neither case was this important. Perhaps in fifty or seventy-five years an historical society would spring up, coaxed into existence by the Ladies' Aid Society of Hurd's Crossing, but if that would happen, no one knew it at this time, and no one would have much cared if they had known, for Hurd's Crossing was a clutch of rough buildings, broad, unshaded, fiercely dusty roadways, and a few reasonably presentable residences on its back roads.

156

But Hurd's Crossing had three business establishments larger, more populous towns could've envied. One was the large and commodious general store owned by John Oberdorf. Another was Hezekiah Wicke's big freight yard, where buggies and excellent wagons were also manufactured, while the third imposing structure was Leverett Hall's Bella Union Saloon. Leverett Hall was a pale-eyed, impassive man of few words. He had good features, offset by an acid tongue, perfect manners, ameliorated by a deadly gun hand and a coldness toward people, the town of Hurd's Crossing, animals, and even the predictably hot weather of desert country Arizona. Leverett was perhaps a shade over six feet tall and weighed two hundred pounds. He had dark hair, scarred fists, and a reputation that said, drunk or sober, Leverett Hall welcomed no familiarities. But Leverett Hall's Bella Union Saloon had just about everything, including a polished bar top, which could have been found in the bars back across the Missouri River where civilization existed, so travelers, freighters, cattlemen, townsmen, soldiers, and even outlaws overlooked Leverett's veiled hostility toward everything and patronized the Bella Union.

It could safely be said of Hurd's Crossing that while it had a town council, merchants, and order, a settled community with a local water supply and a volunteer fire brigade, it did not have either community spirit in the generally accepted meaning of the word or trust between and among its influential citizens. For example, the day Sam Bennington entered town on a dusty horse with a bedroll and saddlebags behind his cantle, a tied-down ivory-butted six-gun, and a hat brim tipped so low it all but hid Sam's blue eyes, one of Charley Jones's soot monkeys went swiftly out back to where Charley was shrinking a wagon tire to say another gunfighter had just ridden into town, and Charley at once hustled over to Dutch John's general store to say that a hired killer had just arrived in Hurd's Crossing, and Dutch John went out the back way, up the alley in a clumsy trot, and told Zeke Wicke at the freight and buggy works, an assassin had just hit town to settle with the men who'd gone over to Fort Jackson to beg aid from Colonel Cross. For the balance of that day the merchants speculated, and watched one another like hawks. If an assassin had been sent for, they reasoned, he had to have been hired locally. Since Emmett Roberts didn't need to hire his killings done because he already had a gun crew to do them for him, the merchants and townsmen reasoned someone right in Hurd's Crossing had sent for this ambusher.

The lanky, sun-bronzed man ambled into the Bella Union, bought a cigar, a glass of cool beer, idly talked with the barkeep, and afterward went along to the local café for some dinner. By evening the rumors were flying, thick and fast. By nightfall hardly a man of any importance in town wasn't making a point of always seeing that his back was well protected.

By the time Sam Bennington returned to the Bella Union after seeing to the care of his horse down at the livery barn, Charley, Zeke, and John Oberdorf were hunched like conspirators over a corner table in

158

Leverett Hall's establishment, trying to convince each other they had explicit trust in one another, while at the same time discussing what must now be done because, obviously, Hurd's Crossing wasn't just turning into a private hunting ground for the Roberts gang, but was also becoming attractive to men like that hawk-like, bronzed, and lanky stranger with the ivory-butted gun.

They had tried to solicit Leverett Hall's interest, on the grounds of common interest in the well being of their town and, failing there, had then darkly hinted that the assassin just might be here to settle Leverett's hash. But that failed, too; Hall had looked down his high-bridged nose in contempt, and had walked away.

Then Sam Bennington walked into the place, talk dwindled along the bar, out among the card tables where men stoically sat concentrating on their games, and over in the gloomy far corner where Zeke, Charley, and Dutch John sat. The sun-layered stranger seemed scarcely to notice the quick ripple of caution that went up and down the room when he entered. He headed straight across toward that far table where the three local merchants sat, and stopped beside it, looking down into three blanched and decidedly uneasy, upturned faces.

He smiled. "I'm Sam Bennington," he said. "I heard a day or two back you folks here in Hurd's Crossing were looking for a town marshal."

The seated men sat still, saying nothing, gazing up at the lean, easy-standing raw-boned man there beside their table. What he'd just said knocked all their hastily constructed theories into a cocked hat, but such was the power of self-delusion none of those three men could at once, or would at once, concede this.

Sam Bennington pulled out a vacant chair, sat down at the table, signaled to the barkeep to fetch some glasses and a bottle, then thumbed back his hat and made a slow, careful appraisal of his companions. They were doing the same thing to him. After the liquor and glasses came, Zeke Wicke cleared his throat, looked askance at Dutch John and Charley, worked up a little smile, and reached over to fill his glass.

"As a matter o' fact," Zeke said, "we were just talkin' about that, Mister . . . Mister . . . ?"

"Bennington. Sam Bennington."

"Yes. Well, Mister Bennington, that there's Charley Jones an' this is John Oberdorf. I'm Hezekiah Wicke, owner of the freight line across the road. We also make buggies an' wagons, an deal a little in harness an' animals." Zeke was magnanimous; since he hadn't called for the whiskey and therefore wouldn't be obliged to pay for it, he filled all their glasses, set the bottle down, and beamed as he raised his glass. "To Sam Bennington," he said. "Hurd's Crossing's new town marshal."

They all drank and smiled. "The pay," said Zeke cheerfully, "is twenty dollars a month an' horse feed, Mister Bennington." Charley and Dutch John nodded. Sam looked amused. He eyed the three men a moment, then reached forward to refill all the glasses again.

"Thirty a month, horse feed, and tobacco," he said, finished filling the glasses, and raised his, held it aloft, waiting for the others to do likewise, and looked straight into their faces, his little faint smile hardening just the slightest bit toward them.

Dutch John slowly hoisted his glass, reddening a little because he knew exactly what Charley and Zeke would be thinking: John was being intimidated by this hard-eyed, half-smiling gun-fighter.

Zeke reluctantly raised his glass. Charley, with no choice, followed suit. They all drank and put their glasses down again. "It's settled," stated Bennington, pushing back his chair as though to arise. "Thirty a month, horse feed at the livery barn, and tobacco from Mister John Oberdorf's store. I reckon the badge, keys, and whatever else I'll need will be over at the jail-house. I'll start work tomorrow morning." He arose, flashed that strange smile of his again, and stood a moment, waiting for someone to speak. No one did, so Sam Bennington stepped back, turned, and ambled on out of the Bella Union Saloon.

The bottle and glasses were still there. Charley Jones reached for a refill. His leathery old cheeks were beginning to sport an almost youthful glow. His eyes were bright with a soft and tender benignity. Charley was not an alcoholic but he dearly enjoyed acquiring a pleasant glow after supper on these warm summer nights. Or on cold winter nights. Or on blustery spring nights or windy autumn nights.

"Wait just a damned minute," said Zeke Wicke, eyeing that half empty whiskey bottle as though it had fangs and rattles. "He come in here and talked us up ten dollars a month when we'd already decided we weren't goin' to pay the next one more'n twenty dollars a . . ."

"Come along, Charley," said John Oberdorf. "Go easy on that stuff."

Charley wasn't perturbed. He refilled his glass, set the bottle down, and hoisted the drink. "To the new town marshal" — he sighed — "Mister Sam Bennington."

Dutch John was reaching when Zeke recoiled. "Hey, he walked out of here and never paid for this whiskey." That alarming statement cooled even Charley Jones's warm amiability. They gazed at one another for a moment, then Dutch John chuckled far down in his chest and picked up his shot glass, nearly losing it in the size of his fist. "Drink slow," he said to Charley Jones, "this is goin' to cost us fifty cents each."

They drank, and put aside their glasses and eyed that offending bottle that was two-thirds empty now. Then Oberdorf smiled again, and chuckled. He dug out a half dollar, tossed it down, and looked at his friends. They dug down, too, but not very graciously until John said: "I tell you boys, this time we may have the man Hurd's Crossing needs. He talked us up ten dollars a month, hornswaggled us into payin' for the whiskey, and walked out of here smiling. I don't know how good he'd be in a shoot-out, but I'll tell you this much . . . maybe, if he can't out-shoot 'em, he can outthink 'em. He sure outthought the three of us."

Charley was thoroughly mellow now, his scrawny frame unwound and loose-draped in the chair, his narrow hatchet face rosy and pleasantly perspiring. "I didn't get no supper tonight," he murmured, grinning at Zeke and Dutch John.

Zeke wasn't impressed. Neither was he drunk. He said: "Charley, why'd you spread that story Bennington was a hired bushwhacker after someone here in town?"

Jones blinked and lost his smile. "I didn't say no such a damned thing!" he exclaimed a little thickly. "In fact, was you to ask me, I'd tell you right to your connivin' face that Mister Bennington's the first real town marshal we've had in Hurd's Crossin', and, by God, I'm a good judge of men."

Zeke grimaced. "You aren't even a good judge of whiskey," he said, and would have pushed back to arise, but Charley suddenly whipped upright in his chair and called Zeke a bad name. John Oberdorf was nonplussed. His blue eyes got perfectly round. He stiffened a little in his chair. Zeke's reaction was much the same. He wasn't as angered as he was startled. But slowly and gradually the wrath came. "Why you shriveled up old devil," he said, "I ought to slap you silly."

Charley, though, had an argument in rebuttal that closed off every avenue of retaliation except one — suicide. He said: "Zeke, I've got m' pistol pointed right at your gut under this table. Listen, I'll cock it."

There was no mistaking that sound. Zeke and Dutch John sat petrified, staring with total disbelief over at old Charley Jones. They'd had their disagreements before; they'd even gotten downright angry at each other, but this — this was an unpardonable thing. They were old men; their days of reaching for a gun to settle disputes were long past. They were slow now, and unsteady, and also they'd lived long enough to understand something about life. Nothing — nothing at all — was worth getting killed over. All that mattered was hanging on for as long as a man could.

Zeke said: "Charley, you put that damned gun up. I'm not goin' to drink with you again. By God, Charley, you reached the age where you can't handle your likker no more. I'm plumb disgusted with you."

Dutch John shook his head mournfully and said pretty much the same thing. "What's got into you, Charley? Zeke's your friend. He didn't say nothing, only that . . ."

"I heard what he said," piped up Charley Jones. "He said I warn't a good judge of whiskey. Why that walkin' totem pole with his silly Adam's apple a-bobbin' an' a-smirkin' . . . I was drinkin' good whiskey when he was still stealin' furs off the redskins he got drunk at the tradin' grounds with that green cactus juice he had the gall to call likker."

Zeke shuddered with rage but he didn't do anything rash. That six-gun under the table wasn't more than five feet, perhaps no more than three feet, from his belt buckle. He placed both hands atop the table, mightily wrestling with his anger, then stood up and leaned over and said: "Charley Jones, you're nothin' but an old horse thief, an' I know that for a fact!" Zeke then drew up very straight, turned, and went indignantly stamping across the room and out through the roadway doors into the soft-scented, dusty desert summertime night.

164

John Oberdorf sighed, wagged his head back and forth, and reached for the bottle. Charley watched briefly, then put up his gun, smiled happily, and pushed forth his empty glass also to be filled. "Fine night," he said to Dutch John. "Nothin' like these summertime nights, I always say. Fine whiskey, too, wouldn't you say, John?"

John didn't say. He just drank, then arose, and went ambling on out of the Bella Union Saloon.

CHAPTER
THREE

For Sam Bennington the ride from Fort Jackson to Hurd's Crossing was uneventful in a sense, and in another way it brought him back in time and space to another segment of life where he'd been something besides a captain in the Army. This was in pre-war Virginia where the cavalier tradition survived, hardy and vigorous, where the gentlemanly tradition was steadfast right up to the time of civil insurrection. Virginia's proud cavaliers had ridden off to tilt with money-grubbing Yankees with plumes in their hats, high jack boots, gallant sashes, shiny swords, and servants to pitch their tents and curry their horses.

Sam Bennington had gone to war like that. He'd seen the blooded drums at Bull Run. He had ridden into the Yankee town of Gettysburg a lifetime later without his plume or jack boots, and with his saber dull and honed, his youth gone, his past a haze of gray smoke, his future destined to go up in flame and fire and deafening shouts as the blue hordes rolled up and over and beyond the gallant men in gray. Sam Bennington's Confederacy died at Gettysburg, and Sam very nearly anticipated it. He was shot through the body and by all rights should have died amid the other

166

gallant hundreds who perished that final day of the Gettysburg carnage. But instead some wagoners, kindly Quaker folk, had put him in their westering wagon, and, when Sam Bennington came around again to the world of the living, he was a long way from old fealties.

He left the Quakers at Scotts Bluff, a scarecrow wanderer. He traded his saber for a piebald horse and kept right on going. He knew no trade but the doubtful one of simply being a gentleman, but he had had nearly four years of warfare, plus perfect co-ordination honed to a bright-hard edge. Sam Bennington was a deadly shot.

For three years he sold his gun, first as a deputy sheriff in bloody Kansas, then as a marshal up in Missouri, and later in Colorado's mining camps and Wyoming's cow country. Finally, as a highly-esteemed deputy U.S. marshal in New Mexico Territory, he'd traded it all for a lieutenant's silver bars, and had been belatedly sent out to Colonel Cross at Fort Jackson, wearing a blue uniform, the same uniform in years past he'd fought so hard to obliterate from his native countryside in Virginia.

But "galvanized Yankees" as the blue-belly officers called former Confederates in blue were far from rare on the far frontier. They were men apart, it is true, men with nothing but ashes left behind, but in this raw new land they could become anything, and they very often did. Sam Bennington had told Colonel Cross before agreeing to this assignment over at Hurd's Crossing what it all boiled down to was simply that a man couldn't close his eyes, lie down, and quietly die, because the will to live was too strong, so he perhaps lost his laughter acquiring in its place an impersonal cynicism, but, still, he was a living man, so he'd go on acting like one.

Colonel Cross who had a Confederate saber scar on one cheek, and a missing finger, too, was a professional like most frontier commandants were. The Civil War was long past. He said: "Tragedy wasn't all on one side, Sam. I know. I've ridden through Virginia towns that made me want to cry. The only answer I can give you is this one. We're a young country, our mistakes are big ones, the healing processes slow, but we're one nation, Sam, and one people, and out here the only thing we've got to concern ourselves with is the maintenance of law and order. I know that's damned trite, but I'm no orator, either, and in simple words or flowery ones it's still the same thing. You go on down there to Hurd's Crossing, see what you think. You've got the perfect background for this assignment. You'll go as a civilian. Then you report back to me with your recommendations, and, by God, I'll take action. But be careful, Sam. Those townsmen down there aren't much better than the outlaws they swear are running wild in their area. I know. I've got files on them all. There's just one man you might be able to rely on if you're in real danger. Leverett Hall. He was a Rebel . . . excuse me . . . a Confederate brigadier general. I think, in a pinch, a man like Leverett Hall would find the old tie still binding, so remember his name."

Sam remembered it. He didn't have a chance to get a good long look at Leverett Hall until the day after he'd

168

gotten himself hired as town marshal, and that look wasn't something to inspire a lot of admiration in Sam Bennington. Leverett Hall was a large, scarred, aloof, cold man. Some lout of an unshaven cowboy slapped him genially on the back and called for him to stand the drinks. It was a bad mistake on the range rider's part. Hall had turned, drawing himself up straight, had called the cowboy every cutting and fierce name he could lay tongue to, then had proceeded to lay the cowboy out with his powerful battering-ram fists.

Sam was across the road when the range rider came drunkenly out through the louvered doors, fell off the plank walk out into the manured roadway, bleeding from the nose and mouth, conscious but dully, stupidly so. He rolled heavily, got both hands braced, and started to arise. Leverett Hall was right there, standing over him. He sledged the weaving, blinking range man across the back of the head and that time the cowboy sprawled out, dripping claret and looking lifeless.

Sam started over. When he was still in the center of the road, he called softly, saying: "Mister, that's enough. He was already finished when you hit him from behind."

Leverett Hall turned slowly, brushing back the long tail of his gray coat to make the holstered six-gun there more readily accessible. He glared flintily out at Sam Bennington, at Sam's badge, and at the cold, capable look of the equally as tall but considerably lighter man out there in the hot and lemon-yellow roadway.

"Don't start on me," he said. "The badge gives you no guarantees, Marshal. Stick to handling the scum, which is the kind they usually hire to wear that badge, because it takes scum to know scum."

Zeke Wicke was up there against the rough log wall of his office, out front of the freight yard. There were easily a dozen others also looking and holding their breaths on both sides of the shimmering roadway when Sam Bennington nodded his head at Leverett Hall.

"Go ahead and draw," he said. "I doubt if you'll do it, mister. A man who'd club down another man from behind can't have any red up his back. It's got to be . . . yellow!"

Leverett stood stiffly thoughtful, his lean, aristocratic features almost serene as he made his deliberate appraisal. To the townsmen he was both inscrutable and unpredictable. He seemed very much that way now. None of the onlookers thought he was afraid, and apparently he wasn't, because he went for his gun, his elbow straightening, his fingers closing swiftly. But the weapon didn't clear leather. Leverett Hall was looking into the dark barrel of Sam Bennington's tilted-up pistol barrel.

Zeke Wicke let out his breath slowly. Elsewhere, other spectators stood stunned by the lightning speed of Sam Bennington's draw. Southward, down the road and out back of the livery barn, a man's angry voice rose, heaping imprecations on a horse down there. That was the only sound for a moment, before Sam Bennington said: "Finish your draw, mister."

Leverett Hall didn't finish it for the best of all reasons. Bennington would kill him if he did. He pushed the gun back down, took his hand off it, and stood there flintily staring. At his feet the battered cowboy groaned, fumbled with both hands seeking for solid footing to raise himself up, and looked around. The first thing he saw was Town Marshal Sam Bennington, and his tilted-up, cocked six-gun. The second thing he saw, by craning around, was icy-eyed and impassive Leverett Hall. He decided and wisely not to try to get up just then, and relaxed.

"What's your name?" Bennington asked.

Hall seemed about not to answer. He seemed about to turn and stamp back inside his saloon. Sam Bennington holstered his six-gun in a smooth move, and stood there waiting, the resolve just as indelibly etched across his bronzed features as before.

"Mister," he called softly, "I asked you your name. You're going to tell me."

Hall turned back, gave Sam that same cold look, and said: "Without the gun, Marshal, do you think you can get it out of me?"

Sam nodded. "I reckon I can, mister. I'm just hoping you don't make me dig that hard . . . for both our sakes."

Hall stood gazing over at Bennington as though something in the leaner and younger man's face intrigued him. Actually it was in Sam Bennington's voice, in his soft Virginia drawl. "My name is Leverett Hall, Marshal. I own the Bella Union Saloon." Hall prodded the man in the dust at his feet with a toe and said: "I don't encourage this type in my place. When they get too familiar, I throw them out."

"Hit them from behind, Mister Hall?"

"Hit them any time and any way I have to, Marshal."

Sam ran his slow, sulphurous glance up and down the older and heavier man very slowly. This was his initial introduction to the man Colonel Cross had said might be sympathetic if Sam needed any help in Hurd's Crossing. He gently shook his head from side to side. "Not any more, you don't," he said, lifting his eyes to Hall's face again. "Not in any town where I'm enforcing the law."

Hall hung there just a moment more, then turned without another word, and passed beyond sight through his roadside saloon entrance.

Sam went over, helped the cowboy to his feet, ascertained no real damage had been done, and told the cowboy to get on his horse and get out of town. The range man was glad to be able to comply evidently because he wasted no time in heading over to Hall's hitch rack, clambering aboard a horse there, and poking the beast into a sloppy trot southward, straight down the main thoroughfare and on out of Hurd's Crossing.

Sam returned to the shady, westerly side of the road and stepped up. He was immediately accosted by Zeke Wicke who had a gray look around the gills. "Marshal, you never should've done that. Leverett wouldn't have hurt that danged saddle bum, an' now you've roiled him up, givin' him an order like that."

Sam fell to making a smoke with perfectly calm hands. He let Wicke talk on until he had his cigarette lighted, then he cut him off with a softly spoken question: "Did you hire me to keep the peace, Mister

Wicke, with exceptions, or did you hire me to keep peace in Hurd's Crossing with no exceptions? If it's the first way, I'll give you back the badge right now. If it's the latter way, you keep your nose out of it."

Zeke had his mouth open to offer further admonitions. He closed it, and squinted his eyes. Several idlers over along the freight office wall were listening. One of them chuckled. He was a dark-bearded, villainous-looking individual with a badly re-set broken nose and the shoulders of a bear. Zeke glared at him. The bearded man kept right on grinning. Zeke turned and went marching into his office and that brought another of those deep-down rumbling chuckles from the bearded man.

Sam Bennington turned. The bearded man's twinkling little eyes didn't flinch. He said: "Marshal, you may not last any longer'n the others, but, by God, while you're around, it's goin' to be a pleasure to see you work. My name's Everett Bull. I drive freight for Mister Wicke." Bull pushed out a mighty hand. Sam grasped it, pumped it once, and dropped it. Everett Bull had the strength of his namesake.

Sam said: "He'll fire you for laughing."

Everett Bull shook his big head. "Naw, he won't. Mister Wicke can't replace me. He may not have a heap to say to me for a day or two, but he ain't goin' to fire me. I've laughed at him before an' I'm still around."

Sam eyed the other idlers. They were watching him with the quiet and subdued caution that seemed to be prevalent among the citizens of Hurd's Crossing. If they admired his deadly draw, his obvious courage, and his willingness to buck trouble, they nevertheless had seen others do the same thing, and the others were no longer around. They would, their patient, cautious expressions said, wait and see.

Sam turned and walked on down to the jailhouse he'd inherited with his job, which was smelly and cramped and musty, but which had one distinct advantage in the summertime desert heat. It had adobe walls three feet thick and regardless of how hot it got outside the temperature inside never got above seventy degrees.

There were two steel cages called cells across the back wall, a battered old desk, a chair that had been ingeniously wired together, several other chairs and benches in the one-room structure, and three small, barred windows, all on the roadway side of the building. There was also an *olla*, a porous clay bulb-like object that, when suspended as this one was, where the air freely circulated around it, kept the drinking water it held always cool and refreshing. *Ollas* were very common in the Southwest. They were part of the Spanish-Mexican-Indian heritage of the desert country, and all true Yankee ingenuity in the world hadn't yet found a way to replace them with anything as simple yet as efficient for their purpose.

Sam Bennington drank, pushed sweat off his face afterward, and crossed to the desk to ease down upon one corner of it, swinging his free leg back and forth. Colonel Cross had said nothing about becoming personally involved in the plight of Hurd's Crossing. All he'd said was for Sam Bennington to make his study and report back what corrective measures Sam thought advisable. Well, Sam had made his appraisal, and would in time report back to the colonel, but in the meantime he'd take the corrective measures himself. He'd done that in Colorado, in Wyoming, and in New Mexico. No one knew better than Sam Bennington what Hurd's Crossing needed, and the U.S. Army couldn't give it: self-respect.

He gazed out into the shimmering roadway. Hurd's Crossing needed a stiffening of its collective backbone. He thought he'd seen the first man to recruit to his side to implement this stiffening process. Everett Bull. He also thought he'd just met a perfect example of Colonel Mike Cross's dismal inability to judge men correctly. Leverett Hall.

As for the others; they were simply men. Zeke Wicke was a product of his time and environment. He wanted to survive, that was all. Like Charley Jones and John Oberdorf, he knew right from wrong, but he was hazy about which was best for him. It wasn't an unusual way for men to be. Far from it. With most men it was the common way to be.

He stepped over for another pull at the *olla*, and turned to step away again. A slow-growing roll of running horses came into the stale atmosphere from somewhere beyond town. He stood a moment, pegging that sound, sorting it from all the other sounds, decided there were at least seven or eight riders in this approaching group, then scooped up a shotgun from the scarred old wall rack and moved over to stand in his shady doorway waiting to see these newcomers.

175

He had an idea who they'd be, and he'd already made up his mind what must be done when the Roberts gang hit Hurd's Crossing again. To put off a showdown never solved a thing.

Somewhere up by the general store a man wailed a cry of warning. The roadway emptied in a twinkling as men and women ducked out of sight into doorways and stores. The Roberts gun crew was riding into town!

CHAPTER
FOUR

Emmett Roberts was a sharp-featured, shrewd, whipcord man with a frame for more weight than he carried and dark eyes to match his black hair. There were enough legends surrounding his villainous name to scare off the most dauntless peace officers. He'd been an assassin since before he'd learned to shave. He'd been an outlaw, bandit, marauder since the year he'd first voted, and after that the stories of his escapades had multiplied until it was no longer possible to separate fact from fiction. But it was very easy to guess, after one look into those muddy dark eyes, that the spirit and soul of Emmett Roberts was impaled upon inner spikes of ferocity, and that therefore he was entirely capable of any heinous act he stood accused of, whether he'd actually done it or not.

The men who rode with Roberts were border sweepings and worse, and, although they frequently died or simply rode away, such was the dark magic of Emmett Roberts's name that he could, simply by passing through a town, attract the weak and dissolute and vicious, so that he never, or at least scarcely ever, rode with less than half a dozen or more men at his back. That's how he rode into Hurd's Crossing — with eight murderous-looking men riding with him. But they didn't look suspicious or lethal or menacing; they looked hot and amiable. They'd been drinking heavily off in the broken country somewhere northward or westward, in whichever direction lay their renegade camp, and they grinned or laughed, or called out to the people they caught glimpses of, as they made their way up toward the Bella Union Saloon.

They were armed like Mexican insurrectionists, with tied-down six-guns and brass-studded shell belts. They had their booted saddle guns slung up tightly at the saddle swell so that the stocks were readily available and within inches of the right hand. Several of them even wore two tied-down sixes. That didn't imply there were any genuine two-gun men among them. Ambidextrous gunfighters on the frontier, except in song and fable, were as rare as upper teeth on a cow. All those two guns meant was that someone — whoever rigged himself out like that — meant to have enough firepower in a pinch to blast his way out of it. It sometimes also meant a man practiced the border shift, which was to fire one pistol empty, then swiftly whip the fresh gun from the left to right hand and continue the firing.

The issue was not so much who would draw fast, shoot accurately, or who would use the border shift. As Sam Bennington saw it, the issue was who — he or they — would make the first issue of the fact that Hurd's Crossing had a fresh town marshal. When in doubt, so the axiom went, attack!

178

Sam was standing in a recessed doorway, watching, his twin-barreled scatter-gun up and ready, both hammers cocked back. Across the road stood the Bella Union Saloon. At Sam's back was Zeke Wicke's log office and large, fenced-in freight yard and wagon works. Up and down the roadway there was no movement, no sound. There were spectators, but very discreet or frightened ones, for although the townsmen of Hurd's Crossing outnumbered Emmett Roberts's bristling renegades by perhaps ten or more, there were neither willing martyrs nor dedicated heroes among them. They were either very ordinary people with a burning desire to go on living, or they were merchants of one kind or another, with a reason for living. In either case, they did not now make and never had made, since the arrival of the notorious Roberts gang, any attempt on their own part to put an end to what they watched and feared and despised — the taking over of their town by bandits, thieves, killers, notoriously wanted fugitives from nearly every territory west of the Missouri and south of Montana.

It was Sam Bennington's choice and his initiative. Thus far, as they slouched in toward Leverett Hall's hitch rack in front of his Bella Union, except for casting a few indifferent, scornful looks right and left, the renegades were not concerned with trouble from a town they'd cowed on each previous visit until there was no backbone left. It was Sam Bennington's choice and he made it. While the outlaws were dismounting, he stepped clear of his recessed doorway. As they trooped around through the blistering heat and stepped

179

up onto the plank walk in front of the Bella Union, Sam Bennington lowered his scatter-gun. They were grouped over there, dark with sweat, loose and confident, when he called out.

"Roberts!"

They turned, eight deadly renegades and their leader, squinting their eyes into the burning brilliance out yonder which was exactly the way Sam Bennington had planned it — the sun in their faces, the sun at his own back.

"I'll ask you just once . . . throw your guns out into the roadway, every damned one of you."

He could see the slow spread of solid disbelief among those outlaws over there. One man with a lousy shotgun was bracing them, and he very clearly meant exactly what he'd just said. It was suicide.

Several of the outlaws looked at Roberts. Emmett and the unmoving ones among his crew kept staring straight across at Bennington. This was absurd; it was insane.

They had been drinking obviously, but not so much that they didn't catch the coldly sobering scent of brimstone in the stale, fierce heat. Roberts said: "Mister, put that damned shotgun down an' walk away from here. I'm handin' you back your life. I see the badge. Well, don't let it go to your head. We eat 'em like you for breakfast every mornin'. Have for years. I'm makin' an exception in your case. You got guts, mister. That's all that's goin' to keep you alive right now. Put that damned shotgun down!"

180

It could have been a stand-off with Roberts refusing to be disarmed, and with Sam Bennington unable to go over physically and disarm that many outlaws without help. But Sam Bennington had been here before. He said: "I'll count three, boys, then I'll open up with both barrels. That'll give you three seconds to kill me before I down at least four of you from this range with my scatter-gun. Or, it'll give you three seconds to decide to shed the guns."

It was incredible. Sam Bennington was forcing a fight with nine notorious killers. At every window and partially closed doorway up and down the roadway where men and women fought to get close enough to hear what was being said, faces smoothed out in purest astonishment. A man had to want to die to do anything as positively ridiculous as this.

Emmett Roberts was standing in front of his bunched-up riders. He'd survived his share of these wild mêlées, but Emmett was alive because he'd always done the choosing and the timing. No one in twenty-five years had ever got the drop on him like this before. He would catch the first charge of buckshot, and from a distance of no more than a hundred or so feet. All the luck in the world wouldn't keep a man alive under these circumstances, once that madman over there yanked a scatter-gun trigger.

"Hold it a minute," he called softly to Sam Bennington. "Marshal, you'll die, too. You can't get all nine of us."

"I don't figure to," Sam said, "but I'm sure going to try like hell."

181

One of the renegades standing slightly behind another one, and using all this time to make his decision, made it. He went for his six-gun and he was fast. He might even have been fast enough under other circumstances to make it count, but no man living, even though he had a lightning draw beat a cocked scatter-gun. Bennington yanked one trigger, then rolled with the violent kick of the sawed-off gun and let himself be carried ten feet southward as he yanked the second trigger. The noise rattled windows throughout town. Men screamed out, over in front of the Bella Union. They staggered, hit hard, or they turned and wildly ran left and right toward the openings between the buildings, or they stood their ground, firing handguns. The sulphurous great cloud of oily smoke from that shotgun blast gave Sam Bennington his greatest asset at first. His personal presence of mind completed it as he whipped sideways to present the smallest target and fired off three fast shots from his .45 at a distance even a novice gunfighter couldn't have missed from, and Sam was anything but a novice gunfighter. Then he sprang away and lunged for the little place where Zeke Wicke's log office stood ahead six or eight feet from the beginning of his set-back wagon yard log fence.

Glass *tinkled*, men cried out in fright from within Wicke's office where they'd been breathlessly crowding up to peer out, and a bull-bass roar of indignation was abruptly followed by the higher and sharper report of a Winchester carbine being fired from inside the freight-line office.

182

The smoke lay like a yellow pall with dazzling sunlight burning against it with a blinding light. Over across the road there was considerably less gunfire than before, and someone over there was crying out in pure agony. There were two men lying face down in the manured roadway in front of Leverett Hall's saloon. Another man, dimly discernible through the smoke of battle, was sitting with his legs straight out, his shoulders up against the front of the Bella Union, evidently knocked backward violently and downward, looking with a stupidly blank expression over where Sam Bennington was firing from around the corner of Zeke Wicke's building. This man had a gun in his hand and his gun hand in his lap. He was making no attempt at all to participate in the battle.

Roberts's survivors backed into the saloon. Finally, from elsewhere besides Zeke's office, where that bull-bass man was yelling curses and firing his Winchester, other guns began opening up on the Bella Union. One of the louvered doors was torn from its hinges and loudly *clattered* to the floor. More and more guns of townsmen swelled the tumult until someone over inside the Bella Union began yelling at the top of his voice, and waved a barman's soiled white apron over the top of the one remaining louvered doors. By then the firing over there was stopped entirely.

It took longer for the guns up and down the yonder roadway to go silent, but after a time they also did. Then came the slow lifting of the dense smoke. Besides those two dead ones out there in the powdery fine dust of the roadway, face down and clearly dead, and that

183

stupidly staring one whose head had now dropped fully forward onto his chest, there was another dead one. He was draped across the tie rack where he'd evidently tried to reach his horse and had failed.

The high, angry voice of Leverett Hall broke across the acrid-scented hush. "Marshal! God damn it, Marshal Bennington, it's all over. They ran out the back the way . . . the ones that're left. Bring some bandages. I got a gut-shot one over here lying atop my bar. Marshal! Do you hear me? This is . . ."

"I hear you!" called Sam. "Step outside, Hall, with both hands over your head. Anyone inside with you . . . bring them out the same way. March!"

Hall stepped over his broken door, arms high, and behind him, using Hall's thick body as his shield, came one of his barmen. He was short and swarthy and looked to be more stunned than terrified. Both those men had their arms as high as they could reach.

Sam straightened up and began re-loading his six-gun. He let Hall and his barman stand over there for nearly two full minutes where the whole town could see them, before he dropped the freshly charged .45 into its holster and stepped forward to the edge of the plank walk. Behind him on both sides, the walls and fence of Zeke Wicke's place were chewed and splintered and gouged by bullet strikes. Here and there a bold townsman stepped out of a doorway, gun in hand. The man with the roaring voice kicked open the front door of Zeke Wicke's office and shouldered through. It was the massive and bearded freight rig driver, Everett Bull. Of them all, he was the only one grinning.

Sam stepped down into the dust and strolled across to halt in front of the Bella Union, surveying the wreckage. There was no mistaking the flat-out position of those two renegades at his feet, but when he gazed at the man propped along the saloon's front wall, he wasn't sure, so he said: "Put your arms down, Hall. Go see if that one leaning on your building is also dead."

Leverett Hall lowered his arms but didn't budge. "He's dead," he growled at Sam, and Bennington raised his eyes. "I said . . . go make sure!"

Hall balanced on the knife-edge of rebellion, then turned and went over, bent down, straightened back up, and nodded his head. "Dead," he said.

"Where's Roberts?" asked Bennington, looking left and right for some sign of another downed man.

"He got away," Hall growled. "He was limping, but I saw him jump behind those two dead ones at your feet just before you cut loose. Afterward, he backed into my saloon with the others, an', when the whole damned town opened on my building, he led the others out back. There were some saddled horses out there."

"That was convenient," said Sam thoughtfully. "You provide 'em, Hall?"

The big saloon man's cold eyes blazed. "You'd better get something straight," he told Sam Bennington. "I sell liquor . . . nothing more. I don't care who buys it as long as they pay cash. I have no more use for the Roberts bunch than you have, or anyone else has."

Sam let Hall get it all out and off his chest, then he walked on past into the saloon where a dying renegade lay atop the bar, composed and barely breathing. As

185

Sam bent to look at this man's face, the renegade expired. Sam stepped back — four dead out of nine, and Roberts evidently wounded. Perhaps another man or two had also been wounded. It was a good day's work. He went back outside where men were congregating in the shimmering roadway, talking excitedly and brandishing weapons. He said: "Brag later, boys. Right now get some shovels, stake out four graves, and let's get these men buried. Incidentally there are four wanted men here. We'll put in for the rewards and start a Hurd's Crossing community fund. Now get your shovels."

CHAPTER
FIVE

Elation is invariably followed by doubt and misgivings and recrimination. Hurd's Crossing was no exception. For the balance of that day, right up until those four dead outlaws had been tamped firmly into place outside town in the local boothill cemetery — reserved for their kind and the unidentified dead — exultation was everywhere. Even Hezekiah Wicke, recovering from the damage done to his log office and wagon yard fence, said it was the best thing that had ever happened in Hurd's Crossing; it'd teach outlaws and renegades they couldn't tamper with things around this town. Then evening came, the solemn reaction set in, and Zeke met with John Oberdorf and Charley Jones, quite forgetting that no later than the night before Charley had outrageously insulted him, and had something quite different to say.

"That town marshal we hired's got me worried. Did you fellers see him ride roughshod over Leverett Hall out there today?"

John and Charley hadn't seen it. In fact, they hadn't seen any of the actual fighting, only the aftermath, for the same reason most other folks hadn't been eyewitnesses, either — the wish to accommodate an overwhelming sense of self-preservation.

"Well," stated Zeke solemnly, "he ordered Hall around like he would draw on him if Hall didn't do as he was told."

Charley, who'd felt the sharp edge of Leverett Hall's tongue a time or two, said: "What's wrong with that? Anyway, how come Roberts to try 'n' hide in this here saloon, if Hall wasn't a friend o' his?"

Zeke looked over at the raffish and sly-eyed other man. "Charley," he sententiously intoned, "Leverett Hall sells likker. The Bella Union is a bar. Damnation. I've seen that colonel from the fort in here drinkin', too, but I happen t' know for a fact Leverett Hall was a Secesh general durin' the war, so you can't hardly say he's a friend of the Yankee Army, can you?"

"The Yankee Army," exclaimed Charley, signaling for a bottle and some glasses, "has got nothin' to do with what happened here today!"

"Wait a minute," broke in Dutch John, "I got a hunch it might have. Four men died here today. That colonel we talked to last month is goin' to hear of this. I'll bet you new money we get at least an Army patrol down here within the next week or ten days."

"*Humph*," grunted Zeke Wicke. "In ten days Roberts could round up another gun crew, come back here, kill Bennington, an' burn this damned town to the ground. I think our town marshal's biggest mistake was not to make sure he killed Roberts."

Their liquor came. They each downed one drink, then Charley carefully refilled his glass while the other two watched with stirring recollections of the last time Charley had gotten smoked up in this very same place. "Listen," Zeke said, "let's go down to the jailhouse and have a talk with Bennington. I think we got to do that because today he sure maneuvered us smack dab into the center of a right hot place."

"Wait a minute," said Charley, brightening a little, turning pleasantly pink up around the gills, "let's not just jump up an' go bargin' down there. Now, personally, I figure Bennington done just right. I'm sorry he didn't salivate Roberts, too, but right now I'd hate a sight worse to interrupt him at whatever he's doing. Now, then, boys, let's just have one more teeny-weeny drink."

"Charley," stated Dutch John, full of careful reproof, "you're going to drink too much of that stuff and . . ."

"No, no, no." Charley Jones chuckled, downing his second straight shot and reaching for another refill. "Boys, tonight I had supper first. One thing I can tell you, old Charley Jones can drink a regiment of dragoons under the table any blessed time he's had his supper first. Now, come on, we've had a rough day around here, so let's all have another one."

Leverett Hall wasn't present this evening to hear the arguments and protests and suggestions for appeasement running up and down, back and forth in his saloon, but possibly they wouldn't have surprised or particularly offended anyone as saturnine as he was anyway, because he'd seen men react the same way when much loftier ideals and greater issues were at stake. Leverett was sitting, all slouched and rumpled in

189

a tipped-back chair down at the jailhouse, smoking a black cigar and studying Sam Bennington from behind the half droop of lids. He was saying that Bennington's ideas were basically good, good for Hurd's Crossing, for the spirit and morale — and jellyfish backbone — of the town, but they weren't going to be enough by themselves.

Sam was diligently cleaning his fingernails with the wicked tip of a big Barlow clasp knife, a little vague smile across his sun-darkened lower face, taking it all in, and privately telling himself that Colonel Cross's estimate of Leverett Hall probably hadn't been incorrect after all. How many men, when they've been bucked up and growled down in front of a whole town, still had the manhood in them to overlook it and go pay a call upon the man who'd done that to them, with a sort of olive branch in their hands? Not very damned many.

"I've got a supporter," Sam said, snapping the knife closed and pocketing it. "That big bull of a freighter who works for Zeke Wicke."

Hall's thin features creased up into a grimace. "Bull," he said "Ev Bull. Just like his name, Marshal. If being a bull could keep you alive another ten days, maybe Ev would be enough. But you and I know a damned sight better. I think I realize why you did that today, and, as totally foolish and misplaced as I believe your high motives to be, I admire your guts. I'll also tell you that except for the Virginia accent I'd have drawn on you, too."

190

Sam finally and openly smiled. "No you wouldn't have, General, because you knew I'd have killed you. As for where I came from . . . or where you came from . . . or what we've done years past which might have shared a kind of outmoded idealism, let's get something straight. This is Hurd's Crossing, Arizona Territory, and it's today . . . not twenty years ago, or even ten years ago. You're no more the man you were then, than I am. As for what I was trying to do . . . you keep right on guessin' about that. Meanwhile, I'll take Ev Bull and go right on trying to achieve what I think this damned town needs, and you can trail along or stand aside. I don't care a damn which it is."

Leverett Hall sucked on his cigar, spouted smoke, and never blinked even once as he kept studying Sam Bennington. Finally he said: "Mind if I call you Sam?"

"Not at all. Mind if I called you General?"

"Yes, I mind. That's nearly all forgotten now. You just said so yourself."

Sam was still softly smiling. "Well, Leverett's a pretty big mouthful . . . General."

Hall puffed and narrowed his eyes. "Damn you," he softly said, "you've got a bad knack for rubbin' folks the wrong way. It's a wonder someone didn't kill you a long time ago. Years back, my friends used to call me Nick. Don't ask me how that got started. There's no relation between my name and that."

Sam nodded. "Nick it is."

"Now," said Leverett Hall quietly, "give me one straight answer, Sam. How in the devil did you ever get

Colonel Cross over at Fort Jackson to let you come down here as a civilian to tame this town?"

Bennington laughed. "Was it that obvious today?" he asked.

"It was obvious to me last night in the saloon. You've been an officer too long. When you talk, you command. Maybe only another man who's used to doing that would see it right off. And today . . . you were half soldier, half gunfighter, and that's a damned interesting combination. In fact, it was this intriguing fact that brought me down here tonight. How did you ever get Cross to allow it?"

"It was his suggestion, Nick. I'll appreciate it if we keep this between us, though."

Hall shrugged and puffed and kept studying Sam Bennington as though he were one of the last of some very bizarre species. "I never volunteer information," he murmured.

"I was a lawman after the war in different places," Bennington explained. "Then I went from the U.S. Marshal's office into the Army . . . became one of those galvanized Yankees. There are worse things, Nick."

"I suppose," said Leverett Hall thoughtfully. "Let me tell you something you've probably already figured out. This wasn't an end to anything today. It was a beginning. If you'd killed Roberts, it might have been an ending. Next time, Sam, you'd better aim exclusively at him, granting, of course, he doesn't aim exclusively at you first." Hall stood up, a big, hard, bold man with much more behind the cold, aristocratic façade that he showed to the world than most people ever suspected.

He sucked back a big gust of smoke, savored it, then slowly let it out. "About that cowboy I cold-cocked out in the roadway," he said, speaking as though making this explanation was something he ordinarily wouldn't have done. "I did that for a very simple reason. I don't like these people. Mostly they're scum like Charley Jones, the blacksmith, and Zeke Wicke, the freighter, or the dozens of shifty-eyed men who come and go around Hurd's Crossing. I've made a point of keeping clear of them all. That's how I've wanted it, and that's how I show them to keep away."

Sam arose and nodded, looking thoughtful. He didn't say anything until Leverett Hall was reaching for the door latch. "I've felt the same way, also, a time or two, Nick. All the good ones I've seen die in my time sometimes make me want to hate all the lousy ones who're still alive. But I learned a long while back brooding doesn't change a damned thing . . . except the man who does the brooding. It makes him in his own way as poor an example of humanity as the scum he dislikes."

Sam reached, hauled the door open, and stood trading a long stare with Leverett Hall. Then the saloon man walked on out into the night, looked back just once, and went slowly pacing his way along the wrong side of the darkened roadway up toward his saloon. But he didn't stop there; he didn't even cross over and enter the building. He kept on pacing along to the far north end of town, and stood up there for a full fifteen minutes, gazing off northward through the pleasant and fragrant desert night, the cigar dead between his lips.

Town Marshal Sam Bennington closed his jailhouse door from the outside and stepped back where darkness laid in black layers to make a quiet, long survey of the roadway. Hurd's Crossing was more alive tonight than he'd seen it since riding into town. The mood of the place had changed. It was half fearful, half proud. Those were things a man attuned to the pulse of towns could sense in the atmosphere. He wasn't concerned with the fear, only with the dawning pride. There wouldn't be much of it tonight, or for the next two or three days for that matter, but at least there was a nucleus, and he asked no more than that to build from.

He watched two men supporting a third man coming down toward the jailhouse from up by the Bella Union. Oberdorf's bulk and Wicke's sparseness were identifiable. The man between them who was having serious navigational problems looked like the blacksmith, Charley Jones. Sam thought he could guess what those three wanted, and he didn't feel very much like explaining, so he drifted southward deeper into the night until he came to an opening between two darkened shops, and stepped down through there into the rear alley. From there it was a simple feat to by-pass those three, cut across to the rooming house where he'd got an upstairs room, and make that entire trip undetected by John and Zeke, who were finding it increasingly difficult to steer Charley Jones along.

From his upstairs roadside window Sam Bennington looked out over Hurd's Crossing. Far out where the desert lay, flat and seemingly endless, a cow bawled.

194

Moments later her calf quaveringly called back, and the cow was silent. There was someone playing a sad song on a guitar over west of the main roadway, probably on a back porch chair. The song was an old favorite of the cow country called "The Cowboy's Lament".

He made a cigarette and smoked in cool darkness, speculating on Colonel Cross's reaction when word reached Fort Jackson of the historic gunfight in broad daylight in Hurd's Crossing's main thoroughfare. He could pretty well imagine the direction that reaction would take. Colonel Cross was a direct and forceful man.

CHAPTER
SIX

Seven days passed uneventfully. About the only noticeable change in town was a cautiously emerging confidence that Town Marshal Sam Bennington, along with the few local men who'd come along belatedly to back him up against the Roberts gang, had inspired. But it was an uncertain thing. Sam knew exactly how uncertain it was in the late afternoon of the seventh day.

There were two of them, unmistakably gunfighters. One was swarthy and hook-nosed with eyes as black as midnight. The other was taller with light blue eyes and a slash for a mouth. They tied their horses at the hitch rack before the Bella Union, ambled up onto the plank walk, stood looking left and right, and then entered, fetching belly up against the Bella Union's bar.

Charley Jones saw them, and so did Dutch John. Zeke, who probably would also have seen them except that he'd gone out with big Ev Bull onto the desert west of town to test a five-span mule hitch someone was trying to peddle him, didn't return to town for an hour after they'd ridden in.

At once the rumors stirred to life again, the confidence began to ooze out of folks' boot soles,

Hurd's Crossing gradually sank back into its cowering posture, and simply because two gunfighters had drifted in. Their kind were two-bits a dozen. The closer a man got to the Mexican line, the more he saw of them. Two-legged rattlesnakes who seldom caused trouble unless someone ruffled them, for the elemental reason that usually, where they'd come from, they'd recently had all the trouble they wanted for a while, and simply wanted a brief rest before hastening on across the border into Mexico.

That did not fit the two gunfighters in Hurd's Crossing however. They had no blanket rolls behind their cantles and very little trail dust on their sleek, good-quality mounts. Sam Bennington saw this while leaning across the tie rail, considering their horses. He saw their outfits as well. Outlaws they might be, he told himself, renegades on the run, but one thing was certain — they hadn't come far since their previous halt, and they hadn't traveled fast, either.

He took his time, but eventually walked in the Bella Union. It was a little early for the after-supper crowd to be showing up. Besides the pair of strangers there weren't more than six or eight men loafing around the room, three at a card table, the others scattered loosely up and down the bar. Leverett Hall was behind the bar himself, which was unusual. He was just finishing taking the pair of strangers refills when Sam Bennington entered. The atmosphere was right; those two over yonder were strangers, and gunfighters to boot; every townsman and range man in the room, so elaborately unconcerned, so totally involved only in his

197

own private affairs, was exuding curiosity and caution like a haze. As Sam approached the bar, he thought that if someone struck two flat boards together just outside the door now, every man in that room would explode as though impelled by tightly wound springs.

Hall brought Bennington a beer, looked him impassively in the eye, and moved on. Hall said nothing and looked nothing; his attitude was very plainly one of cold speculation. If Sam Bennington didn't know what might happen in Hall's saloon this early evening, then Hall wasn't going to tell him.

Sam studied the strangers a moment, sipping beer, then put aside his glass and strolled down to them. He said: "How's Emmett, boys?"

Both the strangers turned and blankly gazed at him. The black-eyed one took a little longer; he ran his eyes up and down, then he said: "Emmett who, Marshal? You sure you ain't got us mixed up with someone else?"

Sam smiled and stood hipshot with both thumbs hooked in his shell belt. He held the unwavering stares of those two and hung fire over whatever he might say next, using all these little things against them, making them uncertain. It was nothing new; the Indians had been doing that with their enemies for hundreds of years. Let a man stand long enough in a town he's not sure of, facing a smile he knows really has no warmth toward him, in front of a man whose prowess he knows of, and the inevitable result is a little chipping away of a man's self-assurance.

"Emmett Roberts," said Bennington. "How many men named Emmett do you know, boys?"

The tall one elaborately shook his head. "Been quite a spell since I've seen Emmett Roberts," he said, turning sly and clever. "The last time was over near Tucomcori. He was sittin' in a poker game with . . ."

"Mister," broke in Sam, "I'm glad to know he's close. No, I don't mean in Tucomcori, which wouldn't be close at all. I meant close enough so that when you boys left his camp you didn't even have to fetch along canteens on your saddles and you never sweated your horses. Now go on back and tell him I'm waitin' just like I was last time, but with one difference. Next time he gets both barrels."

The black-eyed one would have said something but his friend put out a hand, silencing him. He was gazing straight at Sam Bennington, his face cold and skeptical. "Never mind," he quietly told his friend, "I don't like this lyin' anyway. All right, Marshal, we come from Emmett."

"To spy?"

The tall man didn't answer that. He said: "You know what this stinkin' town'll look like if he decides to hit it again?"

"About like it looks right now, mister," said Sam Bennington, "but with one change . . . boothill will have some fresh graves, with Emmett Roberts's grave in a special place right near the front gate, so all the two-bit gunfighters who pass down this way'll have a good look at it first, before they get any fatal ideas."

The tall man gently moved his head from side to side. "Marshal, you may have guts. You may have had luck once, too, but you sure ain't very smart."

199

"Care to elaborate?" asked Bennington.

"Twenty guns, Marshal, not nine, this time. You think a lousy scatter-gun with two barrels would make a dent in twenty men?"

Sam saw Leverett Hall coming slowly along his bar from the edge of his eye. He said: "Nick, three beers." Hall impassively turned and went back the way he'd just come. The black-eyed gunfighter shifted position. Along the bar and out across the room loafing townsmen and ranchmen were about as they'd been before, slouching and gazing at their cards, or the backbar shelves, or at the drinks they were nursing along, straining with all their might to catch every spoken word in the silence of the Bella Union's large room. The black-eyed gunfighter didn't like it, obviously; he looked up a couple of times at his companion, but the tall man wasn't to be diverted. He was making his appraisal of Sam Bennington. He was trying to see weakness somewhere, trying to guess what his chances might be the way one stray dog eyes another stray dog.

Sam said to the tall one: "Twenty guns would make a difference, mister. I'd need ten more shotguns, wouldn't I?"

The gunman's upper lip pulled back in a wolfish, sour grin. "Where'd you get 'em, Marshal, in this yellow-livered place? Not likely."

Leverett Hall brought the beers, set them up, lingered a moment to look at the three men opposite him, then went back down his bar again. Sam rolled his head sideward. "Cool beer tastes good on a day like this. It's hot out. And it could get a lot hotter."

The black-eyed man turned, reaching for a glass. His taller companion did, too, but not right away, not until he and Sam Bennington had traded their last long look. Sam was the last one to reach — he did it left-handed. For several still minutes there wasn't a sound in the Bella Union, then the doors were thrust open, and Dutch John came halfway through the opening. He was profusely sweating. It was a very hot afternoon. He saw those two gunfighters. He saw Sam Bennington watching them, a glass of beer held aloft in Sam's left hand, and he saw the stony expression upon the face of Leverett Hall, and backed out of the saloon without taking one more inward step. When the louvered doors swung back and forth in their decreasing pattern after Oberdorf's withdrawal, the black-eyed gunfighter looked at them over his shoulders, and kept right on watching them until they were still again, then shot his tall companion a plain look of warning.

"Boys," said Bennington, "if Roberts wants to try it, let him, but if you're halfway smart, you won't ride in with him." Then Sam turned and walked across the silent room and out through those same louvered doors.

That was when Zeke Wicke came driving back into town, sweating like a bull in fly time, sitting atop the high seat of one of his freight wagons beside Everett Bull, looking pleased with the sleek hitch he was tooling expertly down the roadway, grinding the powder-fine dust to life as he went along under the fierce

201

summertime sun, which was falling rapidly lower in the reddening west. He and Ev Bull saw Sam and threw him two little casual salutes. He nodded back, leaning upon an upright post out front of the Bella Union.

Charley Jones appeared across the road in the window of Zeke's office. Over by the open gate leading into the wagon yard, John Oberdorf was copiously sweating out in plain sight, but less than five feet from one of the mighty corner posts. Down the road upon a bench in front of the Hurd's Crossing café sat two cowboys, sun-blackened, lean, tight-lipped men. As Zeke tooled his hitch into the wagon yard, he saw John Oberdorf standing there and was surprised. John sunburned easily; he was very pale-skinned. Zeke started to haul back on the ribbons but Ev Bull, pulling at his beard, had also seen those others, including old Charley Jones, and he muttered something quick and sharp under his breath. Zeke drove on inside without stopping, then both he and Ev Bull shinnied down the high side of the wagon and headed without any waste motion, straight across the yard toward the office.

It was about then those two gunfighters strolled out into the soft-lighted dying day and paused out front of the Bella Union, gazing first over where Sam Bennington was leaning and idly smoking, then turned a little at a time to pick up the others, seemingly just happening to be standing or sitting, gazing straight back at them, every one of them, even Dutch John, with a belt gun strapped around their middles.

The tall one said: "Marshal, you figure you got the ten you'd need?"

Sam shrugged and went on smoking, saying nothing in reply.

Across the road Zeke Wicke's front door opened, Everett Bull stepped through, and halted upon the edge of the yonder plank walk in the shade of the warped old wooden overhead awning, looking belligerently straight at those two gunfighters. He didn't have a belt gun on. Ev Bull was two inches over six feet tall and weighed two hundred and twenty pounds; there hadn't been very many times in his life when he'd needed a six-gun, providing he got close enough to an adversary first. He stepped off the sidewalk, shuffled over to Leverett Hall's tie rack, loosened the reins of the only two saddled animals tied there, then stepped back, and beckoned.

Both the gunmen studied Ev Bull from impassive faces. He didn't have a gun on, which simply meant, out there in the eyes of all those witnesses, they couldn't draw on him. He was as big as an Army mule to boot, with muscle bulging under his faded old butternut work shirt; jumping him in a dogfight wouldn't be too wise, either. He continued to beckon. The black-eyed man turned, spat into the roadway dust, then started forward. The tall man had more sand in his craw; he'd already demonstrated that back in the saloon. Still, grit under these circumstances wasn't going to be enough. Neither was a fast gun. He threw a sulphurous glare over at Sam Bennington, who was watching, and stamped down off the plank walk toward his horse.

Bull was solicitous. He stood holding each horse by the cheek of the bridle until those two gunfighters were safely across leather, then he released them, and stepped back out of the way.

Sam Bennington killed his cigarette underfoot and raised his face, saying: "Just remember what I said inside, boys. If he wants to come, try to stop him. Just make damned sure you're not riding with him."

The black-eyed one raised his rein hand. He was patently ready to depart, but the taller man leaned a moment, staring straight at Sam Bennington, then he said in a silky way: "Marshal, you'd be surprised how many ways there are to skin a cat, if the price is right." He nodded, booted his horse, and went loping on out of town with the black-eyed man right beside him.

Zeke Wicke came out, over across the road, and waspishly said: "Ev, you danged fool, why didn't you take the shotgun?" Those were the first loud words spoken since that pair of spying outlaws had ridden into town, and for some reason they evoked mirth. Maybe it wasn't just the words or the complaining way Zeke had said them. Perhaps it was the let-down, the sudden dissolving of all that previous tension. Even John Oberdorf, standing over there mopping off sweat with a limp bandanna, laughed out loud.

Ev Bull, though, only smiled. He was regarding the town marshal with a rueful little expression. He said the only thing that might have even been construed as humorous. "Damned if he mightn't fire me one of these days, at that, Mister Bennington. If he does, you got a need for a deputy town marshal?"

204

Sam straightened up and nodded. "Any time," he answered. "Any time at all, Ev."

That ended the eighth day. It also served notice on the people of Hurd's Crossing that Emmett Roberts was back, recovered finally from the deadly reversal he'd suffered here not too long before, full of unreasoning malice toward the town and against Sam Bennington. Sooner or later — probably sooner, folks whispered — Roberts would come.

CHAPTER
SEVEN

The morning coach that brought mail and newspapers and sometimes an occasional passenger lay over for a change of animals at Zeke Wicke's yard, then went on again, southward through the building heat, leaving behind the only comparatively recent news from the outside world. Hurd's Crossing would have to wait two days hence before another coach would repeat the process. The news was surprisingly good. Sam took the letters he'd received up to the Bella Union and spread them out atop the bar where everyone could see them. The only precaution he took was to station Leverett Hall's day barman right there to make certain no sticky-fingered gent walked off with the bank drafts. Made out to the community fund of Hurd's Crossing were rewards totaling close to $8,000 for four defunct fugitives from the law.

The news spread rapidly. Men came rushing in to see for themselves. Then the Lady's Order of Frontier Mothers, Wives, and Daughters sent in a deputation to demand that those letters be brought outside and posted on the front of Oberdorf's General Store where there was a kind of traditional notice board. They refused to step one foot past the iniquitous doors of

206

Leverett Hall's den of dissolution. Sam obediently took the letters down and posted them. He also put the bank drafts in Dutch John's mighty steel safe.

Hurd's Crossing, Charley Jones confided to Sam Bennington, was a rich damned town, nearly $8,000 richer than any town he'd ever before known. Charley rubbed his hands gleefully over that, and proposed that what the town needed was a splendid community hall, which could also double as headquarters for the volunteer fire brigade. Sam only smiled.

John Oberdorf had a suggestion, too. A fine clapboard Lutheran church. When Sam asked why Lutheran, Dutch John rolled his light blue eyes and said it was the only church he'd ever been in, so he just naturally had recommended it. But he was open to reason about the denomination. "It's the idea," he explained. "This town's never had a church. Since I've been here, it's never had but one camp meeting in fact, and that was three years back when the circuit-riding preacher ran up such a bill at the Bella Union he had had to preach nearly all day Sunday, and pass his hat five times, just to get enough cash to pay Leverett Hall and bail his horse out of the livery barn so he could ride on."

Ev Bull had the idea they eventually adopted. Do nothing with the money for now; just let it lie there in Oberdorf's strongbox. Sam had had that in mind anyway, but he was a tactful man and permitted the bearded big freighter to believe his idea was best and would be acted upon.

Leverett Hall took a stroll that evening, fetched up down in front of the jailhouse where Sam was slouching in the breathless night, smoking and watching his town, and Leverett lit one of those cigars he smoked, dropped down upon the same bench with a cross between a sigh and a grunt, then said: "Sam, it'll be a pity to bury you. For the first time since this lousy place was founded, someone's here who is interested in the town."

"I'm not searching out any pallbearers yet," murmured the town marshal. "When I need some, I'll let you know."

"When you need some," stated the saturnine saloon owner, "you'll be the last man to realize it. I heard what that gunfighter said to you just before he and his 'breed friend left town. If the price was right, someone would get you. That's bushwhack talk, Sam, pure and simple. I think you got the idea across to those men just fine, that Hurd's Crossing would be waiting, when Roberts wants to hit it again. I also think that gunfighter was thinking exactly as Roberts will think. He took a hell of a shellacking the last time he tried bracing the town. No matter how mad he is now, and how much he longs to see Hurd's Crossing burned to the ground, he's no damned fool. He's not going to come charging up the roadway. Not now, and that gunfighter knew it. Roberts is going to concentrate on getting you salted down first. Then, when he's got the one man in town out of the way who has come here and instilled a little pride and spirit into this place . . . then he'll come up this roadway with his twenty blazing guns."

Sam kept on idly smoking and gazing up and down the evening roadway. "Seems you 'n' I think pretty much alike on some things," he said quietly. "I came to that same conclusion this afternoon."

"What have you done about it, besides sitting out here to make a target of yourself?"

Sam killed his smoke. "What can a man do when the initiative lies with the other side, General? Get set and wait."

Hall snorted. "Too bad you weren't a general officer in the Yankee Army during the war," he said. "We'd have cleaned 'em out. Sam, a man . . . or an army . . . strictly defending itself never wins. Offense, not defense, makes a winner in war, in life, in private feuds. You keep sitting here waiting for Roberts to strike, and he'll get you sure." Hall considered the long gray ash of his stogie a moment, then added: "Suppose we got ourselves about twenty, thirty local men, including some of the local ranchers and cowboys, then went hunting for Roberts and this bunch of cut-throats he's collected."

Sam turned to gaze at the heavier, slightly older man. "I'll tell you what would happen. Roberts would be watching and waiting. The minute we were five miles out he'd come in from the south, maybe, or the north, hit Hurd's Crossing like a whirlwind, and from five miles off we'd see the black smoke rising."

For a moment neither of them had anything more to say. Up in front of the Bella Union several cowboys hauled up and sprang down, laughing and loudly talking back and forth. They'd evidently had a long ride

209

from some outlying cow camp to reach Leverett Hall's oasis and were immensely pleased to be there now. Across from Hall's place, behind the high, barred gate of Zeke Wicke's wagon yard fence, someone let out a high, anguished cry, and fell to swearing at a horse or mule. It was a reasonably safe bet to assume some hostler up there had been painfully kicked.

Then Hall said: "Maybe you're right at that, Sam. Maybe Roberts is that smart. Although I sure as hell doubt it. Anyway, why sit out here?"

Bennington shrugged. "The darkness is a good friend to a marked man. A lot better friend than four walls with a lamp lighting them."

Hall slapped his thick legs, and stood up. "Well," he murmured, "what I really came along to say was . . . you did a good thing by turning all that bounty money over to the town. I think that's probably the first decent thing anyone ever did for Hurd's Crossing. Folks are very pleased." Hall gazed straight downward in that impassively aloof way he had, and added: "But, Sam, don't be deluded. When you started your war with Roberts, you bought a pretty lonely chore for yourself. They're all up there agreeing with each other in my saloon what a fine fellow you are, but when the chips are down, you're going to find yourself quite alone." Hall turned and walked off.

Bennington sat a while longer out front of his jailhouse. There was something about being relaxed and alone in the darkness to make a man low in spirit and morale; there always was. He got up and shrugged as though shaking off the effect of unpleasant realities or haunting memories, and went strolling southward toward the livery barn. Before he got into the doorway lights down there, though, he swung right and passed out through to the alleyway. From a dark spot back there he had an excellent view up the lighted runway. There was no activity; a hostler was reading a tattered magazine cocked back against the tack room wall, yawning now and then. There were stalled horses in there crunching hay and grain. The scene was normal enough.

Sam turned and walked northward, remaining in the back alley until he got up behind Zeke Wicke's big fenced-in yard. There, he found a little postern gate from the alleyway into the freight yard and entered. There was a light up in Wicke's log office. There was another light back across the yard where a kind of bunkhouse stood. The only other lights were at intervals, hanging from pegs along the front of the stalls and corrals where animals drowsily moved, here and there.

Bennington crossed toward the office but went along its south wall as far as the fence permitted. From over at the Bella Union sounds of good-natured revelry were constant, sometimes louder than at other times, but never entirely diminishing. Elsewhere, though, Hurd's Crossing was dark; storefronts showed no life at all. Bennington went back to the rear entrance to Zeke Wicke's office and walked in. Zeke was there, wearing a green eye-shade and chewing savagely on a mutilated stub of a pencil while he worked over a large ledger. He looked up, saw it was Bennington and not, as he'd

211

obviously expected, one of his yard men, and took the pencil out of his mouth, put it in the big book, and closed the thing.

"Nice night," said Sam, staying in the shadows back there. "Not much of a moon though."

Zeke looked baffled. He sensed Bennington's call wasn't entirely social because he said: "Sometimes it's better not to even have a cussed lamp lit."

Sam stepped around, staying away from the light and the window, and halted beside the door, which was recessed and dark. He opened it, stepped out, stood out there for a long moment, then returned to Zeke's office.

Wicke put aside his green eye-shade and reached for his hat. "You expecting trouble?" he asked. "Marshal, not in here . . . please."

Sam chuckled. "Zeke, if there's trouble, you've got the stoutest four log walls in town."

Wicke reached out and turned down his lamp. He got up and looked across the intervening distance at Bennington, his prominent Adam's apple barely moving, his gaunt frame and long, hawkish features soft-shadowed in the gloom. "Marshal, who is it . . . Roberts?"

"It's no one yet, Zeke. I'm just not taking too many chances. There's one thing about the darkness . . . it works as good for one side as for the other."

"But you're expecting trouble," insisted the freight-line owner. "Listen, Marshal, I'm a businessman. It's been thirty years since . . ."

212

The gunshot sounded flat and harsh, slicing across Zeke Wicke's words and cutting them off in mid-sentence. It came from southward, down the roadway somewhere in the vicinity of the livery barn, or perhaps not that far south. Zeke was bolted to the floor, but just for a second. Then he lunged for his lamp, violently blew a big gust of breath down the mantle to plunge the office into total darkness, and raised up to squint over at Bennington.

Sam was gone. The office door was ajar. A little gray light filtered in from the roadway, and all that earlier sound of pleasantry from across the road at the Bella Union Saloon was now replaced with a crawling, frightening silence. Zeke tiptoed across to the door to close it, but, when he had his hand upon the latch, something held him back. He muttered something profane under his breath, then moved very carefully around the door, and stepped outside.

Across the road several men were slipping up between the south wall of the Bella Union and its neighboring building to the south. There were guns in their hands. They were also being exceedingly careful. Apparently they were the townsmen and cattlemen who'd been inside there when the gunshot had sounded; they hadn't rushed out the front way — only fools would have done that — they'd slipped out the back way and were now working their cautious way around toward the front roadway again.

Up and down the roadway where heavy shadows lay in shielded places, there wasn't a sign of movement for a long while, then Sam Bennington called out from down in front of his jailhouse. "There's been a man hurt down here! I need a hand with him."

Zeke and the cowmen across the road peered out and around. Bennington was discernible only when he stood up. He'd been kneeling beside something sprawled on the plank walk out front of his jailhouse. He called out one more time, but no one went down to him right away; the men waited and looked around and gripped their six-guns. Finally a massive, thick, and ox-like silhouette stepped forth across the road and started down toward Bennington with a thrusting stride. Zeke recognized Everett Bull. He and the others still hung back, waiting to see whether Ev would make it or not.

He did. Nothing happened. There were no more shots. The frightening silence ran on and on, broken finally when Ev Bull's deep-down voice rumbled very clearly through the empty night: "Good Lord! Who did it, Marshal?"

Those words broke the spell. Zeke and the others stepped gingerly out, looked up and down, then started in a quick rush toward where Bennington and Ev Bull were standing. There was a man lying face down at their feet, one arm flung out, the other arm curled under him, his black hat lying on its top five feet away, and his holstered six-gun still in place with its little leather tie-down thong holding the weapon securely.

One of the cattlemen pushed through the gathering crowd to bend for a better look. "Damn," he said a little breathlessly, "that's Pete Farraday who rides for me."

Sam Bennington put up a hand when several cowmen moved in as though to take hold of Pete Farraday. "No hurry," he said. "He died while we were waiting for someone to get down here."

The men straightened up, looking at one another, at the dead cowboy, and over at Sam Bennington. The only man to move off was Ev Bull. He stepped out into the roadway and went purposefully hiking on across toward the general store. Evidently he and Sam Bennington had speculated a little before the others had arrived.

CHAPTER
EIGHT

They took Pete Farraday to where his horse stood out front of the Bella Union and lashed him across the saddle, head down one side, feet dangling on the other side. Dutch John Oberdorf was there, looking as though he'd jumped up hastily out of a chair somewhere and jumped into his coat and hat on the run. He was wearing a belt gun under his coat. Charley Jones was also there. He was asking Zeke Wicke what in the devil had happened when Everett Bull returned from across the road and handed a bright brass casing to the town marshal. Bennington studied the casing, then dropped it into a pocket as Ev pointed straight across the road.

"From between them two buildings," Bull growled. "He had his horse back at the other end. He smoked a cigarette while he waited."

"Couldn't have been much of a wait," said Sam, recalling that he'd only left the identical spot where Farraday had been shot not more than fifteen or twenty minutes earlier.

Charley said: "Who was he? What'd he have against Pete Farraday? Well, hell, I've known Pete since . . ."

"You're missing the point," said Bennington quietly, and every face lifted toward him in the darkness. "It

216

wasn't Farraday at all, Charley. That bullet was meant for me. Farraday and I were pretty much alike in heft, build, and dress. That's the first thing I noticed when I got here."

"You took a dumb chance, runnin' out of my place like you did," stated Zeke Wicke. "He could've got you both."

Sam shook his head. "I heard his horse leaving before I was halfway down here. He thinks he got me."

Leverett Hall came from over across the road. He'd evidently walked southward down the back alley over behind his saloon. He was carrying the shotgun from behind his bar. Some of the bystanders were beginning to drift away now. The dead man had been removed, the place of concealment for the murderer had been revealed, and now there was just quiet, general talk down in front of the jailhouse. A couple of cowboys recognized Hall and nodded to him as they passed each other. Hall didn't bother nodding back. Charley Jones and Zeke lingered, then Charley said he thought this called for a drink, and hooked Zeke's arm to get the freight-line owner started up toward the Bella Union with him. Zeke went, but he seemed reluctant.

"Well," said Hall dryly, looking straight at Sam Bennington, "I reckon we called the shot an hour or so back, Marshal, when we figured . . . for a price . . . one of them would try it."

Bennington nodded. He was quiet, seemingly withdrawn, had been like that since the others had rushed down belatedly to take away the dead man. Hall jerked his head to indicate the route he'd just traversed

217

to reach this spot. "He was riding a spotted horse. I saw him when I ran out across the alley after the gunshot. Everyone else was working around toward the front roadway. I figured it was an ambush. There was just one shot. I also figured he'd gotten you."

"So did he," said Sam, stepping back to the bench in front of the jailhouse and sinking down upon it. "He had reason to. Farraday looked enough like me from that distance, in the darkness, and he was smack dab in front of this jailhouse."

Hall stepped up onto the plank walk, draped the stubby-barreled scatter-gun across one bent arm, and stood there gazing at the town marshal, his expression sardonic. "One miss," he murmured. "I reckon they're entitled to one miss, Sam."

"Yeah." Bennington fell to making a smoke. He had nothing more to say evidently. He lit up, exhaled, and gazed over at that dark dogtrot between the buildings where his would-be assassin had patiently waited, only to kill the wrong man. "Did you happen to know this Pete Farraday?" he asked Leverett Hall.

"Passably well. As well as I care to know any of them."

Bennington lifted a jaundiced glance. "Someday you're going to grow up," he murmured. "It's like I told you one time, General. All this brooding does is make you as bad in one way as the men you despise are in their way. But for now just tell me one thing. Did Pctc Farraday normally tell the truth?"

Hall was slow to answer. He seemed not very interested in Pete Farraday at all. He seemed more

218

inclined to take hard exception to that other thing Sam Bennington had said. In the end, though, he answered: "Farraday was a truthful man as far as I know. He was a rather decent kind of a cowboy. Why do you ask?"

"Well, you see, Pete Farraday didn't die right away. He didn't cash in until just before that mob of heroes finally got enough guts to poke their heads out."

Hall was interested. "You mean Farraday spoke to you?"

Bennington nodded, and returned his glance to that yonder dogtrot where the fatal bullet had come from. "Yeah. He spoke to me. He said . . . 'Square it up for me, Marshal?'" Sam raised his eyes. "He also said something else . . . that's why I was wondering about his truthfulness. He said the man who shot him was named Esteban, or something like that. Then he cashed in."

Leverett Hall had no difficulty making sense out of the dead man's first statement. "He knew he'd been mistaken for you."

Bennington inclined his head, watching Hall's face crease up from hard concentration. "Who's Esteban?" he asked, and Hall slowly wagged his head back and forth. He'd never heard of anyone by that name locally.

"He either got a good look at the man who shot him," said Bennington, "or he knew in advance this Esteban was going to be over there."

"If he knew, then why did he walk down here to get himself shot?" Hall inquired.

"To perhaps bring a message to this Esteban . . . who knows? Maybe he didn't know anything about the ambush, and just blundered into it, then recognized the bushwhacker."

Hall turned and gazed across at the little passageway where the fatal shot had come from. "Unless," he mused aloud slowly, "Esteban, or whatever his name was, stepped out first, then fired. Farraday or no one else could've recognized him in that dark dogtrot over there."

Sam had already arrived at this same conclusion. "What's bothering me is that, if Farraday knew this Esteban, or whatever the name was he muttered, then some of the other range men must also know him. I'm going to find out. If I can identify one of them, it shouldn't be too much of a chore to locate another one or two."

Hall was skeptical. "What good will all that do you, Marshal? Roberts isn't going to be long discovering you aren't dead. He'll try again. And, believe me, next time he'll do his damnedest to make sure." Hall shook his head grimly. "There's just one way to stop all this. I told you that before. Make up a strong posse and start a dragnet all around, get an inkling where they're camped, then move *en masse* against them."

Sam Bennington softly smiled at Leverett Hall. "That'd be the classical field tactic, wouldn't it?" he murmured. "But this is a different kind of war, Nick. The rules are entirely different. Besides, I don't want to get a lot of cattlemen and townsmen shot up. When I've run down one or two of Roberts's gun crew, I'll sweat it out of them where he's camped. Then I'll send for the troops from Fort Jackson."

Hall heaved a mighty sigh and looked resigned. "You're going to lose your battle," he dourly said. "And you'll be damned lucky if you don't lose your life, too." He turned and went shuffling back up the northward plank walk, shotgun hooked under one arm, both hands thrust into his trouser pockets, and his head low in bleak speculation.

Sam crossed over to the front of Oberdorf's store, paced up and down for a moment, then stepped into the dogtrot where he picked up the horse sign exactly as Ev Bull had said it was. He had no inkling he was being watched until, moving northward away from the dogtrot, he picked up the very faint sound of something back in that gloomy passageway abrasively rubbing. It was the kind of insignificant sound a man might ordinarily hear a dozen times a day and never heed. But this was neither daytime, nor was it an ordinary circumstance, so Sam sprang back against the rough rear wall of Dutch John's building, palmed his six-gun, and waited.

Whoever was in there stopped moving just short of the alleyway. Evidently he'd also caught the aura of peril in the roundabout night. Sam heard him lift a gun from a leather holster. He didn't much speculate on who that might be, although it seemed impossible it would be the man called Esteban returning stealthily for another try, because Bennington was confident Esteban was convinced he'd killed the right man.

He didn't have time to speculate, either, for the man began moving again, placing one foot cautiously ahead of the other foot. Sam waited until he knew the stranger

221

was just two feet from the alleyway exit, then cocked his own gun and said: "Keep right on coming, mister, with that gun straight up over your head. If you don't, I'll cut you down in there, where you can't get away from the lead. Just step right on out!"

There was a rasping, harsh sound of breath being sucked violently inward, then a low growl and hearty curse as Ev Bull walked out, holding his six-gun up above his head.

Sam looked, and made a wry face, and holstered his .45. "That was close," he murmured. "Too close. If you're hell-bent on buying into this fight, Ev, then suppose we come to some kind of agreement and work together. I sure don't want any friends on my conscience . . . nor do I want my killing on your conscience." Bennington smiled. It had been a close thing; he didn't actually feel like smiling, but the hang-dog look of purest chagrin on the mighty freighter's bearded face made him try to pass it off as lightly as he could.

"I saw you walk over here," rumbled the bigger man. "I figured you just might try trackin' him, even though it's almighty dark. An' I figured followin' along just might keep you alive."

Sam said: "Tell you what. Go get a leave of absence from Wicke, then come on over to the jailhouse. If he'll agree to hire you back after this is over, I can sure use you. Now, go on. I think Wicke's up at the Bella Union."

Ev Bull turned and went forging back up through the dogtrot. Sam watched him and thought it was no

222

wonder Bull had given himself away in that narrow place; he completely filled it from wall to wall as he worked his way up yonder toward the roadway again.

Sam had never thought of trying to track down Esteban. It was too dark, there were too many interfering tracks, and Esteban would be miles away by now. All he'd wanted to ascertain was that the man had certainly been hiding in wait, and, as he turned to head back up through the dogtrot the way Bull had just gone, he satisfied himself, by standing clear of the two buildings out front, that someone over there in front of the jail-house would, for a fact, be able to see and recognize and identify someone standing where Esteban had evidently stood.

After that he went down to the livery barn. It was a routine check; he knew, because he'd spied on the barn earlier, that no stranger had ridden into it. Still, he asked the night man about someone on a spotted horse. The night hawk knew nothing; no one had ridden a spotted horse into the barn in weeks. In fact, said the night hawk, spotted horses were pretty rare in these parts. Range men wouldn't be caught dead on them. "Fit only for squaw Injuns an' kids," was the way the livery man put it, and that was how horsemen and range men throughout the Southwest felt about spotted horses. It was nothing new to Sam Bennington.

He then strolled on up to the jailhouse and entered the office, turned up the lamp, and flung aside his hat. He meant to use Ev Bull to run down this Esteban, at least to determine from among the range riders and townsmen where such a man might be working, or had been working. Sam was confident that Farraday had recognized the killer. This also meant, in Sam Bennington's view, that other range men or townsmen must also know this man.

He sat down, made a smoke, popped it between his lips, then didn't get a chance to light it because Ev Bull came in out of the night, broadly smiling. "It's fine with Zeke," he reported. "He said . . . if I'm still alive when this is over . . . he'll take me back."

Sam nodded approval of that, then got right down to facts. The results were a little startling, too, for the first question he asked was about the name Esteban. Ev Bull's candid, short answer came right back with genuine worthwhile information.

"You mean Franco Esteban? Sure I know him. He's worked for two or three of the big cow outfits around."

Sam straightened up in his chair. "Did Franco Esteban know Pete Farraday?"

"He'd have to have known him," stated the big, bearded freighter, going across to a chair and dropping down astraddle of it. "They both punched cows for the Hardy outfit northeast of Hurd's Crossing last fall and all winter long."

Sam studied his new deputy a moment, then reached for his hat. "Can you find this Hardy outfit in the dark?" he asked.

Ev was puzzled but he nodded without asking any questions. "I could find it in a blizzard," he said. "I came into this country drivin' a Hardy chuck wagon. You mean you want to go out there . . . right now . . . tonight?"

224

Sam stood up. "Right now . . . tonight," he answered, and reached for the door as Ev Bull heaved off his chair and ambled forward.

"All right," said the freighter. "But they'll all be in their blankets."

"We'll chouse 'em out," said Sam, and closed the door behind them.

CHAPTER
NINE

The Hardy outfit was extensive. It had to be; so was any other cattle operation using the desert country for the simple reason that it was very often twenty steps for a critter between mouthfuls of grass. Unlike deeper, blacker soil, the desert earth was shallow, gravelly, and very unproductive. It wasn't at all unusual for a large cow outfit to use a full ten to twenty thousand acres. Desert cowmen didn't figure their rate of weight gain on acres of grass. They figured it on how far a critter had to walk to get a drink of water. In other words, if a beef animal had to walk five miles for a drink, he was losing weight because he didn't eat — he walked.

The Hardy outfit had been on the desert a good many years. Old Abner Hardy of Tennessee had been the first to trail a herd through Apacheria — and come out still wearing his headpiece of hair. Since those days his three sons, all middle-aged men by now, controlled and directed the far-flung destiny of the Hardy cow operation. As Ev Bull explained it to Sam Bennington while they were pleasantly cruising through the warm, soft night, there were five or six cow camps where the Hardy riders stayed. There were no buildings at any of them except one roofed lean-to, always erected by the

226

Hardys at their camps to keep the provisions dry in case of an inadvertent rainstorm. Otherwise the men lived on the ground and slept on it, as Ev said, and also ate while sitting on it. Ev also said he wasn't surprised that Franco Esteban had turned out to be a renegade, because the Hardys didn't hire any peach-fuzz-faced riders; they only took on the toughest, sometimes meanest, most saddle-callused men they could find, "Mexicans," Ev Bull related, "have been a favorite of the Hardys for years. Mexicans and . . ." — Ev shrugged big shoulders — "gun-handy gents. When I was with 'em years back, I used to wonder how rich a man could be if he'd just corral a passel of Hardy riders in a jailhouse somewhere, then thumb through the posters on fugitives until he'd matched every man with one of 'em."

Sam Bennington thought Ev was exaggerating but he let his new deputy town marshal talk on. Then, well past midnight when someone challenged them from within a clump of little desert trees, Sam got his first introduction to the excellent probability that Ev hadn't been exaggerating the least little bit. They rose up around him like Apaches, armed and wide-awake.

Ev singled out one older man with leathery hide and a totally uncompromising mouth, and called him Jim. He told the older man who Bennington was, and who they wanted to talk to.

Jim listened, as hostile as a Gila monster, never once taking his eyes off Bennington, then he eventually said: "Franco quit the outfit three weeks back, Ev. I think he said he was goin' to drift on over to Tucomcori." The sparse, grim-faced older man then said, without a break in his verbal stride nor any change in inflection: "How come you to team up with a lawman? Work gettin' hard to find down there in Hurd's Crossing?"

Sam Bennington waited for Bull's reply, and, when it didn't come right away, he said: "Old-timer, it has its advantages. At least he can get a bath when he wants one."

The stiff-standing rugged old range man shifted the hold he had on his six-gun, spat, and said: "Marshal, you aren't very sociable, considering there are eight guns pointed at you from around an' about. Bad enough you come a-slippin' onto folks in the late night like this. Why, if you'd been Apaches an' if we hadn't had our ears to the ground to pick up your sounds, you could've . . ."

"There are no renegade bucks anywhere around here and haven't been for five years," stated Bennington. "As for getting you out of your sougan . . . mister, I'd say you probably hadn't been in it very long anyway."

The man called Jim was silent for a moment, looking straight over at the pair of mounted men. He seemed to be having trouble arriving at a worthwhile assessment of Sam Bennington. Then he said: "Marshal, you're either an ignorant damn' fool, comin' into my camp and talkin' like you don't care whether you live or die, or else you're mighty capable. Y' know, I'm gettin' just curious enough to want to find out which it is."

Ev Bull swung off his horse and looked at Jim. "Don't get too curious," he warned him, "or you just might really find out, Jim. Now tell me something. Who rode with Franco Esteban out here?"

Jim let his breath out and turned reluctantly toward Bull. "I never could whip you, Ev," he growled, "so I reckon I might as well go along with this." Jim turned and carelessly pointed at a short, stocky, half-blood-looking cowboy. "Him," he announced. "That's Shadow O'Brien." Jim smiled. "Don't ask me where a feller as Mexican-lookin' as him got a name like Shadow O'Brien. He and Franco Esteban were ridin' pardners."

Sam Bennington and Ev Bull turned. The man named O'Brien was woodenly impassive and armed with a tilted-up carbine. He looked more Mexican or Indian than Irish. He also looked villainous enough to do anything that might cross his mind.

Bennington said: "O'Brien, tilt that gun down." O'Brien didn't move. Ev Bull's face darkened. He repeated the order in Spanish. Still, O'Brien kept his gun pointed at Bennington. He didn't change expression; in fact, he scarcely even flicked his muddy dark eyes from Bennington to Ev Bull and back again.

Then Jim growled the same order at him, and Shadow O'Brien finally lowered his Winchester, grounded it in fact, and leaned upon it, looking dark and impassive.

Sam had an idea that this camp was like many others; no one would harm a lawman entering the place, unless he tried to make some member of the riding crew ride back to some town with him. Then the place would blossom guns all around. Sam pondered this. He meant to take O'Brien back to Hurd's Crossing with him. He stepped out of his saddle and studied Jim, the range boss.

"I want this man for questioning," he said. "No formal charge . . . just questioning."

Jim's brow darkened. His shaded face looked wary and doubtful. "It's up to O'Brien whether he wants to go or not," he finally said, understanding Sam Bennington's position exactly. "Well, Shadow, how about it?"

O'Brien ran his muddy eyes over to his range boss and shrugged. Then he looked at Bennington and said: "You goin' to lock me up?"

Sam shook his head. "Not the way things stand now I'm not. I don't have any charges against you. All I want is a little palaver."

"Palaver right here," said O'Brien. "That'll save me the long ride back."

Sam made a fast decision. "You'll get paid for the long ride back," he retorted.

O'Brien's eyes brightened perceptibly for the first time. "How much?"

"Ten dollars."

Now Shadow O'Brien's eyes kindled with genuine interest and cupidity. He worked for $12 a month and grub. $10 for a day's ride and some talk was a real windfall. "Wait," he said, "I'll get my horse."

Jim strolled on over finally, out of the brush that had partially concealed him. He swung an arm carelessly at the other Hardy riders. "Go on back to camp an' get some shut-eye," he said. The cowboys lowered their weapons, turned, and dutifully went westerly in the same direction Shadow O'Brien had gone.

When Jim was up close, he was still having trouble placing and pegging Sam Bennington, but now at least he was turning a little amiable. He said: "Marshal, you can figure 'em right, anyway. Shadow'd sell his soul . . . if he had one . . . for ten dollars. If you'd tried takin' him with guns, you'd never have made it. You sized him up about right. Now, tell me, what has Franco done that you want to know where you can find him?"

Sam slowly smiled. Jim was hard and leathery and obviously dedicated, but that didn't mean he was any kind of a fool. A man couldn't be a fool and ramrod a crowd of human two-legged wolves as long as Jim had clearly been at it.

"Tried a bushwhack," said Sam. "You know him, Jim, does it sound like him?"

Jim looked at Ev, winked, then nodded. "We don't hire any other kind at this particular cow camp," he said drolly. "Y' see, Marshal, we never relied on the law from Hurd's Crossing because it never done us a lick o' good. And down here in this particular camp we've been hit by Mex raiders from over the line, Texan rustlers from across the easterly desert, flashfloods, an' the wrath o' God. I just can't hire any other kind of cowboy than what I got . . . the toughest kind that grows legs. As for Franco . . . sure, he'd bushwhack. So would Shadow O'Brien, so don't neglect to hand him that ten-spot when you're through with him."

They talked a little longer about nothing very important until Shadow O'Brien returned astride a ewe-necked, long-legged ugly Grulla gelding that didn't appear to have a brain in his head but that could run a hole in the daylight. As the range boss watched Ev and Sam mount up, join Shadow O'Brien, and all turn southwesterly, he said: "Shadow, don't you forget who that damned Grulla horse belongs to."

O'Brien looked back stonily, straightened forward, then abruptly raised his head and laughed. "He don't figure I'll really steal Mister Hardy's damned horse. He only wonders if I mightn't is all."

They talked a little, about general topics and events, as they rode, but each time Sam Bennington maneuvered the talk around to Franco Esteban, the half-breed cowboy would throw him a dazzling, white-toothed smile, and veer off. Finally, with town in sight down the shank of the night, Ev Bull said he'd lope ahead. He didn't say he thought there might be a bushwhack up ahead somewhere; he just said he'd mosey on, then did so, riding at a walk with his head constantly moving.

As soon as Ev was gone, Shadow O'Brien said: "Lawman, it was Franco who tried to put you down without no chance, warn't it?" Sam nodded. "Well, then, lawman, the way I got this figured, you want him right bad. Maybe for somethin' like attempted murder, maybe." Sam nodded again. O'Brien looked ahead down through the soft-silent, endless gloom for a moment before he spoke again. "Well, then, lawman, if I can help you, it sure ought to be worth more'n lousy ten-spot, hadn't it?"

Bennington felt the rising of distaste and revulsion, but it was dark, O'Brien couldn't see it in his eyes or upon his face. "It might be worth more," conceded Bennington. "That depends on just how good your help turns out to be."

"Suppose, lawman, I took you right to him an' you could make the arrest."

This was precisely what Sam Bennington wanted. He'd only hoped perhaps to get a lead on the whereabouts of Franco Esteban that would enable him to locate the rest of the Roberts gang. He'd hardly expected this much success. "I've got a better idea," he said, not trusting Shadow O'Brien at all. "You go get your old pardner, bring him closer to town somewhere out on the range where I'll be waiting. Then I'll make my arrest. Also . . . then . . . I'll be alive to pay you the bounty."

Shadow O'Brien didn't even hesitate. "Done!" he exclaimed, and swung his muddy, ferret-eyes around. "How much bounty?"

Sam did some fast arithmetic. He'd never get a dime from the town fathers, he was confident of that. They'd find a dozen, perhaps two dozen reasons for objecting to this kind of a deal. He had $100 in his pockets, money he'd acquired at Fort Jackson by cashing in some pay vouchers before riding to Hurd's Crossing. To a man like Shadow O'Brien that was a sizeable fortune, but, if he handed it over, he was going to be broke. If he tried to bargain for any less, he was risking something much more distasteful — total failure. This wasn't the time to bargain.

"One hundred dollars," he said, and saw the swift passage of avarice across Shadow O'Brien's swarthy features. Then O'Brien broadly smiled and stopped his horse.

"You just bought yourself Franco Esteban," Shadow said. "Providin' I see that money now. At least half of it now, anyway."

Sam halted, looped his reins, dug out some money, and peeled off five $10 bills. "Take 'em," he told the cowboy, stuffing the rest of the money back into his pocket.

O'Brien grasped his $50, then said: "Marshal, you promised me ten for ridin' to town with you."

Bennington shook his head. "When you deliver Esteban where I can take him, I'll pay the other fifty . . . and the ten. But not until. You understand?"

O'Brien understood. He held the $50 up close to his face, counting it in the night, then stuffed it into a shirt pocket, grinning from ear to ear. For a man who'd just sold out a friend, he was remarkably happy and jovial. "I like doin' business with you." He chuckled. "Now I'll tell you how we got to work this. Y' see, I don't know exactly where Franco's campin'. All I know for sure is he's with some other fellers either easterly or southerly from Hurd's Crossing. It'll take me maybe a day or two to find him. But due south from town alongside the stage road about seven miles off, there's a big rock about a hundred or two hundred feet from the ruts. Folks used to call it Robber's Rock because so many hold-up men used to hide there an' stop the coaches years back. You know the place?"

Sam didn't know it, but he said he'd find it.

"Sure," agreed Shadow O'Brien. "You jus' keep ridin' south on the stage road until you see it. It's the only big rock anywhere around. All right, Marshal, day after tomorrow sometime I'll come ridin' along down there with Franco."

Sam considered this plan, and finally agreed because he was confident Shadow O'Brien could find Esteban in two days. It would involve a lot of riding, but Shadow had been paid amply for the discomfort and deprivation involved, criss-crossing the summertime Arizona desert in his search. Sam raised his reins. "Sometime day after tomorrow down at Robber's Rock," he said. "And Shadow . . . don't do anything silly, will you? You'll not only lose fifty dollars . . . I'll hunt you down."

O'Brien's big smile soured just a little as he said: "You're talkin' like a man who don't have much trust in me, Marshal."

Sam nodded. He didn't have much trust in Shadow O'Brien. He didn't have any trust in him. "Day after tomorrow," he murmured, and eased his horse over into a lope to catch up with Ev Bull.

CHAPTER
TEN

Ev thought the whole idea was crazy and bluntly said so as he and Bennington drifted back into town a couple of hours ahead of sunup. He particularly objected when Bennington said he'd go down to Robber's Rock alone.

"Marshal, Shadow O'Brien's one of the most totally treacherous men I've ever known. It wouldn't surprise me one danged bit to find out he was a spy for Emmett Roberts, or at the very least maybe a part-time renegade who rode with the Roberts crew. If you go down there alone, sure as the devil they'll have a trap laid an' . . ."

"That road southward," stated Sam, "as far as I recall it, is open. There are no hills or trees or anything else to conceal the fact that more than one man was riding down it. Ev, even if O'Brien is on the level and brings Esteban in, the sight of more than just one man coming toward him would scare him out of the country . . . and there'd go my chance for getting Esteban, and with it my chance for finding out what we've got to know about Roberts's gun crew. It's that simple."

"Simple," growled the big, bearded freighter. "Deadly is a better word, Marshal."

Sam Bennington, though, was far from being the novice Ev Bull thought him. He did not, however, go into this matter; he, instead, parted from Ev at the livery barn — where they were obliged to care for their own animals because the hostler was nowhere around — then went on up to his room, bedded down, and got slightly under two hours' rest before the sun came through his window and someone over at Charley Jones's shoeing shop industriously beat out a ringing tattoo on an anvil.

Bennington got breakfast at the café, went down to his jail-house, and put both booted feet atop the desk, tipped down his hat and slumped in the swivel chair. In this way he got another two hours of sleep. It may even have been slightly more than two hours, because when someone opened the office door and walked in, looking down a thin, slightly hooked nose at him in a caustic manner, it was Dr. Ralph Kleburg from Fort Jackson, and on the fastest horse a rider from Fort Jackson couldn't even come close to Hurd's Crossing in less than five hours.

Bennington sat up, thumbed back his hat, and owlishly regarded his visitor. "You're a far cry from home," he said to Captain Kleburg of the Medical Corps. "Who's with you?"

Kleburg was a beefy, deliberate, shrewd man turning gray around the ears. He removed his gauntlets, went to a chair, and dustily seated himself, looking and acting a trifle annoyed and sardonic. "No one is with me," he answered, fishing inside his blue tunic for a cigar, which he lighted and puffed upon. "Colonel Cross asked me

237

to stop by down here on my way over the mountains to Fort Tyler where I'm due to make the usual semi-annual inspection of dispensary facilities. I always make these trips without an escort on the assumption that Arizona Territory is now pacified." Kleburg removed the cigar, stared past it at Bennington, and added: "But that may not be quite correct, either, Sam. Down at the livery barn a few minutes ago I overhead some frightened men talking."

Bennington said: "I can imagine. Well, it just worked out this way, Captain. I took the job." Sam shrugged. "It seemed the best way to get the job done."

"The way those men were talking, Sam, I think I'd be doing more service if I turned right around, went back and told the colonel to get a company down here fast. According to them you . . . and this town . . . are perching atop a keg of dynamite with a short fuse under it."

Sam thought a moment, then said: "Doc, I don't want any troops yet. I may not want them at all. But if they were to show up around here today or tomorrow, it'd upset all my plans. They'd scare off the Roberts gang, which means Roberts would simply run away, stay away for a few weeks, then return. I want his hash settled one way or another within the next twenty-four hours. Unless it's done, Doc, I'll have failed. Also unless it's done my way, we won't have accomplished one damned definite thing."

"Sam, those men down at the livery barn swore up and down you couldn't last out the week. Now neither the colonel nor I feel there is anything here in Hurd's

Crossing worth that kind of risk, when with a troop or two of . . ."

"Doc," said Sam Bennington sharply, "I'm not threatening you, but get this straight. You butt in now and upset things for me, and I'll lock you up in my jailhouse until it's too late for you to get back to the colonel."

Kleburg sat and puffed and quietly sweated in his travel-stained blue uniform for a long while before saying any more. Then he tiredly wagged his head from side to side. "This is the damnedest thing I ever heard of!" he exclaimed. "There's a full regiment of bored troopers at the fort. Here you sit, dressed and acting like a civilian. And somewhere around here is a band of renegades dedicated to nothing more than seeing you dead. And you're too pig-headed to ask for help. Well, Sam, all right. I won't interfere. But I think I'll postpone my trip over the desert and beyond the mountains for a couple of days, just out of sheer curiosity." Kleburg turned sarcastic. "If you don't mind me hanging around, of course."

Sam smiled and eased back in his chair. "Don't mind at all," he said, and swung his head as the roadside door opened. Big Ev Bull filled the opening, then halted just past the doorway at sight of the uniformed Medical Corps captain sitting there with Bennington.

Sam made the introductions and Dr. Kleburg studied huge Everett Bull with bright, clinical interest. Ev undoubtedly appeared to the medical man as a throwback to caveman times, the way he was built and muscled and darkly bearded.

Sam asked Ev to take the captain across to the rooming house and help him get a room. Ev agreed and went back outside. Kleburg hesitated in the doorway to say quietly: "Sam, David had his Goliath . . . are you sure this big moose isn't the same thing to you?" Then he went on out not waiting for an answer.

The heat was building up when Sam finally left his jailhouse office to cross the road and get a fresh sack of tobacco at Dutch John Oberdorf's store. He got the tobacco without any difficulty from a clerk who was old enough to be his father. He also got something else; Dutch John stepped out of a little gloomy backroom office at sound of Sam Bennington's voice, called and beckoned, then walked on over and asked Bennington to return to the little office with him. Sam went, mystified but not too concerned. However, the second he stepped inside, he lost a little of his nonchalance, for Charley Jones was there, along with Zeke Wicke, and one more man, someone Sam was surprised to see in such a gathering — Leverett Hall.

"Town council meeting," explained Dutch John, and went back to the chair at the big old roll-top desk he'd evidently recently vacated. "We were talking of you when I thought I recognized you out in the store talking to my clerk." Oberdorf gestured self-consciously toward an empty chair. "Please," he said. "Please sit down."

But Bennington didn't take the chair. He looked at all the men in there, Leverett Hall longest because Hall seemed more sardonically amused by all this than any of the others, who were solemnly serious, then Sam broke out his fresh tobacco sack and started twisting up

240

a smoke. "If there's something special . . . let's hear it," he said. "Otherwise, I'd like to make my rounds of the town."

Charley cleared his throat and furtively glanced at John Oberdorf. But Dutch John had no intention of saying whatever was bothering the men around him. Zeke Wicke was suddenly attacked under his shirt, down alongside his ribs by some fiendishly voracious flesh-eater. He scratched and peered between the buttons, and became thoroughly involved in a defensive maneuver against that biting enemy inside his clothing.

Leverett Hall softly laughed. It wasn't a mirthful sound; it was, instead, sardonic and a little harsh. "Sam," he said, "I decided to take that bit of advice you gave me the first week you arrived in Hurd's Crossing. I've decided to come back and join the human race. And look where it's landed me . . . smack dab on the town council of Hurd's Crossing. Now, by God, that's as high as a man's noblest aspirations could hope to obtain, wouldn't you say?"

Sam smoked and dourly eyed the men around him, all seated while he remained standing, then he said: "Nick, cut out mocking yourself and get to the point."

Hall said: "Fair enough. In simple words, Sam, the town council has decided to send to Fort Jackson for a troop of blue-belly . . . excuse me . . . gent of Yankee cavalry. In a nutshell, I'd say the town council, by deciding to do that, has voted themselves not entirely in support of you, nor fully in with your plans, either."

"Hey!" roared Charley Jones, indignantly glaring. "Mister Hall that just ain't one damned bit true an' none o' us ever said he lacked faith in the town marshal. If you'll recall, what we said was . . . it wasn't fair to let one man do everything. Those damned soljers are sittin' around up there on their calluses, Roberts is goin' to hit this town sure, and as citizens o' this here Territory o' Arizona, we got the right to soljer-protection . . . no matter what that stump-legged colonel up there says."

Zeke Wicke piped up. "An' what's more, this town's now got eight thousand dollars of community funds in John Oberdorf's iron box. We've got to protect that. Suppose Roberts heard all about this money. He'd have more reason'n ever to hit us like a band of bronco Apaches. Marshal, we got to have more protection. It's no reflection on you at all. Believe me, it ain't. You're the best lawman we've ever had in Hurd's Crossin', but we'd as leave you stayed alive, which you sure won't be doin' if Emmett Roberts hears tell how much money we got here."

Sam caught Leverett Hall's cynical little grin, and nearly grinned back. "Thanks for your anxiety over my welfare," he told Zeke and Charley. "But it sticks in my craw, boys, that for every time you mention me getting killed once, you mention keeping that money intact at least twice. Mister Hall may be right this time."

"How," snorted Charley Jones. "How . . . right?"

"He thinks as I do. You're worrying about the money." Sam stepped over to the door, grasped the latch, and looked back. "You can have the badge back, if that's what you want," he told them. "That way I'd stay alive. But that way you wouldn't have anyone to guard the money, either."

Leverett Hall laughed, stood up, and pushed past the other seated men to say: "Sam, you're right, in a way, and so am I. But we've overlooked something. These boys will fight to keep that community fund intact, all right. They'd even fight Emmett Roberts. You get my point?"

Sam didn't get it and said so. That made Hall's amused look deepen and broaden as he explained that Sam Bennington had given the men of Hurd's Crossing one common ground for fighting shoulder to shoulder. "That damned blood money in Oberdorf's safe. Not a lofty ideal, not a sense of human decency and honor. None of the grand things good men usually fight and die defending or preserving, Marshal Bennington. Just blood money and a big slice of it. Still, that's a start. At least you've unified this lousy place that much. Come on, I'll walk you up to my saloon and buy you a drink. That's all the recognition you're ever going to get out of Hurd's Crossing, until they bury you. Then Charley and Zeke and fat John will chip in two dollars each and send some wilted prairie roses."

Hall opened the door, ushered Sam Bennington on through, closed the door on three red-faced town councilmen, and strode with the lawman out into the shimmering, harsh-lighted roadway where dust and flies and heat were fiercely mingled.

"They'll fire you off the council for talking like that," said Sam, half amused.

"Let 'em," muttered Hall, setting his hat so that the broad brim shaded his eyes. "They asked me to join. I didn't ask them. Anyway, what I said's the truth. They've been sweating bullets ever since you got that money and turned it over to the town. Furthermore, Sam, I'm convinced that, if there weren't three of them . . . if there were just two . . . they'd bust open Oberdorf's safe, split the eight thousand down the middle, and slope. But a three-way cut whittles it 'way down. It wouldn't be worth it."

Sam didn't believe that. He wasn't convinced Leverett Hall believed it. Hall was one of those people who exaggerated their suppositions to lend particular emphasis to what they said.

They entered the saloon, crossed to the nearly deserted bar, and drummed for cold beer. It was a little shy of high noon; only an occasional cotton-throated cowboy or townsman drifted in to cool off, then drifted right back out again.

When the beer came, Leverett Hall leaned wearily upon his bar and made a wry face. "That was a close thing last night," he murmured. "That's what scairt hell out of Charley and Zeke and 'possum-belly Oberdorf. They had visions of another bushwhacker slipping back and blasting you for good next time." Hall lifted his glass, scanned the bottom for sediment with professional, skeptical interest, then threw back his head and drank. Afterward he wiped his lipless gash of a mouth and softly belched. "Tell me something, Marshal," he asked, twisting a little to gaze at Bennington's profile.

244

"There's a medical officer in town this morning. Did you send for him?"

"Nope."

"Do you know him?"

"Yep."

"He didn't just accidentally come here, did he?"

"He's heard some talk of trouble impending," replied Sam. "His name's Ralph Kleburg. He's a damned good medical man, and he's fair and decent in all other ways as well." Sam paused to drink, then set the glass aside and stepped back from the bar. "We'll have use of him within the next day or two, I think, Nick. Thanks for the beer. Now, I've got some rounds to make . . . then some sleep to catch up on later in the day. *Adiós*."

Hall nodded thoughtfully, and watched Sam Bennington walk out of the saloon.

CHAPTER
ELEVEN

Ev Bull was at the jailhouse the following morning bright and early, looking like someone who'd just been listening to a denunciation of motherhood, clean living, and the American flag. He stood back to allow Sam Bennington to walk in, and didn't even bid the town marshal a good morning. All Ev said was: "This isn't goin' to work. They'll be hidin' down there behind them cussed rocks drawin' a big bead on you for a half mile before you get into range. Now I've been thinking. If I was to take out first an' catch you south of town down the road a piece, we'd then know how many . . ."

Sam said: "Forget it, Ev. In broad daylight they'd see your dust even though they never saw you."

Ev looked stormily rebellious. "I'm tellin' you," he muttered, "I'm tellin' you for a damned fact they're going to be waiting, an' you're goin' to ride right into their sights."

Sam blew out a big breath and surveyed his dogmatic, powerful assistant. "You mind the town," he said. "My chances of coming back are better than you think. Maybe I'll come alone. Maybe you'll be proven right and I won't come back with Franco Esteban, but I'll tell you one thing, Ev. No one dry-gulches an old soldier providing he's got reason to expect being bushwhacked."

He gave Ev his orders for the day. They weren't very complicated because Sam Bennington didn't suspect there might be any trouble in town during his absence. After that, he strolled down to the livery barn, rigged out his own horse, filled a canteen at the public trough, and mounted up to ride southward down the stage road.

It was blazingly hot by the time he left Hurd's Crossing. Out on the pitiless and shadeless desert it got still hotter. But Sam Bennington carried no surplus weight, was accustomed to the summertime desert, and, although he was anything but comfortable in that merciless heat-hazed atmosphere, he did not especially suffer, either. But the main thing that contributed to his somewhat indifferent attitude was that he didn't consider the heat. He had something much more personally important on his mind — survival.

By high noon he was as far southward as he'd ever been on the stage road. After that, he concentrated fully on the lay of the land, the brush and occasional clump of paloverde trees where assassins might be lying in wait, and, when he estimated he'd come far enough to be not too distant from Robber's Rock, he left the road, walking his horse eastward over the stale-scented, dusty, dead desert world. He'd had this in mind long before Ev Bull had mentioned it. He was looking for the dust of riders swinging in from the east, or, failing in that, for some sign on the ground that riders had recently passed.

247

He saw no dust, but several miles out he did come across two sets of tracks. This should have reassured him, but something about the way those tracks stopped every now and then, turning to point backward in the direction from which these two riders had come, made him suspicious. He backtracked nearly a mile before he found what he half expected to see. The sign of a large body of mounted men that had come with the forward pair of horsemen just so far, then had broken off southward, leaving a pair of riders to make their solitary way on toward Robber's Rock.

Sam paused to moisten the nostrils of his horse from the canteen, to take two swallows for himself, then he made a smoke, speculated a little, and finally turned back toward the road. Ev had been right, of course, and Bennington hadn't ever felt that he might not have been correct. Sam had never trusted Shadow O'Brien, either. Shadow's thinking was evident enough. Shadow would still get the other $50 if and when Emmett Roberts's ambushing gun crew cut down Sam Bennington. But Shadow would also come out exonerated and trusted by his old riding partner, Franco Esteban, and Roberts's other renegade riders, too.

Sam smoked and watched, and thought some sardonic thoughts, not just about Shadow O'Brien, who was openly and predictably treacherous, but also about Roberts, who would be down there with his men, straining for the revenge he badly needed to bolster his ego, and also his reputation, for what Bennington had done earlier against Emmett and his swaggering bushwhackers. It was possible, Sam thought, that Roberts would turn careless and reckless in his powerful desire to settle with Sam Bennington. It was also possible, Sam told himself just before returning to the road, that he was being exactly the heroic damned idiot Ev Bull had implied he was, coming down here alone to face twenty guns.

He thought of Leverett Hall and that dryly amused him. If Hall had been along with him in this, it would've been interesting to see how an old Rebel general reacted to being both the staff and the line in a one-sided fight. But Sam Bennington felt no fear. Caution, yes, even some misgiving, for unless he used every trick he'd ever learned, he wasn't going to ride back from this one, but fear, no. When a man's survived two dozen red-flaming battles from which he'd had no reason at all to believe he might ride out alive, the twenty-fifth such impending peril didn't unsettle him as it would have upset someone who'd never been through anything hazardous or deadly. He was cool and thoughtful and perfectly calm, turning to consideration of the ancient patterns of violence to find the ones applicable to this situation. He was certain that, although O'Brien and Esteban would be waiting as bait in the larger trap carefully set by Roberts, that some of Emmett's gunmen would be watching, too, from a careful distance so as not to alarm their prey before Sam rode into the trap, and it was this very delicate matter of distance and timing he decided to turn to his full advantage by seizing the initiative.

249

It wasn't prudent. It wasn't even sensible, from the viewpoint of men like Dr. Kleburg, if he'd known, or of Ev Bull and the Hurd's Crossing town council. But to Sam Bennington the prospect of cowering back there in that dusty little town waiting endlessly was far, far less attractive.

A hard white flash of bitterly reflected sunlight off hot metal alerted him when he finally saw a huge old lonely boulder, larger than a big house, off on his left, to the east of the stage road a hundred or two hundred feet. Shadow O'Brien, he speculated, was atop that mighty rock, looking northward for sign of Sam Bennington. He'd probably moved after seeing Sam approaching, and this movement may have been what caused that hot, white flash of light. Sam reached down, eased off the leather thong holding his six-gun in its holster, leaned to lift and lightly drop his Winchester in its boot, to be assured of an easy and swift withdrawal, then he settled for a swift lope up to the rock, which was part of his little scheme.

O'Brien came out from behind the rock, gesturing for Sam to come on up. Sam lazily raised his right arm to salute O'Brien, dropped his left hand low, and released the right rein with predictable results. At the loping gait he was traveling, when his horse eventually stepped on the rein, it jerked the beast's head violently downward and to the right, making the horse lose balance and fall heavily. Bennington had both feet clear of the stirrups and lit standing astraddle his threshing beast, but he at once doubled over and rolled forward

250

to the very end of the left rein, to which he still held firmly.

He saw Shadow O'Brien sitting his horse down by the rock, still with an arm upraised, look nonplussed at all the abrupt, dusty movement up where Bennington had fallen. Then O'Brien turned, called quickly to someone, and, as a second horseman came spurring around from behind the rock, O'Brien started in a rush up the road where Sam Bennington was lying.

Sam's horse arose, shook itself, and looked perplexedly around. It had broken that right rein a foot from the end, but since Bennington used the customary seven-foot split rein, there was still enough leather remaining. When Shadow O'Brien and the equally dark and compact man with him slammed down to a hard halt near where Bennington was lying face down, both arms curled under him, O'Brien said: "I'll get down an' boost him across his saddle, Franco. You keep watch for Emmett. He won't know what we done, comin' up the road like this."

O'Brien was rocking forward and to the left, ready to step down, when Sam Bennington rolled over and sat up. He had a cocked six-gun pointing straight upward. O'Brien gasped and Franco Esteban's right hand started moving.

"I'll bust your head wide open from this distance like a punky melon," warned Sam, getting to his feet. "Reach down, both of you, with your opposite hands, and drop those belt guns."

Shadow O'Brien's face turned curdled. He'd been outguessed and outmaneuvered. He dropped his six-gun, looking badly upset. When Sam ordered them also to shed their carbines, O'Brien did that, too, looking more than just chagrined about being outsmarted; he began to look afraid, for by this time Franco Esteban, the other burly, swarthy, Mexican-looking man there in the road, was beginning to stare coldly, skeptically over at O'Brien.

Sam remounted his horse, adjusted the reins, then jerked his head at his captives. "Right on up the road in front of me," he rapped out at them, "and push those horses hard. If Roberts overtakes us, you two die first. If you try breaking off, I'll still shoot you. Head for Hurd's Crossing, boys, and you'd damned well better pray hard we three all make it. Now, ride!"

Franco Esteban held his horse back as Shadow O'Brien started his forward. He glared fiercely, saying: "Marshal, you ain't takin' me up there to get lynched."

Bennington had no time to reason or argue with his prisoner. He drew his six-gun one more time and cocked it. The barrel was pointing directly at Franco Esteban's belly. Sam said: "You have two seconds to make your decision. Either you ride . . . or I gut-shoot you right here. I've got no time and no one as worthless as you is going to make me waste more than two seconds of it." As he spoke, Bennington's trigger finger curled and tightened. Shadow O'Brien sat petrified. Franco Esteban tried his hardest to detect something in Bennington's eyes or lips that would give him a hint as to whether this was a bluff or not. Sam's finger continued to tighten around the trigger. Esteban's bravado collapsed, he said — "All right." — and spurred his horse. O'Brien went dashing northward, alongside Franco, saying something to the one who had backed down in ungrammatical, border Spanish.

Sam holstered his weapon and hooked his horse, jumping out in pursuit. Once or twice he twisted to look over one shoulder, but they were a long way northward before he saw the boiling dust back downcountry. Evidently Emmett Roberts's watchers either hadn't quite understood all that had happened after Esteban and O'Brien rode away from the huge boulder, or else they hadn't believed Bennington had turned the tables and was getting away with his two prisoners until the running horsemen were more than a long mile northward.

In such murderous heat this kind of racing haste could be disastrous. It could put men on foot when overridden horses collapsed under them. So Sam called on his captives to slacken off to a slow lope. When they did this, Sam reined down behind them, keeping a careful distance because he wasn't convinced those two up ahead were completely disarmed yet, although he'd made them discard their visible armament. Men like O'Brien and Esteban sometimes carried wicked-bladed knives in holsters sewn into the outside uppers of their boots, beneath their pants legs, or else carried very deadly little stubby-barreled hide-out pistols concealed inside their clothing somewhere.

Bennington watched that furious dust cloud back yonder make a slow but noticeable approach. Roberts and his gun crew were speeding up instead of slackening off, in a frantic effort to gain back that mile

253

or mile and a half they'd lost back at the big rock. Esteban grinned savagely at his captor. Sam just waved him on ahead. It was Shadow O'Brien, in the least enviable position of them all, who said: "We got to go faster, lawman. He'll catch up as sure as hell."

Bennington was saturnine toward Shadow. "You can quit play-acting," he said. "I didn't expect you to keep your word anyway."

But O'Brien wasn't thinking of this latest treachery of his at all. He said: "Listen, Marshal, for lettin' you trap Franco an' me like you done, Emmett'll shoot me the second he catches up. He'll never believe I didn't double-cross him and not you."

Franco Esteban turned his deadly smile upon Shadow O'Brien. "Not just Emmett," he snarled. " 'Cause even if we get away from him, Shadow, I'm goin' to settle with you for this, too."

Bennington watched O'Brien's swarthy features dissolve with self-pity, then he shot a final glance over his shoulder, saw that Roberts was gaining rapidly now, glanced at their own horses to see that the beasts were recovered from their initial run upcountry, then nodded his head at O'Brien.

"Lead out. Head straight for Hurd's Crossing and ride hard all the rest of the way unless I tell you to slack off. Go on, Shadow . . . run for it!"

The three of them on their briefly succored horses swiftly and inevitably widened that heretofore closing gap. They rode with hardly a sound all around them until, with town finally in sight, someone far back tipped up a Winchester carbine and tried a desperate, high-arching shot. It fell short and after that Robert's gun crew finally had to slacken off their killing pace.

Sam saw them doing that, far back, and called to his prisoners to slow down, also. The heat was fiercely punishing both men and horses by then. Franco Esteban eyed Bennington's canteen, so the lawman tossed it over to him. Esteban drank deeply, squared around, and rode stonily right into Hurd's Crossing where people were standing stiffly, watching the three of them approach.

CHAPTER
TWELVE

Ev Bull came out of the jailhouse looking enormously relieved. He scarcely wasted a glance upon the sullen, swarthy, and sweaty captives as he went lumbering forward to take Sam Bennington's horse. He said: "I don't believe my own eyes. Wasn't it a trap like we figured?"

Sam ordered the glowering prisoners to alight. Men, and also a number of women, came ambling down the roadway to stand and stare silently. There were more women, as a matter of fact, than there were men in that growing crowd of hard-faced silent spectators.

"It was a trap all right," Bennington told Ev Bull. "But it backfired. I cut Roberts's sign out a ways, and worked a little trick of my own in reverse to suck these two out of their rocks."

Ev nodded and reached for the reins of the other two horses. He said he'd take them down to the livery barn, then trot right back to the jailhouse to hear all about it. Sam jerked his head and marched his prisoners into the jailhouse. It was blessedly cool inside; at least it was cooler than it was outside, or southward upon the smoke-hazed desert. He tossed aside his hat, blew out a ragged breath, and pointed to his *olla*. "Tank up," he

256

told his prisoners, not unkindly, "then sit over there along the back wall on that bench."

O'Brien drank last. He did not act as though he cared much about getting too close to the venomous-eyed Franco Esteban. When they were seated, profusely perspiring and looking rumpled, soiled, and demoralized, Sam Bennington made himself a smoke over at the desk. Once he finished, he tossed the tobacco sack over. Esteban caught it and woodenly manufactured a cigarette, also. He then tossed it back without even looking sideward to see whether O'Brien was interested or not. Esteban's hostility was a fiercely obvious thing. It appeared he didn't care whether he'd been deliberately or inadvertently captured; he still placed full responsibility for it upon his former riding-partner, Shadow O'Brien.

Sam said: "Franco, how many does Emmett have riding with him? No lies, just the simple truth."

Esteban sneered. "I don't got to lie to you, lawman. He's got twenty men. Countin' himself, twenty-one."

"Not counting you," corrected Sam, "twenty." Bennington inhaled, exhaled, then said: "Where's his camp?"

Esteban raised an arm vaguely gesturing. "Out on that damned desert," he retorted, and, when Sam gazed at him skeptically, Esteban shrugged as though to say Bennington could believe him or not, as he chose.

Ev Bull came back and loomed hugely in the hot little stuffy office. He gazed at Franco and Esteban gazed right back at him. "I didn't believe it," the ambusher sneered at big Ev. "When Shadow said you'd turned lawman, I didn't believe it, Ev."

Bull was indifferent to Esteban's opinion. He said, half turning away in contempt: "Believe what you like, Franco. Nothin' ever bothered me less."

Esteban's dark eyes coldly glittered. He was either a half-breed of some kind or a Mexican, which was to say he was still a half-blood. Like millions of his kind, the uppermost consideration in Franco Esteban's mind was the feeling of inferiority. When Ev Bull turned from him with apparent contempt, Esteban's dark eyes savagely glittered even though his features remained woodenly closed to all show of outward emotion. But Sam Bennington saw that look, and he interpreted it correctly, so he said: "Esteban, where's your spotted horse? I always heard it said only squaws and Indian kids rode spotted horses. I reckon that was wrong, though, wasn't it? I guess it'd be safe to say . . . greasers ride them, too."

Esteban's nostrils flared. With a ripped-out curse he catapulted up off the bench. Sam didn't move; he was wearing a very faint little mocking smile. It was cruel and it was meant to be cruel. Ev Bull, from the edge of his eye, saw the hurtling outlaw and whirled back straight into Esteban's path. The renegade didn't weigh more than a hundred and sixty pounds, although he was heavily muscled and compactly built, as opposed to mighty Ev Bull's excessive two hundred and twenty pounds. It was like bouncing a hard rubber ball off a brick wall. Esteban was reaching, both fists curled into raking claws, when he struck Bull head-on. Ev rocked

258

back just the smallest bit, but Esteban stopped so suddenly his hat flew violently back over where Shadow O'Brien was staring, pop-eyed.

Ev reached and caught the stumbling renegade's shirt front. "Why you treacherous damned little chili pepper," he said, and swung. The blow connected and Esteban's eyes rolled up, his knees turned to water. He hung on Ev's huge fist like a broken old doll. Ev shook him, still indignant, then dropped him.

Now, finally, Sam Bennington arose. He'd engineered all that on purpose. Not because he expected to soften up Franco Esteban at all, but because he wanted Shadow O'Brien to see it happen. He walked to the *olla*, tipped the jar, deeply drank, stepped away, and said: "Shadow, where's their camp?"

O'Brien answered rapidly: "I dunno whether you ever seen the place or not, Marshal, but they's a water hole in an arroyo about six or seven miles east o' Hurd's Crossin' with some trees down in it and some grass where . . ."

"Lynch Cañon," growled Ev, raising his eyes from the unconscious man at his feet to the frightened and completely demoralized prisoner over on the wall bench. "That it, Shadow, Lynch Cañon?"

"That's it," confirmed the cowboy, shooting an unsteady look at Ev, then jerking around to face Bennington instead. "Lynch Cañon, Marshal. They was over there when I rode in. One of their scouts seen me first, though, and escorted me on in."

"And you sold me out," said Sam.

O'Brien looked fleetingly at Franco, lying in a heap on the floor with a little flung-back trickle of blood from his smashed mouth across one cheek. "Yeah," he whispered. "But I had to, Marshal. They'd been sneakin' up here at night an' spyin'. They had this whole country roundabout under watch day 'n' night. They seen you 'n' me 'n' Ev Bull come back from the cow camp."

"Aw," growled big Ev, looking darkly over at Sam. "He's a cussed liar, Sam. No one saw us ride back from that cow camp. It was too dark, in the first place. In the second place, with a bounty on your scalp, if any o' Roberts's men'd spotted us out there, he'd have back-shot you." Ev turned and dropped his smoldering gaze on Shadow O'Brien. He took one big forward step and Shadow sprang up, jumping sideward.

"Marshal," he croaked. "All right, that wasn't the truth. All right, I sold you out an' helped 'em plan a trap. Only Emmett said he didn't think you'd be dumb enough to ride into it, so they'd all go far southward and wait for me or Franco to signal, if you came ridin' down to the rock like you said you would."

Ev turned when Franco Esteban groaned and feebly moved. Sam looked down, also. Shadow O'Brien, desperate no matter what happened now, made his fateful decision. He dropped over, grasped the dagger handle in his boot-top, and was straightening up when Bennington turned. Sam had no time to reach for his six-gun. He was standing less than five feet from O'Brien, who sprang even as Sam turned toward him.

Bennington raised his forearm to parry the blow. The blade, aimed low, missed his arm, but Shadow's arm was deflected. Then Bennington spun sideways and that thirsty length of polished, deadly steel slid past his stomach missing by four inches. Sam struck with his other fist and Shadow staggered sideward. But he was tough, and that blow hadn't been hard anyway, so he swung back and made a sweeping slash. Bennington jumped clear and lunged inward as the blade went past. Shadow tried to catch himself, tried to turn in time to escape Bennington, but he failed completely as Sam caught his knife arm and threw his entire weight backward, yanking O'Brien off balance and in toward him.

They stood toe-to-toe, straining for control of the knife. Ev Bull started to move, but at his feet Franco Esteban thickly muttered as he struggled up into a sitting position on the floor, reaching with a fumbling right hand under his shirt. Ev dropped down, struck away that groping hand, and wrenched the .41 caliber under-and-over pistol from Esteban's fingers

Ev heard a gasp and swung around in his kneeling position. Sam Bennington was moving back. Directly in front of Sam, with both hands clasped around the handle of his big knife stood Shadow O'Brien. The blade of his knife was two-thirds buried in Shadow's chest. He staggered, his eyes sprung wide open in incredulity, staring across at Bennington. Even Franco Esteban sat motionlessly. The only sound, the only movement for a long moment was made by O'Brien as he tried with diminishing strength to dislodge the knife from his body. Then he gave a shudder and fell, landing face down.

"Lord," whispered Ev Bull, seeing what the falling weight of the dead man had done when it came down upon the knife handle.

Sam stood a moment gazing at the body, then shook his head. "I yanked it down," he said quietly, speaking of his earlier struggle with O'Brien. "He tried to swing me around and he lunged forward at the same time. He fell right on his own knife."

Franco Esteban regarded the dead man with a fixed, hard, and cruel stare, then said: "I like it better this way. He did it to himself. I like that even better'n me doing it . . . the double-crossing, lyin' bastard . . ."

"Shut your lousy mouth," growled Ev, catching hold of Esteban's shoulder and dragging the renegade to his feet as Ev also arose. He gave the cowboy a rough push, sending him over against the wall bench where Esteban fell, and squared himself around.

Captain Kleburg opened the roadway door, started to step inside, and halted, staring at the dead man upon the floor. Ev Bull was dusting himself off, looking blackly hostile and muttering under his breath. He shot the medical man one swift look, then went on beating dust off himself.

Sam briefly explained what had happened. Dr. Kleburg went over, gently turned Shadow O'Brien face up, looked, rolled Shadow over onto his side again, and shook his head. "Never did like knives," he said, looking around for a blanket to cover the corpse with, and not finding one. He was the most coolly practical man in the room right then, untouched by rancor or shock, or grim resolve and hatred.

Sam went to his desk, got a key, and walked to one of those little cells across his back wall. He entered, picked up a moth-eaten old Army blanket, and tossed it to Kleburg, who at once flipped the thing out and dropped it over Shadow O'Brien. At the same time Sam jerked his head at Franco Esteban. "Inside," he said. The outlaw glared and didn't move until Ev said one harsh word and started moving. Then Esteban got up, steadied himself, and went over inside the cell. As Sam was locking the door, Esteban said: "What charge you got, lawman?"

"Bushwhacking'll do to hold you for a while," answered Sam. "That'll give me time enough to see where else you're wanted." He straightened up and met the muddy, cruel glare of his prisoner. "If the bushwhacking charge won't stick, Franco, I'll use the murder charge. That man you killed the other night, thinking it was me, was named Pete Farraday."

Franco's dark eyes sprang wide open. "Pete . . . Pete Farraday?" he murmured.

Sam wasn't impressed by either the shocked expression or the stammering. He said: "You knew it wasn't me the minute O'Brien rode into Roberts's camp."

Esteban nodded dumbly. "But I didn't think it was Pete. Hell, Pete Farraday was a friend of mine. We used to . . ." The outlaw raised both hands and gripped the bars of his cell.

Bennington gazed at him, surprised that Franco Esteban had any decent instincts left. Then he turned and went over where Captain Kleburg was standing, talking with Ev Bull. Sam caught just a snatch of that conversation before it dwindled off, but the little out-of-context sentence or two was enough. Kleburg had just said Leverett Hall and his men had ridden north four hours earlier. Ev Bull had replied he'd never believed going north up the stage road was the correct direction.

Those few words struck Bennington like a hammer blow. He stopped, looked at the other two men, and said in a very low voice: "Leverett Hall took a posse out of town?"

Dr. Kleburg nodded, beginning to roll his brows together in mild puzzlement. Ev Bull gazed at Bennington without changing expression at all. "Shortly after you left, going south," confirmed the Army surgeon. "Hall had his posse organized and ready to ride. I was just leaving the general store and didn't get a chance to count them, but offhand I'd say he had at least fifty men in his party."

"Easily fifty men," conceded Ev Bull. "What's the matter, Marshal?"

Sam went to his desk and dropped down upon one edge of it. Now he knew why, when he'd ridden into town much earlier with his two prisoners, there'd been more women among the spectators than men.

"Damn Leverett Hall!" he grated, raising angry eyes to Bull and Captain Kleburg. "I thought I'd talked him out of that."

264

"Out of what?" said the Fort Jackson surgeon. "He wants Roberts as badly as you do, Sam. I think his way's the best method for finding and eliminating that band of thugs. Unless we get troops from the fort."

"Do you?" said Bennington, reaching for his tobacco sack. "Doc, since when is a post surgeon a tactical officer? Let me tell you a couple of the facts of life. One . . . Roberts and his gang are southward, not northward. Two . . . the only thing that's kept Roberts from attacking this town is the number of hostile, armed men in it. How long do you think it'll be before Emmett Roberts hears that Leverett Hall and nearly all the able-bodied armed men in Hurd's Crossing are running upcountry somewhere on a damned wild-goose chase?"

Sam lit up, flung down the dead match, and looked at the other two. They looked back, turning a little gray and slack around the lips.

CHAPTER
THIRTEEN

Sam Bennington was angry. Actually it was more indignation than cold wrath. He privately cursed Leverett Hall up one side and down the other. He sent Ev Bull southward to the edge of the town to see if there was any sign of Roberts or his renegade riders on the shimmering desert, and, while Ev was gone, he gave Captain Kleburg a generous slice of his rancor. Kleburg conceded, eventually, that perhaps Hall hadn't done a very wise thing. But Kleburg was unperturbed. "All you have to do, Sam," he explained, "is send a rider up to the fort. Colonel Cross can be down here in a forced march before midnight. By tomorrow morning Hurd's Crossing will be impregnable. We'll have a full regiment of . . ."

"Damn it, Doc," broke in Sam Bennington exasperatedly. "Can't you understand? We don't have six hours!" Sam got up off the edge of the desk and made one angry circuit of his little office. As he passed the open grille-work of Franco Esteban's cell, the renegade killer grinned wolfishly out at him.

"You sure don't!" he called, and chuckled. "Emmett'll have a couple o' the boys slip in here after nightfall to bust me out. They'll hear about that fool saloon man strippin' the place."

Sam stopped, staring from beneath lowered brows over at Captain Kleburg. "You hear that?" he demanded.

Kleburg had heard what Esteban had said, but he didn't say so. He nodded his head, then stepped to a little barred roadside window, and stood there, gazing out into the yellow sun smash with his back to the room. "Then we'll have to organize the men who are left," he muttered. "Sam, if Roberts has only twenty men . . ." He turned, waiting for Sam's answer. It wasn't very long coming, and Sam swore as he gave it.

"We don't have even twenty, Doc. We don't have even ten. If you saw Hall take fifty men, that would have to include every able-bodied man in Hurd's Crossing, plus maybe some of the cowboys in town for a drink. Take fifty men out of here and you won't have five good ones left . . . including you and Ev Bull and me."

Captain Kleburg turned to look up and down the empty, heat-blurred roadway once more, and this time he didn't say anything even when he saw Ev Bull trotting back up the plank walk.

Ev barged inside and kicked the door closed. His shirt was sodden from perspiration; his beard was dusty and rumpled. He headed straight for the *olla* and deeply drank, then turned, and said: "There's a cowboy down at the livery barn, Sam. A dead cowboy."

Bennington straightened up and Captain Kleburg turned. Over in his cell Franco Esteban made that little wolfish chuckle of his again. Ev turned his head and Esteban's exulting little sound stopped. Ev said: "There was a knife in his back with a note tied to its handle, Marshal. Oh, Roberts is out there all right. It's just exactly as you said, too. He knows Leverett Hall took all the armed men and went chargin' up the stage road." Ev held out one massive fist, uncurled the fingers, and held forth a limp strip of paper edged with blood. "Read it. Roberts says we've got one hour to set Esteban and O'Brien free, let 'em ride out of town unmolested, then he'll decide what he's goin' to do to Hurd's Crossing . . . and you.'

Bennington took the note, read it, and flung it on the desk. Captain Kleburg walked over and also read it. In his cell, Esteban was smiling broadly now, but he didn't offer to make any further sounds. He stepped back to the wall bunk, sat down, flung aside his hat, and leaned far back, gazing exultantly up at the old fly-specked ceiling.

Sam said: "Ev, who was the cowboy?"

"Young feller who rides for a little outfit southwest 'o town. The livery man and his hostler saw him comin' on a loose rein all slumped over. They figured he was either heat-struck or drunk and went out a short ways to fetch him on in. That's when they saw the knife between his shoulders. It looks to me like Roberts has the town surrounded an' cut off, an' this poor darned fool just rode blithely along, and blundered right into someone out there who wrote the note and stuck the knife in him. The livery man said he was still alive when

268

they got him off his horse into the shade of the barn. But when I got down there, he was dead."

Bennington and Kleburg exchanged a glance. Sam said: "Captain, you still think all we have to do is send for help from Colonel Cross?"

Kleburg frowned. "Sam, it was your idea yesterday not to send for troops. Don't put the blame on me."

Ev Bull went over for another drink and Franco Esteban said pleasantly from inside his cage: "Marshal, get smart. Emmett won't care about Shadow. He'll probably salute you for killin' him with his own knife. But, Marshal, Emmett and I are right close pardners. You set me loose an' I'll give you fair odds he won't burn this stinkin' town to the ground an' roast everyone in it . . . including you."

Bennington didn't answer. He waited until Ev finished at the *olla*, then told him to go over to Jones's shoeing shop, Oberdorf's store, and anywhere else he thought he might be able to round up armed men. "Then bring them back here," he said. "And Ev, remember what the note said. One hour."

Bull departed, shaking his bear-like head and dripping sweat. Captain Kleburg stood in the roadside doorway looking out. It was the hottest time of the day so, as usual, the plank walks and roadways were deserted. But it was more than just that; there was a thickening to the atmosphere, a kind of curdling of stale air and fear. It wasn't anything the surgeon could reach out and touch, yet it was very tangible nonetheless. He unbuttoned his tunic, shuffled back inside, and went after a drink of water.

Bennington walked out upon the breathless sidewalk and moments later Kleburg joined him out there. The surgeon said:

"Well, Sam, you wanted him."

Bennington turned as Ev Bull walked out of Dutch John's store hastening on around toward the blacksmith works. Up in front of the Bella Union Saloon someone called, and Ev faced across the road. Zeke Wicke came out to the edge of his sidewalk. Ev said something brusquely and pointed down where Bennington and Dr. Kleburg were standing. Zeke squinted, then started down that way.

"Here comes a bawling out," Bennington muttered to his companion, but when Wicke came up, he looked from one of the solemn, bronzed men to the other, and wanly shook his head.

"Ev's not having much luck," he said to Sam Bennington. "Oberdorf says it's not up to him to try and stop Emmett Roberts." Zeke rolled his frightened eyes southward on down the still empty roadway to the yonder desert. "Maybe the others'll come back directly. Maybe they'll figure out there's nothin' up north and turn back, Marshal."

Captain Kleburg looked away because, evidently, he didn't like what fear did to a man's face. Sam Bennington looked away, too, but he said: "If they come back, Mister Wicke, the general'd better have a strong vedette screen out, because Roberts has his murderers hiding out there, just waiting to spot some dust so they can demonstrate their gunmanship. No. I don't think Hall will come back in time. Roberts gave the town one hour to turn loose the prisoners I brought back, or else."

"Or else . . . what?"

"He'll burn the place and roast us all. That's what his note said. But particularly, he'll roast me."

Wicke turned as the high sound of arguing voices came down the still, leaden air from farther uptown. Sam and the surgeon also turned. Ev Bull hove into sight around a corner up there, pushing and shoving two men, both with rifles in their hands. He'd swear and push. The two men were Charley Jones and his blacksmith apprentice, a younger man but evidently not an especially courageous one, because, like old Charley, he'd brace his feet and loudly protest each time big Ev shouldered into him propelling them both down the dusty, blazing hot roadway toward where Sam and the others stood.

When Ev passed the general store, Dutch John appeared in his doorway, looking on gravely. He seemed unwilling to take that one additional forward step that would place him out upon the scuffed wooden plank walk.

Ev kept growling and bumping his two companions along until the three of them were standing in front of the jailhouse, then he desisted, looking thoroughly hot and disgusted.

"Here's a brave pair of heroes," he snarled. "They had their Winchesters up there in the shop, and both of 'em were scairt to death to touch 'em when I said we needed every man to fight off the Roberts bunch."

271

Charley looked imploringly at Sam Bennington. "Marshal, for gosh sakes I ain't no fightin' man. I wasn't even real good at it when I was thirty years younger an' folks had to fight."

"You have to now," spoke up Captain Kleburg, and Charley turned on him, starting at Kleburg's blue uniform.

"You're a soljer!" the blacksmith exclaimed. "You get paid for . . ."

"Charley," interrupted Bennington, "this is Captain Kleburg from Fort Jackson. He's a surgeon, not a line soldier. On top of that he's got no interest in Hurd's Crossing. He doesn't own a store or a blacksmith's shop, or a freight yard, around here. But he's staying. What's the matter with you anyway? When we got that money for the other outlaws, you were pleased as punch. Do you want Roberts to burn this town?"

"Marshal," gasped Jones, "I'm an old man. This kind of . . ." Charley's faded eyes gradually widened. He painfully swallowed. "Did you say he'd burn the town?"

"That's what Roberts wrote in a note, Charley. Either we set free the prisoners I brought back within one hour, or he'll burn the town and roast everyone in it."

Charley and Zeke exchanged a shocked look. Zeke said: "Marshal, set the prisoners free."

Bennington's reply was blunt. "I can't set one free. He's in there on my jailhouse floor, dead. And I won't turn the other one loose. He's the bushwhacker who killed that Farraday fellow thinking he was me."

272

Zeke started to speak. Dr. Kleburg turned a sober face and said: "Gentlemen, let me make one thing plain to you. If you had ten hostages in Hurd's Crossing right now, and, if you turned every blessed one of them loose, Emmett Roberts would still burn this town to the ground! I'm not a soldier in the strict sense of the word, but I've been through one major war and probably a hundred other battles of one kind and another. I tell you from experience, a man like Emmett Roberts will not keep his word!"

Zeke subsided. So did Charley Jones. Ev Bull and the youthful apprentice blacksmith looked soberly at one another. No one had anything to say; everyone knew very well that Kleburg had spoken the blunt, unpleasant truth.

From up the road a man called down to those standing in front of the jailhouse. It was John Oberdorf, red as a beet and without his usual apron. Dutch John was carrying a spanking new Winchester carbine in one fist and an equally as new double-barrel shotgun in his other hand. He was fiercely perspiring because his trouser pockets were sagging under the considerable weight of bullets. Also Dutch John was badly upset as he waddled on down, stepped in under the overhang in front of the jailhouse, and halted to let off an unsteady sigh

"What the devil you figure you're up to?" growled Charley Jones. "John, you idiot. Them guns'll only be an invite for someone to shoot you."

Oberdorf nodded, shook off sweat, and stooped to lean his weapons over against the shaded jailhouse wall.

273

"Maybe so," he said, turning back toward the blacksmith. "But I promise you one thing, Charley Jones, if he don't get me the first time, I'll blow a hole in him big enough to drive a span of mules through. An' what're you doin', draggin' your feet all the way down here?"

Charley reddened and scuffed a boot toe against the edge of the plank walk. "I wasn't draggin' my feet," he muttered acidly. "I just didn't like Ev Bull pushin' me is all. I was goin' to come along . . . if there was any real danger." He turned on his apprentice. "Wasn't we, Slim?" he growled, and the apprentice bobbed his head up and down like a cork on a string.

"Yes, sir, Mister Jones," he whispered. "Yes, sir, you're plumb right."

Zeke Wicke mopped at his face and forehead with a limp red handkerchief. As he pocketed the thing, he said: "I better go fetch my guns." Then he cursed and said: "I never should've let Leverett Hall take them hostlers and drivers and yard men of mine."

Oberdorf shook his head again. "Go get your guns," he told Zeke. "Marshal, there are a couple of fellers down at the livery barn. There's old . . ."

"Naw," broke in Ev Bull. "Right after they got a good look at the cowboy with the knife stickin' out o' his back, they purely vanished. I tried to find 'em, but they'd hid out too well."

Zeke was fifteen feet away when Ev said that. IIe halted and turned back. "Knife in the . . . back?" he croaked, his face draining of all color. "Who got a knife in the back?"

274

Bennington gestured with one hand. "Just get your weapons and get on back here. We'll talk later. Maybe after this is all over."

"If," muttered the profusely sweating general storekeeper, "there are any of us left to talk."

Captain Kleburg showed them all a tight little smile. No one smiled back at him, not even Sam Bennington, who stood gazing up at the location of the sun. Their hour was up. He said: "Come on inside and help yourselves to guns and ammunition. We shouldn't have long to wait now."

They trooped into the jailhouse, one genuine fighting man, one medical man, a frightened apprentice blacksmith, two elderly merchants of Hurd's Crossing, and a temporary deputy town marshal.

CHAPTER
FOURTEEN

They formulated no elaborate plans. There wasn't any point; there were six men in that jailhouse office armed and waiting to fight off twenty renegades; the only plan they needed was a miracle and that wasn't even remotely likely, so they drank water, checked their weapons, made certain they had pockets full of ammunition, then waited for Sam Bennington to make his disposition of them.

"Charley," the marshal said, "you and Mister Oberdorf get onto a rooftop southward, down toward the lower end of town. Keep a sharp watch all around down there."

Jones was agreeable. He asked about his apprentice, though, and was told the youth called Slim would go with Dr. Kleburg. What Bennington didn't say was that as timid as the apprentice was, he wanted to pair him off with someone who could stiffen his backbone if such a need arose.

Sam then detailed the apprentice, Slim, and Dr. Kleburg to the northerly rooftops, with particular orders to keep a close vigil for horsemen of any kind, and, if they saw Hall's party returning, or even any Hardy cowboys heading toward town, to start shooting so whoever might appear out on the desert would be warned about charging right on into town. Bennington said that he and Charley Jones would keep patrolling the back edges of town on the east and west, from the ground. Beyond that, and admonishing them all to tell any women or children or older people they saw to get inside and stay there, Sam Bennington didn't have much more to say, beyond urging his men to go now and get into their positions.

Captain Kleburg armed himself from the wall rack and told the youth who'd attached himself to him to be certain also he had plenty of ammunition. Aside from those few words there wasn't much said, but the last one to leave was John Oberdorf. He turned in the doorway and said: "When it turns dark, I think they can sneak in on foot and set a fire, Marshal."

Bennington looked at Oberdorf and nodded. "When it's dark, we'll use our ears instead of our eyes, but we'll keep those men out of here, Mister Oberdorf, because we have to."

Charley Jones stood in the doorway, watching them go their ways up and down the hushed and abandoned roadway. As Sam Bennington started toward him, Franco Esteban called from his cell: "You'll never get it done, Marshal, an', if you wing one of Emmett's boys tryin', they'll storm this damned place like a band of Comanches!"

Sam had an answer ready. "Esteban, you better hope they don't get into town, because if Hurd's Crossing goes up in smoke . . . you're sure to be the first one to roast." Bennington followed Charley Jones out onto the plank walk, then turned and locked the jailhouse door, and pocketed the key. From inside came the high and desperate yell of that caged prisoner in there.

Sam pointed across the road. "Keep down as much as you can, Mister Jones," he cautioned. "If there's one good place over there where a man can stand and see all around without being seen himself, find it and use it. The less a fellow moves when everything else around him is still, the better off he'll be."

Charley nodded, rolled up his eyes, then stepped down into the empty roadway and swiftly crossed over where he disappeared between two buildings, heading for the eastward back alley.

Sam waited until he was certain Charley had made it, then turned and went northward until he, too, found a place to pass down to the westerly back alley. He stopped as soon as he was beyond sight of any of the others, removed his hat, wiped off sweat, then leaned upon the rough rear wall planking of a building.

Six who would fight against twenty who could fight. It was a pretty forlorn situation they were in. He made a smoke, lit it behind his hat, kept the red glow hidden by cupping the cigarette in his fist, and he privately blamed himself for this mess. If he'd sent to Fort Jackson as Dr. Kleburg had suggested the day before, Hurd's Crossing would be perfectly safe now.

Still, no man can accurately predict events, although at times he can surmise how they might occur. The trouble was that Sam Bennington had thought, if the worse came to the worst, he could organize the townsmen and cattlemen himself, and lead them against the Roberts gun crew. But where he'd failed had been in not finding out where the renegades were until they, not he, had seized the initiative. It was, he tried telling himself, one of those situations men whose trade is war and weapons find themselves in now and then, and it wasn't actually hopeless until the last shot had been fired, the last defender of Hurd's Crossing sprawling lifelessly in the dust.

But none of that boosted his spirits at all. He finished his smoke, studied the waning sky, and ran a careful glance up and down the back alley, before he hoisted his Winchester and started walking carefully northward, keeping close to the buildings, if the sudden need arose for him to dive for shelter.

There wasn't a sound anywhere. Even the usual barking dogs, yelling boys, bawling milk cows, and neighing horses were silent. It seemed almost as though even the dumb brutes understood that after a generation and more of survival against all enemies, human, animal, and otherwise, the town was facing its final moment of truth. For Sam Bennington the private recriminations were bad. But he didn't allow them to influence him as he made his careful patrol up the shadowy back alley. Once, a woman came to the back door of a small clapboard house and silently watched him walk past. He saw her and she saw him, but neither of them said a word or so much as exchanged a nod. Up near the northward limits where the heat was fiercest and the yonder desert lay in a sharp blur of mustard light, Bennington thought he saw a rider loping easily from east to west, far out. He stepped into the lee of a building, shaded his eyes to make certain, and in that brief interval the rider vanished.

Roberts's men would have canteens, of course, but they would suffer out there, for even in the places where there'd be shade from scrub brush or the little shallow arroyos that fierce heat would punish them unmercifully. Still, he reasoned, their kind could be patient; sooner or later they were quite convinced, they'd have a town to sack and demolish. To their kind the inconvenience would be worth it.

An old man cracked a door across the alley. He'd evidently been watching Bennington through a window for some time before he did this. He was stooped and gaunt but had a thick mane of white hair and bright blue eyes. He also had an ancient muzzle-loading big-bore musket in his hands, upon which he leaned as he said: "Young feller, you show me one of 'em, an' I'll do the rest. Just point him out to me."

Sam crossed over and asked for a drink of water. The old man pointed to his *olla* under the eaves where circulating air passed around the thing constantly, then, as Bennington went over to drink, the old man said: "I counted my share o' coup on the bloody hands years back, Marshal. I'm a might unsteady on my legs nowadays, but if you'll point out the direction they'll be comin,' I ain't lost a bit of my sharpness in the eyes. I an' Eloise here, my musket, we can pick 'em off at over a hunnert yards on the wing."

Sam turned, wiped his chin, and said: "How did you know?"

The old man chuckled. He didn't have a tooth in his head. "Funny thing about word gettin' around," he confided. "Nothin' beats the old moccasin telegraph, Marshal. We heard they were scoutin' up the town right after you rid in with your prisoners. The word just got around. You know how that is."

Bennington smiled at the old man. "Stay inside," he said, "and watch through your northerly and westerly windows, pardner. If there are any around on this side of town, they'll skulk in closer as soon as the sun goes down. If they're going to fire Hurd's Crossing, they've got to get in pretty close."

The old-timer listened and nodded, then made a wry observation of his own. "You bet I'll watch, Marshal, an', if I see a skulker, I'll salivate him, too, don't you fret none about that. But y' know, when I was young, they wouldn't have tried gettin' into gun range to shoot fire arrows." He thought a moment, then cackled again. "Good thing they got guns instead o' bows an' arrers, ain't it?"

Bennington agreed that it was a good thing, indeed, then turned and started back down the alley toward the southerly end of town. He got as far as the rear of his jailhouse before he heard someone shout from down toward the livery barn. The cry didn't sound particularly desperate or anxious. He stopped, waited for a repetition or whatever was to come next, and all he heard was the settled, strained silence once more.

He continued along, keeping closer to the walls of buildings now, and had almost reached the livery barn when another yell erupted over beyond town on the east side. He could imagine that frightened youth with Ralph Kleburg jumping half out of his skin every time one of those howls erupted. He waited again, and, when nothing further happened, Bennington began to suspect what was happening. Still, he went on down to the livery barn, which was empty except for some stalled, unconcerned horses eating hay, and there he remained for a few moments in the blessed shade.

Another of those unnerving screams erupted. This one came from up at the northwesterly edge of town. Bennington stepped back out into his alley and looked. As he did so, a rifle up there somewhere let go with a tremendous explosion. Bennington thought of that sharp-eyed old man up there in his shack, and waited to see whether his gunshot drew an answering one, or another shout, and, when the silence ran on again, Bennington smiled to himself. Evidently that old man had tipped the scales. Obviously Roberts's renegades had been instructed to shatter the nerves of the town's defenders with those screams from all around, and it probably was working right up to the moment someone made the mistake of thinking there wasn't going to be any retaliation at the north end of town. But instead of terrifying that old Indian fighter up there, the yelling renegade had instead given the old man a direction to shoot in. And that, since the silence now settled down again, appeared to have ended this particular phase of Roberts's strategy of demoralizing and terrifying the town so it would be softened up sufficiently when he and his men crept up to finish him off.

Sam started patrolling back up toward the northern end of Hurd's Crossing one more time. He was beyond the jailhouse, striding along, keeping a close watch ahead and all around, when a carbine viciously snarled up there on the northward desert, then another one opened up from off to the west, out where there was ample chaparral and sage to hide the shooters. Bennington heard window glass *tinkle*. He started trotting forward, was almost up to the old man's shack when that big-bored old musket cut loose again, rattling every door and window for a hundred feet in all directions. For a second after that the two renegades out yonder were silent, as though awed by the sound and flash of that long-barreled gun in the shack. That was when Sam reached the door and wrenched it open to jump inside. The old man was sitting on a nail keg using his wiping stick as he reloaded. When Bennington came though the door, he grabbed for a huge old horse pistol in his belt, then eased off as he recognized his new ally, went back to recharging his musket, and said: "Son, I winged that one out there who figured to stampede me with his caterwaulin'. But when he commenced groanin' and rollin' around, them other two come up on horseback and commenced attackin' me. I'd be obliged if you'd lend me a hand for a few minutes. You take one an' I'll take the other."

Sam went to the broken window, stood aside, leaned down, and looked out. The desert was turning shadowy out there. Nothing moved anywhere. He was pulling back when a carbine thundered off to the north, and lead struck the shack hard behind the old man, who was finished reloading now and was priming his weapon as he got to his feet. He grinned at Bennington. "Dang' good thing I got log walls," he said, and approached the northward window with great caution, bent forward and holding his rifle with both hands, cocked and with the trigger set.

Sam stepped wide, went forward upon the opposite side of the same window, and risked a peek out. At first he saw nothing, then the old man, also peeking out, said: "You'll see him. He's got to raise up to fire, an' there'll be a flash o' sunlight off his rifle barrel. But y' got to be quick, son. Y' got to be right smart at your work."

The renegade raised up exactly as the old man had predicted, but Bennington, beginning to straighten away, wasn't ready when the outlaw fired. The old man was, though; he squeezed his trigger no more than a fraction of a second after the renegade cut loose. The deafening roar of that old musket drowned out the higher, sharper sound of the Winchester's rifled barrel. Sam saw a man spring straight up out there, fling his gun violently to one side, then go backward end over end as though he'd been struck head-on by a sledge-hammer. Where the renegade fell, a sturdy bush grew; it held him half suspended until his dying reflexes made him shake free and roll out into a little clearing where he expired, looking straight up at that pitiless, faded sky.

The old Indian fighter chuckled and moved back, shuffling on over to his nail keg to sit down and reload his weapon. Bennington moved over to the other window. There was still that other one left out there, to the west. He didn't see the man, though; he never did see him again, that he afterward could be sure of, but a minute or two later he heard sounds of a horse far out somewhere, heading straight southward. Apparently the surviving outlaw had had enough, and was going down where Emmett Roberts was to warn his companions about approaching that shack at the far northerly end of town where two men had died.

Bennington leaned upon the wall, gazing at the old man. He was sitting there working at the recharging of his old gun as though he hadn't been so pleased with himself in years, which he probably hadn't. Bennington decided they had one more defender. He crossed to the door. "I'll be back," he said. "Keep an eye peeled." The old man looked up, winked, and grinned.

CHAPTER
FIFTEEN

After that costly exchange at the north end of town, Roberts's renegades seemed to pull in their horns a little. Charley Jones came halfway across the road and met Bennington to find out what had happened. Sam told him, and Charley bobbed his head up and down.

"That's old Cheyenne Willard," he said. "He's been livin' in that old tumbledown shack o' his forgotten by the whole town for years."

Bennington had some private thoughts about the comparative courage of old Cheyenne Willard and some of the other townsmen, but he kept them to himself and inquired whether Charley had seen anything on the eastward plain. Charley hadn't, but he said he'd better get back because with the sun departing, the shadows thickening all around Hurd's Crossing, there was no way of telling when Roberts would try something new. Charley also said he thought Roberts was a fool, holding off like this, trying to snipe a little, trying to scare folks out of their wits with that caterwauling. "He should've hit us full strength when he had the chance."

Bennington had some thoughts on that. The last time he had tried that he got some buckshot in one leg and lost more than half his men. "I think, as badly as Roberts wants to exact vengeance from Hurd's Crossing, he's got a little fear in him, too, Charley. Now get on back to your post."

Long after the blacksmith had departed, long after Sam went back to his westward alley to patrol up and down again, dusk began to stalk the town, but because this was midsummer, darkness itself wouldn't arrive until about 9.00 at night. The way Bennington figured things, the longer a full-scale clash could be postponed, the better, for once Roberts either burst into the town firing left and right, or infiltrated after nightfall, Hurd's Crossing's defenders were going to find themselves badly outnumbered and perhaps outgunned as well.

He went back up to the old Indian fighter's shack but it was dark and he did not want to call out. He was satisfied Cheyenne Willard was crouching in there, waiting. He went back down the southward alleyway again, stepped in alongside a shed once, and stood perfectly motionless for a long while trying to sight movement out upon the yonder desert, but failed, so he walked on down as far as the jailhouse again.

From over across the main roadway and northward, two carbines suddenly opened up with several angry rounds each. For a moment there was no answer, then it also came, more furious gunfire. Apparently some of the renegades had gone across through the northward dusk from in front of Cheyenne Willard's shack toward the building where the northward vigilantes were crouching atop the roofs, and perhaps they'd gotten a

287

little careless, rode in too close, and started that firing up there.

At least that's how Sam Bennington assessed it, because as abruptly as the fighting began, it also ended, and for nearly ten more minutes there wasn't a sound anywhere. But when that ten minutes elapsed, Charley Jones, directly across from Bennington in the yonder alleyway, opened up, too. That meant the renegades out there, probably mounted, were completing a big circuit from northwest to northeast, then on down Charley's southeastern route. No gunshots came back at Charley, though, and Bennington grinned in the shadows. Charley had heard them, no doubt of that, but he probably hadn't seen them at all. Charley Jones was a high-strung man, easily upset.

Bennington stood a while, listening and thinking. Roberts was starting to move. There probably hadn't been more than two or three of those scouts riding around upon the yonder desert, their purpose to test the defenses of Hurd's Crossing. They hadn't tested Bennington's westerly defenses yet, so they probably would complete their big circle, coming up from the southward desert. He waited, expecting to hear Dr. Kleburg and the apprentice blacksmith who was down there also fire, but it never happened. Either the doctor hadn't seen those scouts, or hadn't considered them any real threat, if he had seen them. Bennington knew Ralph Kleburg; he was no Charley Jones. If he fired, it would only be because a real threat was at hand.

Of course, that didn't help Sam Bennington any. He wanted Kleburg to fire, so he'd be sure of his surmise that the town was being tested by scouts. When there were no more gunshots, Sam was tempted to believe the scouts had given up before getting anywhere near were he was waiting. Still, he had nothing better to do, so he walked across the alleyway and out through the gathering night toward a distant outhouse. From the shadowy wall of that old structure he'd been able to see a fair distance across the desert, without himself being seen, unless, of course, those scouts were riding close in, which he doubted after they'd been fired on. Then he dropped to one knee and waited.

The stars were faintly discernible. The sky was turning a soft velvet hue. The night was hot but at least the direct rays of that hazy molten disc were gone. He wondered what Roberts would decide to do, once he knew how many defenders there were in Hurd's Crossing, and about where they'd elected to make their stands. Infiltrate, Sam thought; if the conditions were different and that was Sam Bennington out there with a troop of soldiers, he would choose to infiltrate, then charge the town's defenders from behind them.

He caught the light scuff of a shod horse down the southward night, forgot his previous thoughts, and concentrated his full attention upon this sound of peril. For a moment there wasn't any additional sound. Sam craned for a rearward look. He was a goodly distance from the nearest shelter if he had to leave this spot. A rein chain musically rang, and a man's spur rowel got hooked in a wiry sage bush, and twirled. The stars weren't much help and the moon hadn't firmed up yet, so it was no help at all. Unless those scouts out there

289

curved in closer to the town, Bennington wasn't going to get a shot, either. He thought this was probably the same reason Captain Kleburg hadn't fired. He may have heard them out there in the thickening night, but hadn't seen them.

A horse shuffled along and blew its nose noisily. A man's quick, indignant curse followed that previous sound. Sam had their location pegged. They were south of him no more than three hundred feet, moving cautiously northward. They would come within a hundred or a hundred and fifty feet of the outhouse where Sam was kneeling. He lifted his carbine, eased back the hammer very softly, and got set. He had no intention of giving these men any warning whatever; all he meant to make certain of was that they weren't townsmen or cowmen. That would be apparent from their weapons and the way they wore them, as soon as they got into view.

He heard a man say, in a hushed tone of voice: "Hell, they're all up along the north end o' town. We could slip in right here an' set one of them old shacks afire, Ace. Look yonder. There's an old outhouse. We could set fire to it and it'd light up the whole blessed back end o' town."

The renegade called Ace said: "Yeah? It's so dang' far from every other buildin' around it'd burn itself out an' the town still wouldn't catch fire."

"In that case," muttered his unsuspecting companion, "let's just mosey in a little closer."

"No. You heard what Emmett said. First we make sure where they're waitin'. Then we split up an' one

290

bunch hits the place from the east an' the other bunch charges in from the west. We go settin' fires now an' Emmett'll have our cussed hides."

They were now close enough. Sam Bennington could make out their shadowy silhouettes in the night. He drew a careful bead and called softly: "Someone's goin' to have your cussed hides." Then he fired. The nearest man screamed and went drunkenly off his horse sideways. Both the horses out there responded with panic; the one whose rider had been shot from the saddle bolted and hit the other horse head-on nearly knocking both animals off their feet. Sam levered and tried to catch the surviving renegade down his gun barrel, but that man was spurring savagely to keep his mount on the far side of the riderless horse for shelter, while he went for his six-gun. He got off a wild shot that didn't even strike the outhouse. Sam fired at the flash of his gun, missed, and levered up another load. The renegade finally got his animal turned to race away. What saved him was that riderless animal. It fell in behind, head and tail up, sped along between Sam and the hunched-down, fiercely spurring outlaw, and in this manner kept Sam from ever getting a good shot.

He lost the badly shaken outlaw across the darkening desert, lowered his gun to lean upon as he listencd to the horse's diminishing hoof falls turning southward, out there somewhere, then he leaned the gun aside and made himself a smoke, lit up behind his hat, and remained right where he was until the cigarette was finished, a length of time involving perhaps ten minutes. Finally, then, he arose, scooped up his

Winchester, and walked out where the man he'd shot was lying.

It was an old hunter's trick. Never rush right up after a successful shot. Always sit quietly and wait until the victim was fairly well bled out before approaching. Many an eager or novice hunter had been gored to death by wounded bucks or bears, or shot to death by wounded outlaws, when they were too anxious to examine their kill.

The man wasn't dead when Bennington walked over to him. He wasn't unconscious, either, but he had no will left to reach for his six-gun. He simply lay there breathing in a fluttery way and gritting his teeth against the intense pain caused by a smashed right upper arm. The blood was gushing. The outlaw was feebly trying to staunch it, but he was too badly shocked; there was no grip in his left hand to cut off the spurting claret.

Sam bent down, tossed away the man's six-gun, took his trouser belt, and set it very tightly above the broken bones, stopping the flow of blood. He didn't say a thing and neither did the outlaw, who was as white in the face as a sheet, all except his eyes; they were dry, hot, and nearly black with pain. At the close range that he'd been shot, if that bullet had hit him anywhere else, in the chest for example, it would've plowed a hole as big as a man's fist. As it was, the man's right arm was irredeemably shattered.

Bennington finished tying off the bleeding, made a smoke, and stuck it between the man's tightly held lips, lit it behind his hat, and held the man's head up while the outlaw greedily inhaled and exhaled. Then Sam roughly grabbed the man and hoisted him to his feet. "Walk," he said, supporting his prisoner.

They got back into the dark alleyway before the renegade's legs began to go rubbery on him. The shock was wearing off; intense pain would shortly come to take its place. Sam put the man's good arm around his own shoulders and half supported, half carried, the groaning renegade down to the jailhouse. He had no intention of going after Dr. Kleburg at this time, so he took the man into the darkened jailhouse, snarled at Franco Esteban to get back against the rear wall of his cell, then he put the wounded outlaw in with Esteban.

"Keep that arm from bleeding any more," he told Franco, "and, when this is over, I'll fetch him a doctor. You two better hope like hell it ends with the doctor . . . and me still alive." Sam went back out, locked the door, and picked up his carbine.

He returned to the roadway just in time to hear the distant drum roll sound of mounted men splitting off on either side of Hurd's Crossing as they swept up toward town from the southward desert. There was no time to warn the others of what he knew, of what he'd heard the wounded man and the outlaw who escaped say. How Roberts planned to divide the town between his two groups of hard-riding outlaws. In fact, there was no time for Sam Bennington to do anything but run swiftly back down through and out into the rearward alleyway where he was supposed to be patrolling.

There was a quick, sudden burst of gunfire down where Kleburg and Charley Jones's apprentice were atop a building. For a moment that sustained and evidently unexpected gunfire seemed to slow the oncoming outlaws, seemed to disconcert them. Bennington stood out in his alley barely breathing, hoping everyone else in town would be alerted by what was unmistakably going to be a fierce attack.

A third gun joined those other two, down toward the southerly end of town. That, Sam thought, would be Charley Jones. He'd been patrolling down there, possibly, and was now supporting Ralph Kleburg and the youth. Finally, though, the answering roar of gunfire came from out upon the southward desert. It sounded to Bennington like volley firing by a troop of pony soldiers. He turned to run on down to the south end of town for the purpose of aiding the other three defenders.

Roberts and his men seemed unwilling to break off as planned. Now, they seemed more inclined to stand and fight it out right where they were with those three desperately battling defenders down there. By the time Bennington reached the livery barn he could see orange bursts of gunfire like huge fireballs, here and there, always moving, down across the yonder night. He went inside the livery barn, struck the lighted lamp in there with his carbine butt, broke the thing, killing the light, then slipped back out into the alleyway again.

The noise was thunderous. Some of the attackers were using deep-throated six-guns; they were the dismounted renegades creeping always closer through the shielding darkness. But, mostly, the gunfire coming from the desert was from saddle guns.

Sam tried twice to anticipate muzzle blasts and catch the gunmen before they could afterward jump away, but both times he failed. Roberts and his gun crew were seasoned, battle-toughened night riders from a dozen states and territories. In their trade, novices either learned fast or were buried early. These were the wily, scarred survivors of that pitiless school. They knew every trick and every ruse.

Bennington had to pause to reload, where he was kneeling against the back of the livery barn. As he did this, he strained to determine whether all three of the other defenders were still firing. It was impossible to tell in all that tumult, but he hoped and prayed that they were, then raised his reloaded carbine, and joined the fight again.

CHAPTER
SIXTEEN

Dr. Kleburg and his youthful ally atop the roof overlooking the southward desert were in an excellent position except for one thing — Roberts and his outlaw gunmen were determined to dislodge them because of the advantage they had up there, looking down over and across the sparsely sheltered desert. Sam could see, by risking a quick look out from behind the livery barn wall every now and then, that the renegades were literally chewing that building up over there with their angry shots. He tried to determine whether Kleburg and Slim, the apprentice blacksmith, were still firing, but that was impossible. Sam couldn't remain exposed long enough, and the way that building's upper story was being peppered, Kleburg and his companion wouldn't be able to raise their heads except very rarely.

Bennington settled down to swap lead with the outlaws. Once, he heard someone shouting orders. He thought that had to be Emmett Roberts but wasn't at all certain. Nonetheless, he fired three rapid sound shots in the direction of that voice, and thereafter the man did not yell out any more orders.

Someone in the overhead loft of the livery barn opened up with a carbine. Bennington looked quickly upward to determine which way that man was firing — into the town or out over the desert. He wasn't sure an outlaw hadn't preceded him to this place. But the muzzle blast, when it came, was pointing downward and forward, toward the desert. Bennington grimly smiled. He recalled Ev Bull's saying the livery man and his hostler had fled after they'd seen that cowboy die with the knife in his back. Well, if Ev were here now, he'd know where those two had gone. A second carbine opened up from the loft, also. That accounted for both the livery man and his assistant. That second gun also diverted some of the wrathful gunfire from Ralph Kleburg's rooftop; Sam could hear — and feel — the vicious striking of lead against the upper portion of the barn.

He got down prone, inched ahead until he was clear of his protective wall, and waited with infinite patience for a target. When he eventually got one, it was a pair of slyly crawling men approaching the dark alleyway entrance from far off to the west. Those two had detached themselves from the raging battle for the obvious purpose of infiltrating the town. Their purpose would be to set fire so that the attackers would have their enemies backgrounded with bright light.

Sam waited, not moving at all, until he thought the oncoming men were close enough, then he swung his carbine and fired at the nearest man. At the last possible moment that renegade leaned to look around for his companion. Sam's bullet struck the brim of the man's hat violently ripping through and startling the outlaw into a loud squawk as he flopped over onto his side. At once the second man fired at Bennington's muzzle blast. The bullet hit wood within four inches of Sam, making him flinch and slowing his reflexes as he fought to lever up his next bullet.

The hatless renegade didn't try to swap bullets; he concentrated upon frantically rolling, log-like, until he was back in the darkness again. Then he straightened around and began angrily firing. Sam had to press flat down until this minor fusillade was over. The gunmen fired alternately, keeping him pinned to the ground, until the second man also escaped in the darkness. After that, though, the gunfire began to slacken somewhat. Several hooting outlaws hiding out upon the dark desert taunted the defenders, promising them a grisly end when the town was finally taken. At first they elicited no replies, then Sam heard the bull-bass roar of Ev Bull, and it dawned upon him that the north end of town was unprotected, for if Ev was down at the south end fighting, too, that meant Dutch John would probably also be down there. He swore under his breath. What Roberts was doing now would be apparent to trained soldiers, but men like Ev Bull and Charley Jones, who also began giving curse for curse with the renegades, evidently had no idea that when all the defenders began answering from the south end of town, Roberts and his wily gunfighters would realize there was no one defending the north end.

He started to arise. Instantly a bullet clipped into wood below and in front of him. Apparently one of those men he'd surprised and routed a few moments earlier was vindictively lying out there, waiting to even up the score. Sam flattened again, began cautiously working his way backward crab-like, and was within ten feet of the barn's dark back alley opening when someone hissed at him from farther up the alley. "Steady now, son, keep a-crawlin' an' keep your head down." It was the old man; the one Charley Jones had called Cheyenne Willard. Sam eased back into the livery barn runway and looked back. The old Indian fighter was difficult to make out. He was leaning upon a weathered shed with his horse pistol in his belt and his bigbored old musket grounded in front of him. He was chewing something with an easy rhythm, and, although Sam couldn't see his face very well in the darkness, he would have bet money the old gaffer was grinning about all this.

Sam got up and called gently across their separating distance: "Mister Willard, there's no one guarding the north end of town. Come along. You 'n' I'll go back up there."

Cheyenne Willard kept on chewing whatever it was he had in his toothless mouth, and nodded his head, turned without a word, and groped his unsteady way back up the alleyway, staying always where the shadows were darkest and thickest. Sam watched a moment, gave his head a hard shake, then stepped out and faded ahead into the same kind of gloomy darkness.

The moon was beginning to brighten the roundabout desert. Its support seemed to give the stars a brighter sheen. Down along the south end of town there was still some occasional sniping, but mostly the attackers and defenders were satisfied, at least for the time being to hurl fierce threats and insults back and forth.

When the old man reached the jailhouse, which was midway, he halted, turned, and spat amber. He was chewing tobacco. He was also breathing reedily. "More cussed exercise'n I've had in thirty y'ar," he muttered, and gave Sam Bennington a bright, blue-eyed smile. "Well, son, I figured to lend a hand down there, but 'pears like some of the local cowards found they had some guts after all."

They went on, Sam accommodating himself to the older man's rickety gait. They had to pause one more time for Cheyenne to rest, then they made it all the way up to his bullet-marked shack, and there Cheyenne cackled again as he sank gratefully down upon an old chair out front, facing the alleyway. "All right, boy, we're here. Now let them skulkin' devils come, eh?"

Sam had to leave Cheyenne to go farther out, then over eastward, seeking enemies. What he found was Dutch John covered with dust and sweat, frightened half out of his wits but grimly crouching at the farthest end of the plank walk, protected by a recessed doorway where he was keeping his lonely vigil.

John was enormously relieved to see Sam, but that was true in reverse, also. Sam said he thought John had gone down where the fighting was in progress with Ev Bull, but the storekeeper shook his head. "Someone had to stay up here!" he exclaimed, then shook his head until his jowls quivered. "But if they'd come, I don't know what I could have done alone."

Sam told Oberdorf he'd be over to the west, near Cheyenne Willard's shack, also watching, so if trouble came, John would have support, then he started away. He hadn't gone more than ten steps when a woman's unpleasant, waspish voice twanged out at him from beside a partially opened doorway. When Sam turned, he caught the unmistakable glitter of moonlight off a blue-steel gun barrel.

"He warn't alone, Marshal. He never was alone. There are seven of us members o' the Ladies' Aid Society in here, all with guns. If those varmints aim to come . . . let 'em!"

Sam stood a moment gazing over toward that faintly seen, blunt-jawed, middle-aged face. The steady hand she had on her blue-steel six-gun dispelled any doubts he might have had. "We're obliged to you ladies," he responded. "But if they come, don't expose yourselves. Those men are professional gunfighters, ma'am. They'd shoot women about as quickly as they'd shoot men."

The woman said: "*Humph!* Just so happens, Marshal, we ladies talked this over, and we decided that there's never been a gun that didn't have another gun to match it." She closed the door softly and once more the roadway looked as emptily deserted as it always had. John Oberdorf looked from the door over to Sam Bennington, then said: "I never even heard them gathering in that house, Marshal. Never saw a one of 'em." He turned as a thought struck him, gazing wonderingly up and down the roadway. "I wonder, Marshal . . . ," he murmured, and didn't finish it, but

301

instead asked a question: "You don't suppose the folks still in town are banding together, do you?"

Sam nodded, remembering those two down in the livery barn loft, and old Cheyenne Willard with his big-bored old buffalo gun. "Odd thing," he murmured, "but sometimes this is what it takes to get some spirit and backbone into a town, Mister Oberdorf." Then he turned and slipped back around the corner heading over toward Willard's cabin. He was halfway there when he heard the gunfire down at the lower end of town brisk up again. He paused to cock his head, trying to determine whether the outlaws were past the defenders, finally decided they were not, and resumed his way. As he stepped down into the alleyway opening, a six-gun flamed up toward him from several hundred feet southward. He felt the disturbed air as that heavy slug sang past his head. Someone had infiltrated; that was no friendly gunshot. He dropped to one knee, swinging his carbine. He couldn't see the man down there but he knew about where he was. Cheyenne Willard's rifle crashed and roared. A flame two feet long gushed from the mouth of that old weapon. Down the alley something hard struck wood with a resounding blow. Sam was nonplussed; he hadn't been able to see that renegade down there in the darkness at all, and he was almost three times as young as the man who had been able to draw a bead on him and fire.

Bennington stood up very gingerly. He was certain that noise had been made by a man's body being knocked violently against the back wall of a building. But he couldn't be certain, so he started easing along,

302

keeping both shoulders against rough planking as he went.

He made out old Cheyenne sitting over there recharging his rifle. The old man didn't look up or speak until Sam was directly opposite him on across the alleyway, then he said: "No use you slippin' down there, son. When Eloise hits 'em square, they're dead afore they hit the dust. But you go look, if you're a mind. I'll sort of mind things up here till you traipse on back."

Bennington went down and looked, but he didn't even have to bend down in the watery, weak light of the shadowy alleyway. Cheyenne's bullet had caught that renegade right over the heart. It was no exaggeration at all to say the man was dead before he bounced off the wall and fell into the churned dust at his own feet.

Bennington thought he knew who this one was. The man hadn't been wearing a hat. It was that same vindictive outlaw who'd made a personal vendetta out of the fact that Bennington had almost cashed him in down near the south end of the alleyway earlier.

He returned to Cheyenne. The old man had his cabin door open at his back apparently so he might have a quick way to retreat if the need arose, but he was still sitting in that old chair out there, his rifle cradled across both arms. When Sam came up, Cheyenne waited for a lull in the southward fighting, then drawled that he'd sure admire to have a little snort of whiskey about now. Sam smiled. "I'll buy you a month's supply when this is over," he promised.

Old Cheyenne lifted his seamed, parchment-like face with its startlingly youthful, bright eyes and said: "Y'

303

know, son, up until yestiddy that's about all I figured I'd need to last me up until folks stuck me in the ground. But today I'm feelin' a sight better. A month's supply now just might kindle some of the old fire, and just to be cantankerous I might hang on for another eighty-eight years."

Sam had no reply, which is just as well because the firing seemed to be shifting from straight southward out upon the desert to over along the southwesterly curve of town. Sam was anxious about what that might mean. Cheyenne Willard, who'd evidently been in dozens of these skirmishes, said he thought the renegades were giving up trying to storm in from the south, and were gradually easing around to the west where they'd stand a better chance of getting in among the town's buildings. After that, the old man said, it would only be a matter of picking one another off. "The best shots'll end this thing, Marshal. Not the fellers who throw the most lead. I reckon you 'n' I'd best get on down there."

Sam was torn between the desire to go, and the need to stay. He balanced the decision for twenty seconds, trying to make the correct judgment, but in the end what Cheyenne Willard said influenced him.

Cheyenne got unsteadily to his feet, hooked the big old rifle across the bend of one arm, and looked at Bennington. "Marshal, we're just a-kiddin' ourselves if we figure them devils won't fight past four or five men. Maybe one or two'll slip in up here after we leave, but it's the big body of 'em we got to stop. Even if a couple o' us get killed from behind, we got to keep 'em out as long as we can. Until sunup if possible. By then I expect just the stink of all this here gunpowder'll fetch us some help. Let's amble on down an' sort o' lend a hand."

Bennington paused to check his carbine, making certain its magazine was still fully charged, then he nodded at the older man. "Let's go, Cheyenne. And if we come out of this, I've got something to tell this damned town about lettin' one of its best citizens live in a shack facing an alleyway."

They started down through the darkness. When they came abreast of that hatless, dead man, old Cheyenne patted his rifle affectionately.

CHAPTER
SEVENTEEN

The gunfire was increasing as both townsmen and renegades jockeyed for their fresh positions west of the town. Roberts had evidently found himself bogged down south of town with less and less chance of fighting on in. Sam thought he was perhaps trying to revert to his earlier plan of hitting the town from both east and west simultaneously, but that proved only partly right, for the moment old Cheyenne Willard and Sam Bennington got down where the battle was shifting and raging and shifting some more, it immediately became apparent Roberts still had nearly all his guns with him out there in the night. He hadn't detached any significant number of guns to go around and hit Hurd's Crossing from the east. The reason he hadn't was plain enough; there were just too many fiercely firing defenders facing him. If he weakened himself, even though it might mean access to the town, the chances were excellent that the defenders would overwhelm him before he could get inside.

Cheyenne faded back out of sight, as he seemed always to do, then he fired. Just for a moment that startling crash and roar surprised everyone on both sides so much they looked, holding off with their own weapons. Sam broke the spell by dropping low, easing around a building, and letting drive with two fast carbine shots. At once rifles winked up and down Emmett Roberts's crude line. Splinters of parched, dry-rotting wood flew in all directions. Sam had to jump away, and quickly. He'd had no reason to suspect, in the darkness, that the building he'd chosen as his rampart was so musty with that bane of the arid lands — dry rot — it was on the verge of collapsing.

He encountered a hulking large shape. Ev Bull. The mighty freighter squinted, then called something over to Sam that Bennington could not hear because of the deafening gunfire, and Ev melted away northward.

The fight seemed to be fluid now. Roberts wasn't actually confining himself to one place. He'd gotten around the lower end of town out upon the westerly desert, but he was still moving, sliding northward as he fought. For a while Sam kept pace. It was slow going for both sides, and, while there wasn't much protective covering for the renegades, except some occasional sage and scrub brush, the townsmen had buildings to utilize for protection. But the primary ally of both factions was the night. The moon had passed across overhead and was away now, which increased the gloominess all around. Except for muzzle blasts there were actually very few visible targets on both sides.

Ralph Kleburg walked up beside Sam Bennington. The doctor had a red-splashed bandage tightly knotted above the knee of his left leg. He paused where they were both sheltered, looked at Sam, and shook his head. When he spoke, he had to place his lips close to

Bennington's ear, and, when Bennington replied, he had to do the same.

"If they had any sense," said Kleburg, "they'd give up."

Sam said: "Doc, they're probably thinking the same thing of us."

Kleburg nodded. "I lost the apprentice blacksmith, Sam. He was on the roof with me. He raised up at the wrong time. He never knew what hit him. He's still up there."

Sam slowly nodded. This was, as far as he knew, their first fatality. "What happened to your leg?" he asked.

"I was climbing down off the cussed roof. One of them was in a lot closer than I thought. He tried to skewer me up there like a spider on a wall. Jones . . . Charley Jones . . . settled his hash for him right after he winged me in the leg. It's nothing. Sam . . . ?"

"Yeah?"

"Somewhere along the line we've picked up reinforcements. The livery man and his hostler are here with us."

"There are others," stated Bennington. "There's an old Indian fighter with a cannon for a rifle. He caught two of them north of town and one right here in this same alleyway. Killed two of them. Doc, they're moving northward again out there. We'd better stay with them."

Kleburg nodded, and limped over among some buildings where the other defenders were stubbornly trying to force the renegades to halt, to stand and fight in one place. They weren't successful; each time an outlaw fired, he also moved northward again.

For Sam Bennington this tactic was a mystery, and yet he had no doubt at all but that Emmett Roberts had something in mind. Roberts was not a reckless or imprudent man, whatever else he was. If he was moving northward up along the west side of Hurd's Crossing, he had a very good reason for doing it.

There was a brief lull, one of those inadvertent and spontaneous interludes that unpredictably occur in every battle. That was the first time Sam Bennington had a real opportunity to look right and left to see who all was there with him. Charley Jones was there, and that annoyed Sam but he didn't say anything, for Charley had evidently abandoned his post over in the eastward alleyway the same as Ev Bull had, because he felt his presence and his gun were needed more repelling the attackers to the west of town, and of course he was right. So was Ev Bull, but it also left their former positions fairly vulnerable. Sam hadn't forgotten John Oberdorf up there, nor those determined women in that house. But neither was he convinced they could stop the outlaws if Roberts's scheme was to get out upon the northward desert, then charge the town. And certainly, if Roberts decided to strike from over to the east, there wouldn't be anyone over there to stop him. But, his reason said, even if Charley Jones had been over there, he wouldn't be able to stop them by himself anyway, so perhaps it was just as well he was with the others on the west side of town. Actually, he decided in a calm moment, whatever happened from here on, was no one's fault, not Charley's, or Dutch John's, or even his own fault. The tragedy was simply that they just did

309

not have enough guns, even though they'd gained three since the fighting had begun. They just were not strong enough to do any more than they were doing.

Ev Bull ambled over. He had a welt across his shoulders he hadn't had when Sam had seen him earlier. The shirt was torn and the flesh was puckered as though Bull had been seared with a hot iron. "Crease," he growled, as he saw Bennington looking at his wound. "Don't amount to anythin'. Marshal, we're holdin' 'em, but if the damned Leverett Hall don't get back here right soon, we aren't goin' to be able to keep this up a whole lot longer."

Sam nodded. Ev looked gray and bone-tired. His hair and big beard were dusty; his eyes were sunken from strain and exhaustion. "We'll keep it up as long as we can," he said. "Ev, why's he trying to work his way up to the north end of town?"

Bull had the answer on the tip of his tongue. "That's easy, Marshal, that's the only place the brush ain't been cut away from behind the buildings. He can send a couple of his fellers scuttlin' through the sage up there where we can't see 'em at all, then they'll set the brush afire and duck back again. We're holdin' him out so far on the desert it's the only way he can hope to fire the town."

Bennington pondered that a moment, recalling that the greasewood, sage, and chaparral did indeed grow right up and around a number of old sheds and buildings up there, and that, as Ev said, it had been chopped away from everywhere else around he town.

310

Bull gave his big shoulders a little shrug and spoke again.

"Outside of old Cheyenne Willard no one still lives in those shacks up at that end of town, Marshal. Just a bunch of old deserted cabins and shacks. Folks never paid them any mind, the brush come back, an' now it's too late to try an' hack it down."

"Maybe too late to hack it down," said Bennington, "but it's not too late to get it for our side before Roberts gets it for his." He looked around where stealthy shadows were reloading or checking bandages, or drinking greedily from *ollas* and canteens, or just plain lying flat to get a little respite during this little interlude. He'd had in mind taking two or three of those defenders up to the brush patch with him, but one good look told him there just weren't enough men as it was, so in the end he said: "Ev, stay with them here. I'll get up into that brush alone. Pass the word they're not to fire into the brush, that I'm out there."

Bennington was moving away when Bull said: "Hey, wait a minute, Marshal. You can't do any good by yourself. I'd better . . ."

"I can do fine myself," called back Sam in a low, soft tone of voice. "I'll have plenty of brush cover and they won't know I'm up there. Now do as I said, Ev. Stay back with the others."

He was halfway up the dark alleyway with its strong stench of burned gunpowder when the firing back where he had been started up again, and at once he understood what Emmett Roberts had been doing during that lull. He and his men were farther northward and were beginning to creep in closer. For Sam Bennington this confirmed what Ev Bull had predicted. The outlaws were trying to reach the brush patch up north to start their fire.

Bennington ran on, slowed out front of Cheyenne Willard's place, turned in, and eased cautiously around the north side of the shack. He had no idea whether or not Roberts had detached a man or two for the express purpose of getting into the brush first. Where the first spiny limbs brushed his trousers was at the back wall of Willard's cabin. From there on outward, both northerly and to a lesser extent southerly, the thorny, flourishing scrub grew to a height of a man's waist; in some places, farther out, it was even higher.

Bennington dropped down until only his head was above those surrounding, wiry limbs that grew profusely in all directions. He saw nothing directly ahead, and besides the crashing gunfire southward but moving up toward him, he heard nothing. This did not mean he was alone in this tangle of dark green underbrush. For a moment he studied the way Roberts was advancing inward and northward. He could also tell by flashes and explosions, that the townsmen were easing northward, too, running from house to house, from shack and shed to shack and shed. Finally he poked his way forward, eased aside the nearest thorny limbs, and crawled ahead on all fours.

He went nearly a hundred feet before he found a little clear place where he could briefly settle, hoping for something, another lull perhaps, that would let him hear anyone else in this place with him. No such lull

312

materialized. He got out of the little clear spot, found a meager little trail of some kind, perhaps made by town dogs on the prowl for jack rabbits, and went along this another hundred feet. By that time he could distinctly hear the renegades up ahead and across his line of advance, swearing and furiously firing. He even heard someone give an order for someone to get into that damned brush. That was what he'd been waiting to hear.

He eased up, hatless, held sage limbs close to his head, and peeked out. The gun flames were turned slightly away from him, southward, but nevertheless they were blinding. He looked back. The same kind of gunfire was being returned. He was not in a very enviable place, being halfway between both factions, but also slightly northward of them, so only an occasional wild shot came into the brush anywhere near. But he had no illusions on that score, either; as both sides crept closer to the brush, they would straighten out their bullet trajectory. Then Sam Bennington would be directly between both lines.

He squinted, trying to sight the renegade Roberts had sent into the brush, but the moon was nearly gone now, darkness lay thickly all around, and until, several minutes later, he caught the quick, bright sputter of match flame less than fifty feet ahead through the sage, he had no idea where that other crawling man was. He still couldn't see the outlaw even when that little flame guttered down to a wisp, then winked out altogether, but he didn't wait. Fortunately, because of all the crashing gunfire southward, he didn't have to be careful of the sounds he made as he charged through the underbrush, seeking to reach that outlaw before he could get another match lighted. Fortunately, too, the darkness was his friend now; neither his friends nor enemies could see him as he plunged straight ahead. The renegade was bending over, half turned away, when Bennington finally spotted him. The man was concentrating on his lowered, cupped hands, where he was coaxing the next match to stay lighted. Not until Bennington was rising up, lifting his carbine, which caught in the brush and set up a wild quivering as Sam wrenched it free, did the outlaw feel the reverberations through the intermingled limbs, and realize he wasn't alone. Instead of springing up as perhaps another man might have done, the alerted renegade threw himself downward and sideward, burrowing desperately into the nearest bank of brush. Bennington jumped forward as the renegade went for his holstered six-gun, striking downward with his carbine. He caught the outlaw's right wrist under his Winchester barrel, half pinning the man's arm to his side. He leaned his weight on the carbine even as the renegade caught his first full view of Sam, and simultaneously tried to whip sideways again to free his neutralized right hand.

Bennington leaned harder, pushing that pinned wrist and hand with his solid weight. The renegade got hold of the Winchester barrel and tried to tug it free. Bennington put his full weight forward as he leaned and with his own right hand went for his six-gun. As the outlaw looked across his shoulder, upward, he saw the six-gun swing up not more than fifteen inches from his face, saw Bennington cock it, and the man's features curdled with terror. He cried out in a gasping whisper: "I give up. I quit right now. Don't pull that trigger, mister!"

Bennington balanced on the raw edge of judgment for five full seconds, then finally eased off with his weight, dropped his carbine, and sank to one knee, pushing his six-gun straight forward. "Turn around," he snarled. The outlaw obeyed at once, although he couldn't but have known what was going to happen. It happened, too; Bennington raised his gun barrel and chopped downward with it, striking through hat and hair and crunching over bone. The renegade slumped forward without a sound.

CHAPTER
EIGHTEEN

Sam Bennington was moving back, taking his carbine and the weapons — and matches — of that unconscious outlaw, when someone far off let out a high yell that was abruptly bitten off in mid-cry, as though one of the renegades had been trying to shout a warning and had been cut down before he could complete it. That unexpected but compelling scream had an immediate but uncertain reaction upon the renegades. Their gunfire slackened a little. Bennington couldn't see any of them but he imagined they were raising up to look backward, out where that yell had come from. Then that moment passed when a furious volley of gunfire broke out up and down among the buildings and sheds facing the westerly desert, and this, much more than that outcry, brought everyone's attention forward again. Bennington dropped like a stone. Bullets snipped off sage branches around him and sang overhead, heading westward. At once that furious voice out in the desert darkness bawled for more gunfire from the renegades. Another volley erupted, this time going from west to east. This time, too, although there were one or two close misses, Bennington was safer than he'd been from the initial volley. The outlaws were much more seasoned gunmen obviously.

He was starting to crawl back toward Willard's shack with the intention of getting inside, over near that broken back wall window where he'd be able at least to command a partial view of the brush patch, when another of those furious volleys broke out from the yonder alleyway, and this time a bullet kicked up a big gout of dirt and sand straight into Bennington's face. He sank flat down, digging at both eyes and cursing whoever, up there among the defenders, was so damned inexperienced with firearms that ... He suddenly stopped digging the sand from his eyes. The gunfire was swelling up and down the yonder alleyway. Through tears he saw at least fifteen muzzle blasts. When he'd crawled away, there hadn't been more than five or six defenders. Now, that yonder alleyway was flashing with more gun flame than he could catch sight of all at the same time. Not only that, but those shooters up there were keeping it up; they were pouring lead straight out across the desert with scarcely any let-up at all.

Those women! It couldn't be anyone but those women who'd been holed up in that house near where John Oberdorf had been keeping watch of the northward desert. A man's bull-bass voice roared out a mighty cheer. Sam began crawling forward again. He was within sight of Cheyenne Willard's shack when that bull-bass voice bellowed out once more, rising above the deafening crash and roll of gunfire.

"Give it to 'em, girls! Give 'em hell with the compliments of the Hurd's Crossing Ladies' Aid Society!" Then Bull's booming deep laugh rocketed up and down the gunsmoked alleyway, echoing high and low.

Sam got to Willard's shack, raised up, and found himself looking straight into the tunnel-mouthed barrel of old Cheyenne's big-bored musket just for a second. Cheyenne was kneeling, sighting down his long barrel. He lowered the gun, spat aside, then waggled his head back and forth. "Son, that's the second time I damned near salivated you."

Sam got into the lee of the shack and used a handkerchief to massage away gently the last of the dust and grit under his eyelids. Finally, with his sight clear again, he looked around. That hail of lead was still being hurled westward, and, although there was some return fire from Roberts's renegades, it was nowhere nearly as fierce or savage as before. Cheyenne chuckled over that.

"Got 'em pinned to the ground," he declared. "Them ladies teamin' up with us about now got them whelps out there scairt to raise their noggins, Marshal."

Sam blinked and turned his head. That was when he first noticed something old Cheyenne either hadn't noticed, or hadn't felt constrained to comment about. The sky was turning pale. Dawn was approaching.

Also, something had happened out there on the desert; there was a sudden dwindling of the gunfire toward town. At least it seemed to Sam Bennington this was true, for although he continued to detect the pale flash of guns out there, the weapons were not sending their lead toward the town; they were firing in two other directions — northward and due westward.

Old Cheyenne stopped ruminating to pucker up his bright old eyes in puzzlement. "They fightin' amongst themselves?" he softly asked, as the defenders up and down the rearward alleyway ceased also to fire as townsmen — and townswomen — peered out there where the watery dawn was breaking, just as perplexed as Cheyenne Willard was.

Sam heard a distant note rising high through the cool air, and jumped up to stand against Willard's cabin, staring. He heard it again, but evidently old Cheyenne's ears weren't as sharp as his eyes, because he glanced upward, saying: "Marshal, you better set back down here. Whatever's happenin' out there ain't likely to be in our favor, an' them lads still got a heap of fight left in 'em."

Sam bent low, caught old Cheyenne by the shoulder, and bodily hoisted the astonished old Indian fighter to his feet. "What do you see out there a mile or more?" he demanded, pointing with a rigid arm to the west.

Old Cheyenne looked, scratched his matted hair fiercely, and looked again, then said in a whisper: "It can't be. M' danged eyes are finally playin' tricks on me. It's . . . soljers!"

Cheyenne had scarcely said that when they all heard the swift pounding of many hoofs flashing down from the northward desert. Someone in among the bullet-scarred buildings let off a keening, high shout.

"Hall! It's Leverett Hall comin' back with the posse men!"

Old Cheyenne threw back his head and let off a high, short series of barks, like wolves make when they are ready to fight. It was an old Indian custom, giving that kind of a victory yell.

Ev Bull and Charley Jones came rushing around the side of the shack. They shouted and pointed, as though Bennington hadn't already also seen what was happening out there. Sam, in fact, earlier when it had still been dark, had thought someone had crept in behind Roberts and his gun crew. That sudden, shrill cry of alarm someone had bitten off in mid-shout had sounded very much to him as though an outlaw out there had turned, caught sight of soldiers crawling up on him through the night, and had tried to warn the others before he'd been struck down.

Three men on excited horses swerved inward where that little clutch of men was standing beside Cheyenne's cabin. One of them was Leverett Hall. As he slowed, Hall sent the others on out where a large force of blue-uniformed mounted men were sweeping inward toward the town from the west. Hall saw Sam Bennington and reined over closer. He was about to speak when Bennington beat him to it. "Hall, for two-bits I'd haul you off that horse and stamp you into the ground. I told you what'd happen if anyone stripped this town of its fighting men."

Hall blinked. He hadn't quite expected this kind of a reception. "It didn't happen, though," he said. "Sam, we saw the gun flashes from miles off and turned back right after nightfall."

A number of wounded, bedraggled men including Dr. Kleburg came walking silently up to look and listen as Sam said: "If you'd remember your tactics, General, you'd have put scouts out to cut fresh sign of Roberts. You wouldn't have just gone riding out to make a big sweep of the whole blessed country with just fifty men." Sam looked around and saw that hard-faced, middle-aged woman standing with the others. She had a dozen more armed women with her. "There are the real fighters of this siege," he told Leverett Hall. "These women. If they hadn't jumped in when they did, Roberts would've finished us for sure within another hour. General . . ."

A swirl of galloping horsemen cut Sam off before he could say more. They were blue-uniformed and hard-eyed men. The foremost one was a short, thick-set individual with the shoulder boards of a colonel on his heavy shoulders. He looked down his nose at Sam Bennington without uttering a sound, then switched his attention to Dr. Kleburg and said: "Well, Ralph, what happened to you?"

Kleburg stroked his jaw and gazed at the soiled bandage he wore on one leg as he answered: "Got caught in a very interesting situation, Colonel Cross. Someday I'll tell you all about it. Right now I'd better go set up a dispensary and start patching up the injured."

Kleburg turned and limped away. Colonel Cross watched him departing briefly, then turned his attention to Sam Bennington. "Looks as though you didn't quite get this place pacified, Captain. Also looks to me as though, if we hadn't arrived when we did . . ." Colonel Cross slowly drew one finger from right to left across his own throat.

That granite-faced middle-aged woman made a sniffing sound and glared upward. "If you hadn't come," she said with fierce spirit, "we'd have cashed them all in anyway, Gen'l. This isn't the first time in my life I've seen the Army come gallopin' up after the fighting's just about over to take the credit."

Colonel Cross gazed at the women silently. He studied bedraggled Charley Jones and mighty Ev Bull, and all the others including Cheyenne Willard, who was rhythmically chewing another cud of tobacco and smiling raffishly straight up at him. Then Colonel Cross said: "The Army's not taking any credit. All we did was intercept some heliograph signals sent by Mister Hall's forward scouts yesterday noon, and decide we'd ride down and see what was going on around Hurd's Crossing. The credit belongs to you folks . . . and Captain Bennington."

Cheyenne Willard spat amber, pouched his cud, and squinted his eyes. He wasn't the only one who turned to gaze at Sam Bennington, but he was the first one to say: "Captain Bennington. An' all the time I calculated he was too smart to be a soljer. I figured him to be a real gun-packin' peace officer. Now I got to go an change all them good opinions I had."

Charley Jones laughed. It was infectious. They all laughed. Even Colonel Cross and the escort riding with him smiled. Sam Bennington turned and threw a mock scowl at old Cheyenne, who rolled up his eyes and added: "Well, I never expected to collect that whiskey he promised me anyway. Only I figured both of us'd be dead, that's why I wouldn't collect it."

Over across the brightening desert Hall's posse men and a band of mounted cavalrymen were herding a number of dismounted men toward the town. The dismounted men were walking along with their arms high above their heads, and with their holsters empty. Sam Bennington stepped clear of the crowd to look for Emmett Roberts. Leverett Hall leaned from the saddle and spoke softly: "He's not there, Sam."

Bennington whirled. "He got away? You're sittin' that horse and Roberts got . . . ?"

"Simmer down," said Hall. "He got away all right, but not like you mean. You see, when my men and I got back last night, we didn't try to join the boys . . . and ladies . . . over here in the alley, because you were doing a good job without us. We tried stalkin' those renegades while the darkness was still down. I jumped one of 'em back where their horses were. I thought it was a horse guard. It was Roberts himself. He'd decided he was losin', and figured to slip away before his men caught on that he'd led them into a lot more of a fight than he'd told them it'd be. We had a little scuffle. I shot him. He's out there . . . dead."

Sam looked around for confirmation of this. Colonel Cross soberly inclined his head. "Roberts is out there exactly as Mister Hall said. Dead." Then, in his usual perfunctory and unemotionally efficient manner, the colonel added: "There's a sizeable reward on Roberts, Sam. Who gets it . . . Hall?"

Bennington looked up. Leverett Hall shook his head. "The community fund gets it," he told Colonel Cross. "The community fund gets all rewards and bounties collected hereabouts from now on. Hurd's Crossing needs a school and a church and a community hall, Colonel. It seems to me that since a couple of ex-Rebels with their guns finally whipped up some pride and spirit . . . and backbone . . . in Hurd's Crossing, it should be those same Rebel guns who say what's to be done with the money."

Colonel Cross shrugged, turned his horse, jerked his head at his escort, and rode on around through the bullet-scarred alleyway toward the front of town. One of his accompanying troopers split off and loped out where those crestfallen renegades were being herded along, with orders for the captives to be taken directly to the jailhouse under guard. Apparently Colonel Cross wasn't too certain a lynch party might not get organized among the injured and battered and victorious defenders of Hurd's Crossing.

"Well," said Leverett Hall, watching Sam Bennington, "what about it . . . Captain?"

Sam wiped his face and nodded, then he slowly smiled as he said: "How could an ex-Rebel major win an argument against an ex-Rebel general, Nick? Sure, the bounty money goes into that community fund. And one more thing, folks. You see those whelps being herded along out there? Looks like we whittled 'em down a little. Originally they were twenty strong. There are nine men still walking. Well, between the walking, the wounded, and the dead, I'd make a wild guess that there must be another five to eight thousand dollars in rewards. I'd say that ought to build a mighty fine set of new buildings in Hurd's Crossing." He paused, seeing flushed and sweaty John Oberdorf standing far back in the alleyway. "And I'd also say that, when it comes to backbone and common spirit, Hurd's Crossing has got all it's likely ever to need, if any more hotshot gunfighters and renegades try to take the town over."

Charley Jones said: "Amen!"

But it was Leverett Hall, who dismounted and started strolling back toward the center of the morning-lighted, battered town beside Sam Bennington, who had the final word. When they were well clear of that crowd, Hall tapped Sam lightly upon the shoulder and said: "Captain. You did it. I didn't think you had a chance of a snowball in hell at getting some community pride and spirit instilled into this town. But you did it. You brought out the best in every man jack in Hurd's Crossing."

Bennington stopped and turned. "In you, Nick? You still feel they're a bunch of scum?"

Instead of answering right away, Leverett Hall resumed walking. They were emerging into the yonder main roadway when he finally and quietly said: "All right, Captain, you've been right straight down the line, and I've been wrong. It's not easy to admit it, but I reckon that's part of the price a man my age has to pay for being so late at growing up. No, they're not scum.

325

They're good people underneath. Crude and rough, but good folks." Hall pushed out his hand. "Shake, Captain?" Sam Bennington stopped, smiled, and shook.

About The Author

Lauran Paine, who under his own name and various pseudonyms has written over 1,000 books, was born in Duluth, Minnesota. His family moved to California when he was at a young age and his apprenticeship as a Western writer came about through the years he spent in the livestock trade, rodeos, and even motion pictures where he served as an extra because of his expert horsemanship in several films starring movie cowboy Johnny Mack Brown. In the late 1930s, Paine trapped wild horses in northern Arizona and even, for a time, worked as a professional farrier. Paine came to know the Old West through the eyes of many who had been born in the previous century, and he learned that Western life had been very different from the way it was portrayed on the screen. "I knew men who had killed other men," he later recalled. "But they were the exceptions. Prior to and during the Depression, people were just too busy eking out an existence to indulge in Saturday-night brawls." He served in the U.S. Navy in the Second World War and began writing for Western pulp magazines following his discharge. It is interesting to note that all of his earliest novels (written under his own name and the pseudonym Mark Carrel) were published in the British market and he soon had as strong a following in that country as in the United States. Paine's Western fiction is characterized by strong plots, authenticity, an apparently effortless ability to construct situation and character, and a preference for building his stories upon a solid foundation of historical fact. *Adobe Empire* (1956), one of his best novels, is a fictionalized account of the last twenty years in the life of trader William Bent and, in an off-trail way, has a melancholy, bittersweet texture that is not easily forgotten. In later novels like *The White Bird* (Five Star Westerns, 1997) and *Cache Cañon* (Five Star Westerns, 1998), he showed that the special magic and power of his stories and characters had only matured along with his basic themes of changing times, changing attitudes, learning from experience, respecting Nature, and the yearning for a simpler, more moderate way of life.

ISIS publish a wide range of books in large print, from fiction to biography. Any suggestions for books you would like to see in large print or audio are always welcome. Please send to the Editorial Department at:

ISIS Publishing Limited
7 Centremead
Osney Mead
Oxford OX2 0ES

A full list of titles is available free of charge from:

Ulverscroft Large Print Books Limited

(UK)
The Green
Bradgate Road, Anstey
Leicester LE7 7FU
Tel: (0116) 236 4325

(Australia)
P.O. Box 314
St Leonards
NSW 1590
Tel: (02) 9436 2622

(USA)
P.O. Box 1230
West Seneca
N.Y. 14224-1230
Tel: (716) 674 4270

(Canada)
P.O. Box 80038
Burlington
Ontario L7L 6B1
Tel: (905) 637 8734

(New Zealand)
P.O. Box 456
Feilding
Tel: (06) 323 6828

Details of **ISIS** complete and unabridged audio books are also available from these offices. Alternatively, contact your local library for details of their collection of **ISIS** large print and unabridged audio books.